Praise for the Isabel Dalhousie Series

"Charmingly told. . . . Its graceful prose shines, and Isabel's interior monologues—meditations on a variety of moral questions—are bemused, intelligent and entertaining."
—*The Seattle Times*

"Genial. . . . Wise. . . . Glows like a rare jewel."
—*Entertainment Weekly*

"Full of his insightful but gentle examinations of human nature. . . . Paints [a] rich portrait of Edinburgh."
—*Rocky Mountain News*

"Endearing. . . . Offers tantalizing glimpses of Edinburgh's complex character and a nice, long look into the beautiful mind of a thinking woman." —*The New York Times Book Review*

"Habit-forming. . . . Leaves plenty of time for pondering moral conundrums, the drinking of steaming cups of hot brew (coffee, in this case) and . . . gentle probing into the human condition." —*The Oregonian*

"Whimsical. . . . [A] memorable cast of characters. . . . McCall Smith's assessments of fellow humans are piercing and profound. . . . [His] depictions of Edinburgh are vivid and seamless. . . . His fans . . . are sure to embrace these moral peregrinations among the plaid." —*San Francisco Chronicle*

Alexander McCall Smith

THE LOST ART OF GRATITUDE

Alexander McCall Smith is the author of the international phenomenon The No. 1 Ladies' Detective Agency series, the Isabel Dalhousie series, the Portuguese Irregular Verbs series, and the 44 Scotland Street series. He is professor emeritus of medical law at the University of Edinburgh in Scotland and has served on many national and international bodies concerned with bioethics.

www.alexandermccallsmith.com

BOOKS BY ALEXANDER MCCALL SMITH

THE LOST ART OF GRATITUDE

THE LOST ART OF GRATITUDE

Alexander McCall Smith

VINTAGE CANADA

VINTAGE CANADA EDITION, 2010

Published in Canada by Vintage Canada, a division of Random House of
Canada Limited, Toronto, in 2010. Originally published in hardcover in
Canada by Alfred A. Knopf Canada, a division of Random House of Canada
Limited, in 2009, and simultaneously in the United States of America by
Pantheon Books, a division of Random House Inc., New York. Originally
published in Great Britain by Little, Brown Book Group, London.
Distributed by Random House of Canada Limited.

Vintage Canada with colophon is a registered trademark.

www.randomhouse.ca

Excerpts from poems by W. H. Auden appear courtesy of Edward
Mendelson, Executor of the Estate of W. H. Auden, and Random House, Inc.

Library and Archives Canada Cataloguing in Publication

McCall Smith, Alexander, 1948–
The lost art of gratitude / Alexander McCall Smith.

(Isabel Dalhousie series ; 6)
ISBN 978-0-307-39702-7

I. Title. II. Series: McCall Smith, Alexander, 1948– . Isabel Dalhousie
series ; 6.

PR6063.C326L66 2010   823'.914   C2009-906723-4

Printed and bound in the United States of America

10   9   8   7   6   5   4   3   2   1

This book is for Roger Cazalet—with gratitude

THE LOST ART OF GRATITUDE

IT WAS WHILE she was lying in bed that Isabel Dalhousie, philosopher and editor of the *Review of Applied Ethics,* thought about the things we do. Isabel was a light sleeper; Charlie, her eighteen-month-old son, slept deeply and, she was sure, contentedly; Jamie was somewhere in between. Yet Isabel had little difficulty in getting to sleep. Once she made up her mind to sleep, all that she had to do was to shut her eyes and, sure enough, she would drift off. The same could be done if she surfaced in the course of the night or in those melancholy small hours when both body and spirit could be at their lowest ebb. Then all she had to do was to tell herself that this was not the time to start thinking, and she would quickly return to sleep.

She had wondered about the causes of her light sleeping and had spoken about it to a friend, a specialist in sleep disorders. She had not consulted him professionally, but had brought the matter up over dinner; not before the whole table, of course, but in the intimacy of the one-to-one conversation that people have with those sitting beside them.

"I don't like to ask about medical things," she said.

"But . . . ," he said.

"Well, yes. But. You see, you doctors must dread being buttonholed by people who want to talk about their symptoms. There you are at a party and somebody says: I've been having these twinges of pain in my stomach . . ."

"Have you?"

"No, I haven't."

He smiled. "The old cliché, you know. Somebody comes and says, A friend of mine has this rash, you see, and I wondered what it was. That sometimes happens. Doctors understand all about embarrassment, you know."

Isabel nodded. "But it must annoy you—being asked about medical matters."

He thought for a moment. "*Nihil humanum mihi alienum est,* if I may lapse into Latin. I don't set my mind against anything human. Doctors should subscribe to that, I think. Like priests."

Isabel did not think the comparison quite fitting. "Priests *do* disapprove, don't they? Doctors don't—or shouldn't. You don't shake your head over your patients' behaviour, do you?"

"If doctors see self-destructive behaviour, they might," he said. "If somebody comes in with chronic vascular disease, for example, and you smell the nicotine on his fingers, of course you're going to say something. Or a drinker comes in with liver problems. You're going to make it clear what's causing the problem."

"But you don't ladle on the blame, do you? You don't say things like, This is all your own stupid fault. You don't say that, even if it patently is his stupid fault."

He played with his fork. "No, I suppose not."

"Whereas a priest will. A priest will use the language of

right and wrong. I don't think doctors do that." She looked at him. He was typical of a certain type of Edinburgh doctor; the old-fashioned, gentle Scottish physician, unmoved by the considerations of profit and personal gain that could so disfigure medicine. That doctors should consider themselves businessmen was, Isabel had always felt, a moral tragedy for medicine. Who was left to be altruistic? Teachers, she thought, and people who worked for charities; and public-interest lawyers, and . . . in fact, the list was quite long; probably every bit as long as it ever had been. One should be careful, she told herself, in commenting on the decline of society; the elder Cato was the warning here—a frightful old prig, he had warned that everything was in decline, forgetting that once we reach forty we all believe that the world is on the slide. Only if eighteen-year-olds started to say *O tempora! O mores!* would the situation be *really* alarming; eighteen-year-olds did not say that, though; they no longer had any Latin, of course, and could not.

"You were going to ask me a question," he said. He knew Isabel, and her digressions, her tendency to bring philosophical complications into the simplest of matters.

"Why are some people light sleepers?" she began, and added hurriedly, "I'm one, by the way."

"So am I, as it happens," he replied. "It's often respiratory—sleep apnoea, where you keep waking up because you're choking. If not, it may be an idiosyncrasy of the brain. Is it a problem?"

"Not for me. Not really. I go back to sleep."

He nodded. "You could get yourself checked for sleep apnoea. It's pretty easy to monitor sleep patterns. You don't look at risk to me, though—it tends to affect heavier people."

That had been the end of the conversation, as another guest

had addressed the table at large and private conversations had trailed off. But now, lying in bed, in one of these brief periods of nocturnal wakefulness that she had decided were the product of brain idiosyncrasy rather than breathing problems, Isabel turned and looked at the sleeping form of Jamie beside her. She still experienced a sense of novelty, even if they had been together for a couple of years now; a sense of having been given a precious gift. And he felt it too; he had expressed it that way, too, when he told her that he was grateful for her. "I feel that I've been given something," he said. "Somebody has given me you. Isn't that odd? Because it doesn't happen that way, does it?" She watched him breathing. The sheet that he had drawn up to his chest and that lay crumpled about him like a Roman toga moved almost imperceptibly, but still moved. The act of breathing was not really an act at all, as the will played no part. We did not tell ourselves to breathe—except sometimes, in yoga classes and the like—and when we were asleep, as Jamie was now, the system itself remembered to do what was required. And how many of the other things we did fell into that category?

Isabel wondered what a detailed record of our day's activities would look like—not a record of the sort that might appear in a diary: *Went into town. Had lunch.* That kind of thing gave a broad-brush account of what we did but did not list the really particular, the hundreds—tens of thousands probably—of little actions in a person's day. We did such things all the time: tiny movements of the limbs as we sat in a chair or lay in bed, as she did now; little twitches, the flickering of the eyelids, the touching of the fingers, the inclining of the head. Those were nothing really—background noise, one might say—but they would all be religiously entered in this record of the day. And then there were the things we said—the speech acts, as philosophers called them—which ranged from the *um*s and *er*s, the muttered phrases of apology on bumping into somebody in a crowd, the meaningless expressions that lubricated our social dealings with one another. A transcript of our speech over the space of a day would make sobering reading, Isabel thought; and over a life-time? What would we have said? What would it amount to? How much energy would we have wasted on the smallest of small talk; how many months would be filled with sheer non-sense?

And then, as often as not, when the time came to talk, really to talk, we were tongue-tied, as could happen to people at the bedsides of the dying, when there was an urgency that cried out for big things to be said, and we found that we could say very lit-tle, or that tears made it impossible to speak. Isabel remem-bered once visiting an aunt on her father's side who did not have long to live; she had wanted to thank her for her generosity to her as a girl, and although she had managed to say the words that expressed her gratitude, the aunt, known for her coruscat-ing wit, had simply said, "Flattery will get you everywhere," and later that afternoon had died. But at least she had been thanked. "Flattery will get you everywhere" were memorable last words, if indeed the aunt had said nothing more after Isabel left her bedside, which she thought was probably the case. It would be a perfectly presentable final sentence, although not as witty, perhaps, as Oscar Wilde's gazing in dismay at the decora-tion surrounding his deathbed and saying, by way of farewell, "Either that wallpaper goes or I do."

If a transcription of our day's speech would make uncom-fortable reading, how much more dismaying, perhaps, would be a record of our thoughts. For a moment she imagined how it would look. A mixture of memories, fleeting and prolonged, what-if speculations, idle observations, regrets—that would be its shape for most of us, and for most of us, too, the leitmotiv would be . . . Isabel paused, unwilling to reach a conclusion so solipsistic, but unable to avoid it: the leitmotiv would be *me*. It was that simple. Most of us, most of the time, were thinking about ourselves.

But was that really bleak, or just human? We were, after all, ourselves; that was all we really knew, and the only point from which we could act. We could think of others, of course, and did, but such thoughts were often about others in the context of ourselves—what they had said to *us,* what they had done to *us*.

She looked at Jamie, who stirred.

"Jamie," she whispered. She had not intended to, but did. She uttered his name, as if to confirm the fact that he was there; we named things and they became more real.

He stirred again. A person's name is the one thing he hears even in sleep.

"So . . . ," he muttered drowsily.

"Are you awake?" Isabel whispered.

"Am now . . . ," although his eyes were still shut.

"Sorry," she said. "I won't talk to you any more."

He reached out a hand. There was a three-quarters moon outside and an elongated rectangle of light came in through the chink in the curtains. She would have to replace those curtains; Grace, her housekeeper, had been going on about that for years now. "Those curtains, they're ancient, Isabel, and the lining has rotted, you know."

She gazed at Jamie's forearm in the moonlight; flesh made silver. She took his hand in hers and held it lightly. She wanted to cry, from sheer happiness, but he would really wake up if he heard her crying those tears of joy and think that something was wrong. Men, on the whole, did not understand crying for happiness, as women did. There were so many different sorts of tears.

She thought: I shall not think. And that thought, a prompting that denied itself, worked as it always did—she drifted off to sleep, holding Jamie's hand. When she awoke to the sound of Charlie gurgling in his cot in the next-door room, she found that miraculously Jamie's hand was still in hers, as lovers will sometimes find that through the night they have cleaved together and are still thus arranged in the innocent light of morning.

THAT DAY WAS A FRIDAY, a day that Isabel always enjoyed very much, although Saturday was her absolute favourite. She had the usual feelings about Monday, a day that she had never heard anybody speak up for, although it must have had its defenders; workaholics, perhaps, found Monday intoxicating in its promise of a whole week of work ahead, but for others, in her experience, it was more commonly Fridays or Saturdays that were favoured. In her case, Friday had been further boosted by Jamie's usually being free on that day, which meant that they could do things together, taking Charlie off on an outing somewhere, or she could use part of the day to catch up on *Review* affairs while Jamie entertained their son. Whichever of these she chose, there was a very satisfactory feeling of making a choice that was unconstrained by necessity. If she worked on a Friday, she did so because she wanted to, not because she had to; and if she went off somewhere with Charlie, it was similarly a matter of doing what she wished.

Occasionally Jamie had to work on a Friday evening, if he

was summoned to play with the chamber orchestra that relied on him when a bassoon was called for. Sometimes he would also be needed on a Friday for session work—a recording of music for a film, perhaps—but that rarely happened, and Fridays had remained more or less free ever since he had given up taking pupils on that day. These pupils were his bread and butter; he taught some of them at the Edinburgh Academy, the school on the north side of the city where he gave music lessons part-time, and others had their lessons in his flat in Saxe-Coburg Street, round the corner from the Academy. At the moment, he had told Isabel, they were not very good, although one or two of them could be competent players if they tried. But they did not practise, in spite of the exhortations he wrote in their notebooks about scales and exercises.

"Of course, Charlie will practise diligently," Isabel had said. "When he starts playing his . . ." She looked at Jamie. He had said something once about miniature bassoons—something called a tenoroon. Somehow she could not picture a reduced bassoon, with miniature levers and shrunken key-work, being played by Charlie in his Macpherson tartan rompers.

Jamie understood her hesitation as a sign that it would be for him to decide the shape of Charlie's musical education.

"Violin," he said. "Let's start him on strings. And anyway, they can't blow wind instruments until they're much older. Nine is probably the earliest. Before that their lungs aren't strong enough and they can easily damage their lips. The muscles around the lips are still forming, you see."

She smiled at the thought of Charlie with his unformed lips and a violin. He would attempt to eat it if she gave him one now, but they could start when he was three, which would come soon enough. And then, after the violin, when he was old enough, ten or so, he could learn the Highland bagpipes, starting on a practice chanter before proceeding to a real set, ebony drones and all, to the full, primeval wail that sent shivers down the spine. He would wear the kilt—Macpherson tartan again—and play the pipes; oh, Charlie, dear little Charlie.

That Friday, Jamie had no commitments and Isabel decided that, although she might take advantage of his presence to do some work in the earlier part of the morning, she would suggest that they should all go into town for lunch together. She had promised to see her accountant, but she had been putting it off; he had telephoned with an offer to come and see her if she would not come to him. She felt guilty about that, as he was a mild man with the air of one who was long-suffering, as no doubt he was.

"I can only do so much with the figures I'm given, Isabel," he had told her. "I can't make things up, you know; we don't work that way." She wondered whether this implied that *she* worked that way—making things up.

She had assured him she would give him what he wanted, and had dutifully put printing bills and postage receipts for the *Review* into a folder . . . until she had somehow forgotten. She had scrambled around and a few missing receipts had turned up, but not everything, she suspected.

"I have to see Ronnie," she said to Jamie. "I have to give him some papers. It shouldn't take too long. Then we can go to Glass and Thompson for lunch. Charlie likes their quiche." And he had indeed liked it on their last visit, even if most of it had ended up on the floor around the table. Charlie had sophisticated likes, his parents were finding out to their surprise; he enjoyed olives, and would wave his hands at the sight of quail eggs. It was almost a parody of the tastes of the privileged baby and Isabel felt slightly embarrassed at the thought of it. She did not remember giving him his first olive—it would never have occurred to her to do so; had Jamie done that? And quail eggs? Would it be oysters next? It was Jamie, she decided; he tended to feed Charlie with whatever they were eating, and Charlie never refused anything from his father.

Jamie was happy with the suggestion. Isabel could make an early start in her study while he took Charlie down to the canal in the jogging pushchair, the one that allowed him to run while pushing. Then Charlie could have his mid-morning sleep and be bright and ready for the outing into town.

They breakfasted together. Jamie, who did not like to eat anything very much before a run, had a cup of milky coffee and a slice of toast spread with Marmite. Charlie had rather more: a small carton of strawberry yoghurt, mashed-up boiled egg on fingers of toast, and an olive, stoned, of course, and cut into four minute parts.

Grace arrived before they had left the table. She fussed over Charlie, who waved his arms enthusiastically, his unambiguous signal of pleasure.

"Pleased to see me?" cooed Grace, hanging her hemp shopping bag on the hook on the back of the kitchen door. "Of course you are, you wee champion! And what's that they're giving you to eat? An olive. Surely not? Bairns don't like olives, no they don't."

Isabel glanced at Jamie, who smiled, and looked away; disagreements between Isabel and Grace were not his affair, and he tried to keep out of them. Privately he sided with Isabel and she knew that she had his support, but they were both aware that it did not help to declare it.

"Some bairns do," said Isabel. "This one, for example."

Grace ignored this. Still addressing Charlie, she continued, "It'll be quail eggs next, my goodness! And caviar after that."

"Small children like all sorts of things," said Isabel. "They're people, after all, and people have peculiar tastes and beliefs." The reference to beliefs slipped in; she had not really intended it, but it rounded off the observation nicely, and was tossed in rather like a depth-charge, thought Jamie. He looked at Isabel with concern. There had been a discussion between the two women the previous week about feng shui, in which Grace had enthused about chi forces and Isabel had expressed the view that they simply did not exist. If they did, she said, then surely we could detect them with some sort of electronic apparatus. This reference to peculiar beliefs was about that, Jamie thought. The debates about olives and chi forces were minutely intertwined.

Grace had stood her ground during that discussion. "There are plenty of things nobody can see," she said. "What about that particle thingy that they're trying to find. That Higgs bison, or whatever."

"Boson," Jamie had interjected. "Higgs boson. It's a sort of . . ."

"Boson," said Isabel. "I saw Professor Higgs the other day, you know. He was walking along Heriot Row looking down at the pavement."

"He won't find his boson down there," said Grace.

"He wouldn't have been looking for it," said Jamie. "It exists only in the mathematics he did. It's a theory."

The argument about unseen forces had continued for some minutes and remained unresolved; both sides were sure of their position and both were sure that they had won. This reference now to peculiar beliefs threatened to reopen the issue, which Jamie did not think was a good idea. Fortunately, Grace paid no attention to it and changed the subject. There was a load of washing to be put in the machine, and did Isabel want Charlie's clothes dealt with now or later? And there was the question of the vacuum cleaner, which had stopped working the previous day; had Isabel phoned, as she had promised, about that?

"I shall," said Isabel. "Today. Definitely. I'll put it on my list."

Grace had nodded, and gone off to begin her tasks.

"Quail eggs," whispered Jamie. "She really disapproves."

Isabel nodded. "Mind you, it *is* outrageous," she said. "What sort of child have we produced, Jamie? Quail eggs!"

He smiled. He loved her. He loved Charlie. He even loved Grace, in a way. It was a perfect morning, the best sort of early summer morning, and all he felt was love.

CHAPTER TWO

FROM HER STUDY WINDOW, Isabel watched Jamie and Charlie disappearing down the street. She gave a wave, but Jamie was looking the other way and did not spot her. It always made her feel proud seeing the two of them together. She used to think that her major achievement in life had been the editing of the *Review,* or perhaps her doctorate; she no longer thought so—now she felt that the most important thing she had done was to give birth to a whole new life, a whole new set of possibilities. She had *made* Charlie, that small, energetic and increasingly opinionated bundle of humanity, that tiny, olive-eating person; she had *made* him.

But, more than that, she had given Charlie just the right father—she could be proud of that as well. Jamie was good with children, although in his modesty he made little of his talents in this direction. But Isabel had heard it from the parents of his pupils. One mother had said of her son, "He never practised his bassoon. Never. We spent all that money on the instrument—three thousand pounds, would you believe—and the little devil never practised. You know what they're like at that age. Then

Jamie took him on and everything was different. He inspired him—it's as simple as that; he inspired him."

Isabel had passed on the compliment, and Jamie had been diffident. "Oh well, we're getting somewhere with him."

He would be good with Charlie—she had known it right from the very first time he held him in the hospital. The nurse had passed him his new-born son wrapped in a towel, and she had seen the tears in his eyes, and she had known. For her part she had thought this briefly, and then, through the residual, euphoric haze of the painkiller they had administered, she had entertained one of her habitual odd thoughts, on this occasion about the towel around Charlie. In the past it would have been swaddling clothes; they wrapped infants in swaddling clothes, did they not? They swaddled them in strips of bandage-like cloth to stop them moving too much. She was grateful that Charlie would not be swaddled. He had not come into this world to discover that he was bound against movement, against freedom. Little Charlie would be free to move, to kick his legs, to live in liberty. She hoped.

She went into her study and gazed at the array of books and papers. The room was on the side of the house that did not get the sun until mid-morning, yet even at this point in the morning the large windows let in a good amount of light. As she surveyed the room she thought that the scene before her could be a still life, *Study with Books,* of the sort painted by seventeenth-century Dutch artists. They liked rooms like this, and they liked the stillness hanging in the very air of such places. Vermeer, perhaps, might have painted this room, or de Hoogh, inserting the figure of a woman sewing or playing a lute—one of those quiet domestic scenes that they did so well. And such an artist would look, as the Dutch painters often did, through the room into the space beyond, in this case Isabel's garden, the square of lawn outside the window bordered by its bank of rhododendrons and azaleas—a sort of courtyard, rather like an outdoor room. Somebody had told her—she had forgotten who, or whether she had read it somewhere—that the essence of a good still life was the feeling it inspired that something was just on the point of happening. What was about to happen here? Her eye wandered to the pile of letters on her desk, put there by Grace the previous day. That was suggestive of the beginnings of something—an exchange of correspondence, perhaps. Somebody was about to enter the room and deal with the letters and then leave again, and the stillness would return.

She sighed. She could have gone off to the canal with Jamie and shared Charlie's delight in the ducks. He squealed with pleasure now when he saw them, waving his arms about in uncontrolled excitement; he loved to watch them swimming for the breadcrumbs Jamie tossed into the water. There would come a time—and it would not be long in arriving, she feared—when ducks would cease to amuse Charlie quite so much. The thought brought regret. Charlie would grow up only too quickly, as all parents said their children did; already she found it hard to remember what he was like as a tiny baby. She remembered the smell, of course, that very particular, soft smell that babies have, a mixture of animal warmth and milk, and blanket, which gave way so soon, in a young child, to something else, as individual and every bit as indefinable, but not quite the same.

She crossed to her desk and switched on the desk lamp. There were at least ten letters in the pile—and four of them looked as if they were manuscripts. Isabel stipulated that prospective authors submit articles for the *Review* on paper, a policy that led to grumbling from at least some of her would-be contributors. "Haven't you heard of electronic submission?" wrote a professor of philosophy from a college in the American Midwest. "You really should accept electronic files, you know. Everyone does." She had written back to explain that she did not read on screen—something for which she felt he should be thankful. "I give far more considered attention to something on paper," she said. "I find that I can *weigh* it. I would have thought that contributors would appreciate this." A day or two later his reply had arrived. "You could print things out," he said. "Why not?" And after that he had inserted in the message a smiley face, winking.

Isabel might have left it at that, but, puzzled by a motivation that she could not explain, she decided to make a concession. Then, after she had made up her mind, she looked for a reason for her decision. She imagined the professor in Iowa sur-rounded by a sea of cornfields and fresh-faced students, waiting for a message from somewhere beyond the vast horizons that bounded his world. "I'm sorry to have to get back to you on this," she wrote, "but printing everything costs money and, as I'm sure you'll appreciate, takes time that I may not have. However, since this means so much to you, I'll be happy for you to submit your paper electronically and I shall print it out."

There was no reply to this, and so a week later she sent an enquiring message, asking if the paper had perhaps been lost in the ether. This time there was a reply: "Sorry—paper not yet written. Perhaps next year some time." She had smiled at this; the whole exchange had been hypothetical. She wrote back to him—a real letter—and said, "I do hope that we get something from you, but I don't want to put you under pressure. The summer, perhaps, might be a good time to put pen to paper, once the students have packed up and gone home. Until then, I remain, in hope, Isabel Dalhousie." She folded the letter, put it into an envelope and wrote out the address. Why had she bothered? It had been a pointless exchange with a man she neither knew nor imagined she would ever meet, and yet for a short while they had engaged with one another. *Treat everyone you meet as if it's their last day, and while you know that, they don't.* She remembered the advice given her by her mother, her *sainted American mother*, as she referred to her. And it was good advice—a childish aphorism, perhaps, but none the less true for that.

And then the memory came back. Iowa: yes, she had been there, and she had forgotten all about it. Years ago, when she had been on her fellowship in Washington, she had been invited to a conference in a college town in Iowa, and there had been a young associate professor who had shown her and one or two others around the town; yes, she remembered now. And he had pointed out a large house on the edge of a river where, he explained, one of the members of a local philanthropic family had lived. He had said, "That is where Miss Ellie lived, and she believed in fairies with all her heart—with all her heart." And with that he had looked at Isabel wistfully, and she had been struck by the thought of anybody believing in fairies with all her heart. To live in a house by a river and to believe in fairies with all one's heart—that was enough, surely.

She could not remember the name of the man who had shown her round, but it occurred to her that this was the same person, which meant that they were not strangers to one another—not really—and that chance, pure chance, had brought them together twice. What was more interesting, though, was the fact that she had decided to make an exception in his case and offer to print out his paper for him. She had thought that this was because he was somehow isolated in his Midwest fastness, but now she knew otherwise: she had been prompted to do it because her subconscious mind recalled their meeting even though her conscious mind was unaware of it; she knew him, although she did not know that she did.

Now, seated at her desk, she began to deal with the letters. Usually she indulged herself in picking out the ones that interested her and attending to those first, leaving the mundane and the bills until last. But today she felt she should be sensible and force herself to deal with them according to their order in the pile; lunch with Jamie and Charlie would be her reward. So if she opened the electricity bill before anything else, it was because it was on the top of the pile, and for that reason deserved to be opened.

The next letter was from the printers of the *Review*—a technical enquiry about the quality of paper. They had bought a supply of superior Finnish paper, they revealed, and would keep some of this for Isabel if she wished; a sample was enclosed. The offer reminded her of her obliging butcher, who from time to time would pull something out from under the counter and say that he had been keeping it for her; some delicious cut that he thought she would particularly appreciate; small acts of commercial friendship binding together customer and provider. She looked at the paper and held it up to the light. She rubbed it between her fingers, and thought of where it had come from, somewhere in those wide forests where . . . where *the ports have names for the sea.* The line of Auden came to her, and made her think of how typographical errors may lend a certain beauty to a line; Auden had written of sea-naming *poets,* in Iceland rather than Finland, but *poets* had been misread as *ports.* That was a creative misunderstanding, she considered, and it made the thought behind the line much better, much richer, as some of our mistakes will do.

Isabel had put the electricity bill to one side—not the same thing as paying it, she said to herself. The admission made her reach for the cheque book kept in the top drawer of her desk and write out a cheque for the requisite sum—an estimate, she noticed, based on what the electricity authorities had deemed a household such as hers likely to have used. That was not the same thing as what she had actually used; parsimony might have overcome her, for all they knew. Or its opposite might apply: she might have taken to growing cannabis and consumed those massive quantities of power that cannabis growers use to force their crop. It happened, she knew, but not in Edinburgh, not in this tree-lined street . . . which would be perfect cover, she realised, for just such a thing, or for a counterfeit currency operation, or for anything, really. And how the newspapers would revel in the unveiling of something like that in the very home of the *Review of Applied Ethics.* Perfect villains have to live somewhere, and even the most innocent-looking suburb can conceal its surprises. *But they were so quiet and considerate, said one of the neighbours; who would have guessed that he had been a dictator?*

She slipped the cheque into an envelope and put it to the side. Not the same as posting it, she thought; and put on a stamp. Now the next letter: a rather bland-looking envelope with her name written on a label that had then been stuck on. *Miss Isabel Dalhousie, Editor, The Review of Applied Ethics.* There were several things about this that made her pause. Firstly, she was addressed as Miss, which now had a dated sound to it in a professional context; most people who wrote to her in her editorial role called her Ms., or, if they knew, Dr., which she had never really got used to. The problem with Dr. was that it made her think of Dr. Dalhousie, her father's brother. He had been such a large Dr. Dalhousie, such a suitable and entirely proper Dr. Dalhousie—a country doctor in East Lothian, breezy, much loved, avuncular to his patients—that it seemed to her there could not be another one. This correspondent, though, had chosen Miss, which might be a statement, an attempt to put her in her place. And then there was the emphasis with which the word *Editor* had been written, with heavy down-strokes of the pen, again suggesting some sort of hinterland of meaning—a sneer perhaps. Or was she imagining things?

Isabel thought for a moment of how somebody who was truly paranoid would view the morning's mail—looking for signs on each envelope of possible slight or of a message beyond the clear meaning of the words. Ridiculous; absurd . . . But when she opened the envelope she immediately saw the letterhead: *Professor Christopher Dove, Chair, Western Thought.* She gasped. How could anybody, even a man like Dove, claim to chair Western Thought? She read on; the address of Western Thought was given, and then its telephone number, as if so great an intellectual movement should establish that it was always at hand, contactable by those who needed, by telephone or post, the reassurance of the Western philosophical tradition.

She read the letter, and then read it again. She stood up.

She had expected something like this from Dove; she had not imagined that he would let matters rest after his toppling—richly deserved—from his brief spell as editor of the *Review;* payment for his coup, as she thought of it. And now he had broken cover; unambiguously, with all the ill-concealed satisfaction of one who had long awaited his moment, and having finally found it, had now made his move.

Isabel replaced the letter on her desk. There had been a time when she would have brooded on it, when she would have been unable to think about anything other than the contents of the letter. This was no longer the case. Charlie, oddly enough, had freed her of that; Charlie had taught her to think of more than one thing at a time, as small children inevitably teach their mothers to do. So now she thought of what Charlie would have for supper and then of his shoes, which she suspected he was already growing out of, and would need to be replaced. It was preferable to thinking of Dove, whose shoes, she suddenly remembered, had been green. It was a curious thing to remember, but the image came back to her of the last time she had seen Dove, which had been in Edinburgh, when he had come to the house wearing green shoes. Was that a new precaution she would need to add to the list of irrational propositions by which we live our lives, in spite of knowing that they are indefensible: that men who wore green shoes were not to be trusted? Of course that was nonsense—perfectly reasonable, trustworthy men wore green shoes, men such as . . . No, she did not know a single man who wore green boots, apart from Dove. And then she remembered: Charlie had a pair of little green shoes, given him by Grace. Well, the next pair would be red.

"NO," said the accountant, "this really isn't good enough."

He looked reproachfully at Isabel over the top of his half-moon glasses, and then glanced across the room at Jamie, who was bending down over Charlie's pushchair, tickling the small child's palm. The accountant had a quiet voice and these were strong words for him.

"Oh, Ronnie, I know," said Isabel. "It's just that paper-work—"

Ronnie cut her short. "It's not paperwork any more, Isabel. A simple spreadsheet. They're not hard to set up. Perhaps Jamie could . . ."

"Jamie is not all that good with computers," said Isabel.

Ronnie looked doubtful. "These days anyone—"

"I'd be perfectly capable of doing it," said Isabel firmly. "There are manuals, aren't there?"

Ronnie sighed. "Yes, there are. And if you simply entered everything on the spreadsheet as sums came in—or went out—then the program would do the work for you. It really is that simple." He took off his glasses and polished them on a hand-kerchief. "Running totals."

"Running totals?"

He replaced the glasses. "Yes. Running totals are a possibility."

Isabel tried not to smile. There was a wistfulness in his voice as he spoke about running totals; as a Bedouin might speak of an oasis in the desert, she thought, or a shipwrecked sailor of safe anchorage. She made up her mind. She would do as Ronnie suggested; or she would try to, at least. "Then that's what I'll do," she said. "Spreadsheets it will be."

"From now on?" asked Ronnie.

"From now on," Isabel confirmed.

They left the accountant's office and began to make their way down the hill to the top of Dundas Street.

"You made a promise back there," said Jamie, as they passed Queen Street Gardens. "Look, Charlie. Trees. Trees."

Charlie looked, and gurgled—he saw only green, and movement, and blue above that—the high blue ceiling of his small slice of the world, his tiny part of Scotland.

"I know," said Isabel. "It was like promising one's dentist to use dental floss."

Jamie did not approve of the comparison. "You should take it seriously," he said. "Ronnie only wants to help. And he has to make up the accounts for the tax people. He puts his name to them."

Isabel nodded. She had taken it seriously, and she had meant what she had said to Ronnie; she would start a spreadsheet and try to stick to it. She felt slightly irritated that Jamie should think that she had tossed words about carelessly, when his own accounts, if they existed at all, were probably little better than hers.

"You keep a spreadsheet, I suppose," she said.

He had been about to say something, but hesitated.

"No?" she pressed.

"It's different," said Jamie. "I don't have . . . well, I don't have much money."

She looked steadfastly ahead. She regretted her remark, and turned to him to say sorry. He was looking at her, smiling. "What a ridiculous conversation," he said.

She was relieved. "Isn't it? One should never let spreadsheets come between one and one's . . . ."

"Friends," he supplied quickly.

"Exactly." He was more than that, of course, but she had not used the word *lover* to his face, nor he to hers. Significant other, she thought, and smiled—if some others were significant, then were the *other* others insignificant? Teenage argot, she knew, had a word for them: *randoms,* who were the people one did not really know. Eddie, Isabel's niece Cat's young assistant at the delicatessen, had used the term to describe the other guests at a party he had attended. "I didn't know anybody," he said. "The place was full of randoms."

"Randoms?" said Isabel.

"Yes," said Eddie. "Just randoms. Who could I talk to? So I left."

"You couldn't talk to the randoms?"

He looked at her with amusement; one did not talk to randoms.

They crossed Heriot Row. "Robert Louis Stevenson's house," Jamie said, pointing to one of the elegant Georgian ter-raced houses that ran along the north side of the street. "I went to a party there once with . . ." He stopped, and Isabel knew what he had been about to say.

"With Cat," she prompted.

"Yes. With Cat."

"I hope she enjoyed it."

He shook his head. "She didn't. We fought."

Isabel thought, *It wouldn't have been his fault.* But she did not say it; instead she made a remark about the Queen Street Gardens, which Stevenson would have seen from his window, and about how you never saw anybody in them, except ghosts, perhaps.

They went into Glass and Thompson, the place they both favoured for lunch, leaving Charlie's pushchair outside. Charlie was wide awake and showing a close interest in his surroundings, delighted by the colourful display of olive oils and pastas that dominated the shelves on one side of the café. He was easily pleased by colour or movement and waved his little arms in approval and a desire to embrace the things he saw.

It was just before the lunchtime rush and there were several free tables at the back of the café. While Isabel settled Charlie on her lap, Jamie went up to the counter and ordered—mozzarella salad for him and Isabel, and a piece of quiche for Charlie. In the display below the counter he saw a bowl of olives, and he added some of these to the order as a treat for Charlie. They were large and unstoned, and he would have to dissect them for Charlie, but they would add to his already considerable delight.

Their order came quickly. Charlie saw the olives from afar, or smelled them perhaps, as he started to gurgle in anticipation even before they arrived.

"He has some sort of sixth sense when it comes to olives," said Isabel. "An intuitive knowledge of olives."

Jamie laughed. He took an olive from the plate and cut the flesh from the stone with his knife. A small drop of oil fell from his fingers; Charlie watched intently.

"Olive," said Charlie.

Jamie dropped the knife, which fell on the plate below with a clatter. Isabel's mouth opened wordlessly, and she reached out to grasp Jamie's forearm. "Did he?"

Jamie beamed at his son. "Olive, Charlie?"

Charlie looked at his father briefly, and then transferred his gaze again to the fragments of black olive on the plate. "Olive," he said again. It was unmistakable.

"At last," said Isabel, and bent her head to plant a kiss on Charlie's forehead. "You spoke, my little darling. You spoke!" They had been waiting for Charlie to say something and, although they had been reassured that first words at eighteen months, even if late, were still within the range of normality, they had been concerned. His gurgles were expressive, but they were impatient to hear *Mama* or *Daddy; olive* was a surprise, but a welcome one.

Jamie grinned with pleasure. "I wouldn't have guessed it would be *olive,*" he said. "What a clever little boy."

They tried to coax more out of him, but Charlie, now engrossed in the large quartered olive passed on to him by Jamie, was having none of it.

"He doesn't need to say *olive* again," said Isabel. "He has what he wants."

They began their own lunch, while Charlie investigated his quiche, quickly reducing it to a pile of sodden fragments.

"I don't want to spoil the party," said Isabel, "but there was a rather unpleasant surprise in the mail this morning."

Jamie raised an eyebrow. "A bill?"

"Well, there were two of those. One for much more electricity than I think we've actually used, but that'll be sorted out. No, something to do with the *Review.*"

Jamie frowned. He enjoyed reading the *Review,* or the readable bits of it, and he took pride in Isabel's ownership of it, but he was concerned about the burden it represented. Isabel worried about her *Review*—he knew that from her occasional muttering in her sleep—fragments from anxious dreams: *revisions, proofs, deadline,* words that revealed the tenor of at least part of her subconscious. He thought of the *Review* as some sort of presence in the house, rather like a demanding domestic pet that required to be fed and exercised and was always causing difficult dilemmas. By contrast, Jamie's working life seemed to him to be so simple: he taught his pupils, he played the music put in front of him by the conductor, and when he put his bassoon back in its case then he could put it out of his mind.

"You worry too much," he said. "There's always something, isn't there?"

She picked up a small piece of quiche and handed it to Charlie, who examined it, cross-eyed; he was looking for olives. "Maybe. But then it's the sort of job that never seems to finish. You get one issue off to press and then there's the next one to think about—and the one after that. It's a bit like Sisyphus and his rock—pushing it up to the top of the hill and then having to do the whole thing all over again once it's rolled down."

Jamie shrugged. "Yes, I can see that." He thought for a moment. It seemed to him that just about everyone's job was a bit like that; repetitious. He glanced at Russell Glass, the proprietor of the café, serving customers at the counter. It was the same for him; he served one mozzarella salad, somebody ate it, and then he had to come up with another one. Or if you were a judge, for instance: you decided one case, disposed of it, and there was another one in front of you.

"We're all Sisyphus," he said. "Don't you think? So isn't the answer not to allow our jobs to prey on our minds too much? Sisyphus doesn't have to think too much about what he's doing—he just has to do it."

Isabel laughed. "You're suggesting that Sisyphus could be happy?"

"Well, he could be, couldn't he? There are plenty of people

who have repetitive jobs who are perfectly happy." He came to this view without thinking; he would have to justify it. "They're happy about other things. Yes, that's possible, isn't it? Horrible job, but other things to think about."

Isabel thought this was probably true, but she wanted to tell him about Dove. "Christopher Dove," she announced.

"Ah."

"Yes. He wrote me a letter. A bombshell."

Jamie looked alarmed. "What did he . . ."

He did not finish his question. He noticed that Isabel had suddenly turned sharply to look towards the café's front door. He followed the direction of her gaze.

"It's her," whispered Isabel. "See?"

Jamie looked. "Her over there?"

Isabel did not reply.

"Olive," Charlie said suddenly, clearly, decisively. "Olive."

CHAPTER THREE

MINTY AUCHTERLONIE."

It was said with as much intensity as if Sisyphus himself had walked into the café. Jamie was momentarily distracted by Charlie's further pronouncements on olives, but then he looked again towards the door and saw the figure of a woman outlined against the light flooding through the café's front windows. She was carrying a child and was looking around for a table.

"Her?"

"Yes," whispered Isabel. "I'm sure it's her." She lowered her voice even further; the woman, having failed to find an unoccupied table near the window, was making her way towards their part of the café. Jamie watched her; Isabel looked away. He saw that the child she was carrying, a boy, was roughly Charlie's age, perhaps a little older, and was wearing a simple tee-shirt with a polar bear on the front and a pair of corduroy trousers. The woman said something to the child, who was looking about him with curiosity.

Isabel raised her eyes at the same moment as Minty looked down. For a moment, neither moved or said anything. Then Minty smiled. "Isabel Dalhousie?"

Isabel felt a fleeting urge to pretend that she had not recognised Minty, as one occasionally does when one wants to avoid
engaging with a vague acquaintance—when one is too tired for
small talk, or in a hurry, or when one has forgotten a name. But
this was not such an occasion, and she said, "Minty. Of course."
She saw Minty's eyes slide to Jamie—appraisingly—and to
Charlie.

"This is Roderick," said Minty. "And you've got . . ."

"Charlie," said Isabel. "And Jamie." It was an unfortunate
juxtaposition; she should have said, "And this is Jamie." Yet they
were both hers, although in a different sense, of course.

Minty smiled at Jamie and then turned back to Isabel. She
looked around her and saw that the remaining tables had all,
rather suddenly, been taken. "You wouldn't mind, would you?"
she asked.

Isabel could not refuse. She did mind, of course, as she had
planned to tell Jamie about Dove's letter and she wanted to talk
to Charlie about olives. Such promising lines of conversation
would now be impossible with Minty and Roderick there.
"Please join us," she said, "I'd be delighted." And she thought, as
she spoke, of how often what we say is the exact opposite of
what we really mean.

Minty had a portable infant's seat, which she fixed to a
spare chair before strapping Roderick in. "Could you watch him
for a second while I order?"

As Minty went up to the counter to place her order, Isabel
whispered to Jamie, "Remember her?"

He glanced in her direction. Minty was elegantly dressed
and was being attended to by the young server.

"She was that woman who told you about that man? Quite a
long time ago?"

"Yes," said Isabel. "I thought that she was the one who was doing the insider trading, but it was really . . ."

"The other one? That man?"

"Yes."

"So she helped you?"

Isabel nodded. "I think so. But I was never really sure about her."

Minty, having chosen her food, returned to the table. "Roderick has a very sweet tooth," she said. "I try to control it, but he takes the view that if he comes out for lunch with me, he's entitled to something sweet. So I cave in, I'm afraid."

"Charlie's the opposite," said Jamie. "He likes savoury things. Olives in particular."

"They're funny," said Minty. "Little individuals from day one."

Roderick was staring suspiciously at Charlie, who seemed unaware of the other child's presence. "Look," said Minty. "They're making friends."

Roderick now reached forward and grabbed at Charlie's small green boot, which he tried to pull off its owner's foot. Charlie, vaguely aware that something was tugging at an extremity, looked to Isabel for clarification.

"He wants to play," said Minty.

Isabel struggled not to show her astonishment. This was not play; this was an alpha baby trying to take her son's boot from him by brute force. She had noticed this sort of behaviour in the playgroup that she took Charlie to three times a week. They were two-hour sessions, held in a local church hall and marked by an astonishing level of noise. Charlie, she had observed, was tolerant and put up in a good-natured way with the grabbing and pushing of his coevals. It was a quality he had inherited from Jamie, she thought.

"Aren't they sweet!" Minty remarked. They were not: Charlie was sweet; this Roderick, it seemed, was his mother's son. She remembered Minty as a ruthless high-flyer in the world of finance; her son would be heading in the same direction, no doubt. But the thought, she decided, was an uncharitable one, and she checked herself; Roderick had not chosen his mother, and, besides, all babies were little psychopaths in their early years. Only later would there emerge the finer aspects of the personality—if there were to be any.

"I wonder what they think of one another," mused Jamie. "Presumably they see somebody like themselves."

Roderick, at this point having abandoned his attempt to remove Charlie's boot, had grabbed hold of his ankle, which he was trying to twist. Charlie watched, wide-eyed, but impassively. Gradually Roderick gained purchase and began to dig his tiny fingernails into Charlie's skin. It was too much; Charlie turned red and opened his mouth to cry.

"He gets a little rough sometimes," said Minty, moving Roderick away. "He doesn't mean it. Sometimes I think he doesn't know his own strength."

Isabel made light of this assault on her son. "Boys . . . ," she said.

"And girls," said Jamie. "I knew a girl who used to pull my hair when I was small."

Minty was looking at Jamie again, and Isabel found herself thinking, *She's undressing him.* And how would she feel if Jamie returned a look like that, as some men would, flirtatiously; but he did not. He looked away; he was used to this, she thought, and was probably vaguely bothered by the admiring glances of women. Such things could become irritating to those who had them all the time; the turned heads, the quick glances. Women used to be discouraged from overt manifestations of interest; but not now, not now that the male body was presented for admiration on posters and in magazines. Men were being given a dose of their own medicine.

She knew, of course, what Minty was thinking. She was calculating the difference in age and wondering how she, Isabel, had managed to catch a young man like this. This amused her. Minty was a type who would condescend to Isabel, but she could not do so on this. She's envious, thought Isabel.

Minty turned to Isabel. "It's a long time, isn't it?"

"Yes," said Isabel. "And here we are with Roderick and Charlie. How's Paul?"

Minty stiffened. "Paul and I are no longer together," she said. "I see him from time to time, of course—professionally. He's fine."

"I'm sorry," said Isabel. "I didn't know . . ."

"There was no reason for you to know," said Minty. "I'm married now to Gordon McCaig. He runs a whisky broking business."

"Ah," said Isabel. Minty, she reminded herself, came from a world where people were immediately interested in knowing what business others were in; she and Jamie did not. Particularly Jamie: his main interest was in the sort of music that people liked. "That man," he might say, "that man who's keen on Wagner. I saw him today." Or, "That pupil of mine—the one who likes Chopin—left his rugby boots in the flat. Covered with mud."

"He has his own blend," went on Minty. "One that he bottles himself. The Lochaline."

Isabel knew very little about whisky—no more, really, than she had picked up from her occasional attendance at a talk by her friend, Charlie Maclean. She had never heard of the Lochaline, which sounded rather obscure to her and not really deserving of a definite article, or at least not yet; a definite article took time. Some whiskies, she knew, adopted a definite article, as an affirmation of their fame. The Macallan was one; a practice justified in its case by habit and repute. And some Scottish clan chiefs did a similar thing. There was a MacGregor who simply called himself The MacGregor, which had the virtues of simplicity and clarity even if it implied that other MacGregors were, by contrast, *indefinite*.

So Paul Hogg had been disposed of . . . no, she should not assume that. Paul Hogg may well have disposed of Minty, or indeed they might even have disposed of one another in an act of mutual emotional suttee. "And you?" asked Isabel. "Are you working?"

Minty nodded. "Rather hard, actually. This is one of my rare days off." She paused. She was looking at Jamie again, and it seemed to Isabel that her answer was directed to him. "I run a bank. An investment bank."

Jamie looked impressed, or tried to; Isabel could tell that investment banks meant little to him. And she liked that. There was nothing essentially wrong with investment bankers, but they were usurers, after all, and she was not sure that she would want to *live* with a usurer. A reformed investment banker, of course, would be another matter.

She immediately reproached herself for that thought. It was immature, unjust, and above all uncharitable. She knew bankers, and liked them. There was an ocean of difference between a usurer, properly so called, and a banker. Usurers exacted excessive interest, whereas bankers extracted . . . moderate interest. We needed bankers, and they were entitled to the same moral respect as anybody else. Most of them did their jobs with integrity and care; some did not, of course, but there were plenty of greedy people in other professions, and philosophers were in no position to claim the moral high ground that they spent so much time and effort identifying for others. Look at Rousseau, who was so rude and ungrateful to David Hume in spite of all that Hume did for him. Look at Schopenhauer, who refused to speak to his mother for years. And look at me, she thought, who has just thought uncharitable thoughts about an entire section of commercial humanity . . .

"Well done," said Isabel.

Minty's pleasure at this compliment was manifest. "Thank you," she said. "It's hard, you know, for a woman. They claim that the playing field is level, but it isn't really. The men still do private little deals amongst themselves. They still . . . *huddle.*"

"And women?" asked Jamie, in a tone of innocence. "Isn't there an association of professional women in Edinburgh that's women-only? I played in a quintet for them once—at a dinner. All women. I was the only man there."

Minty laughed. "Yes, there is. There's more than one, in fact."

"So women huddle too?" Jamie had a sense of fairness and little time for the hypocrisies of the age.

Minty was not ready to concede so easily. "We have to. We have to do it to make up for past injustice."

Jamie nodded. "I see."

It was clear that Minty now regarded the topic as

resolved—in her favour. Jamie might be an attractive young man, but he was still a man. She turned to Isabel and asked her about the *Review*. Isabel explained that she still edited it, but as owner. Minty had the good manners at least to return the compliment that Isabel had paid her. "That's something," she said.

Minty's order arrived and they continued their lunch. The conversation flowed rather well, Isabel thought, and when, at the end of the meal, Minty suggested that they exchange telephone numbers, her views on the other woman were beginning to change.

"Roderick is having a second birthday party on Sunday," said Minty. "I know it's no notice, but why not bring Charlie? They seem to get on very well."

They do not, thought Isabel, but did not say it. She accepted, and Minty, who had some shopping to do, left.

Jamie, who seemed relieved that Minty had gone, now said, "So, what did Dove write?"

Isabel's mind was elsewhere. She was thinking of the invitation; it would be Charlie's first party. Would there be olives? "What?"

"Dove. What did he write? You said it was a bombshell."

Isabel nodded. "He accused me of plagiarism," she said. "Or of aiding and abetting it."

Jamie's eyes widened. "Let's sort him," he said. Then he laughed. "I don't mean physically. Or maybe I did. But if I did, then I don't mean it any longer. It just slipped out."

Isabel reassured him that she had not taken him seriously. "We all say things like that," she said. "Or think them."

Jamie looked thoughtful. "Revenge fantasies. There was a

conductor once—I wanted to . . ." His thoughtful look turned to one of shame. "I wouldn't ever have done it."

Isabel put on a look of mock censure. "I should hope not."

"It would have been very therapeutic, though," mused Jamie.

LUNCH—and defending himself against his new friend, Roderick McCaig—had exhausted Charlie, who was now sitting quietly on Isabel's lap, fighting a losing battle to keep his eyes open. He would sleep, of course, in his pushchair, and Jamie now lifted him gently into it and strapped him in.

"I'll take him for a sleep-walk," he offered. "You go to the gallery. Half an hour?"

Isabel accepted the offer. The Scottish Gallery, run by her friend Guy Peploe, was a few doors down the road from Glass and Thompson, and she wanted to talk to Guy about an auction that was coming up in London. Isabel appreciated art and made the occasional foray into the art market—something she did with discretion and a degree of embarrassment. She sensed that Jamie did not entirely approve of the buying of expensive paintings, and she usually shielded from him the sums she actually paid for her acquisitions. In her view, of course, they were entirely justified; surely it was more selfish to leave money squirrelled away in a bank account than to recycle it? The people from whom she bought the paintings spent the proceeds no doubt—that was the reason they were selling them in the first place. And was it not generally better that money should circulate—which was, after all, its fundamental purpose?

She had mentioned this to Jamie—gently—and he had

listened carefully. "I suppose so," he said. "I don't really under-stand economics though. If you left it in the bank, wouldn't it be working anyway? Being lent to people?"

"But this is going even further," argued Isabel. "I'm effec-tively giving it away. Nobody will be paying me interest once I've parted with the money."

Jamie frowned. "But you're not really giving it away. You're getting something in return."

"Those paintings have to hang somewhere," Isabel retorted. "What point do they serve if they're doing nothing?"

The conversation had petered out after that. Neither really knew anything about the subject; all Jamie knew was that he did not really have any money and was not particularly inter-ested in acquiring it, while Isabel, who had money, knew that it was not only an opaque subject but a rather dull one too. If money could be changed into art, that at least made it more interesting.

Guy was summoned from the back office when Isabel came into the gallery.

"I don't suppose . . . ," Isabel began.

"I do," said Guy. "I've got Lyon & Turnbull's catalogue. And one of the London catalogues too."

They went downstairs and into the small garden at the back of the gallery. Seating themselves on two French ironwork chairs, they began to page through the London catalogue. It was the usual mixture for the day sale, where the cheaper pictures were offered; the evening sale brought out the higher bidders, the collectors who would pay hundreds of thousands, or even millions, for pictures which the artists might well have ex-changed for a square meal. Isabel was not in that league; she was interested in the day sale, and the less expensive end of it too.

"Elegant company enjoying themselves again," said Isabel, pointing to a French picture of a well-dressed group of people picnicking under a tree.

Guy read out the description that the cataloguer had prepared. "Circle of François Boucher. *Elegant company at ease under a tree, musicians in the background.*"

"I love the term *elegant company*," said Isabel. "I wonder how one qualifies? And here, look at this. This is the opposite. *Roughs drinking in a tavern.* Frankly, the roughs seem to be having a better time."

Guy laughed. Turning the page, he came across another allegorical work. "Big," he said. "Seventy-two inches by fifty-four. And not a bad frame. But look what it is."

Isabel studied the painting in the photograph. "*The Parable of the Wise and Foolish Virgins.* Oh look, Guy. See the wise virgins. Look at them."

The painting, by an obscure Flemish artist of the late seventeenth century, showed two groups of young women in a landscape. Six wise virgins, seated on the left, were demurely occupied in reading and sewing, while behind them a number of lissom figures danced on a patch of grass before a church. In the sky above the church, a small group of angels, illuminated by convenient shafts of light, looked down benignly on the edifying scene below. Had these angels turned their heads slightly and glanced to their left, they would have seen a very different set of young women—six patently foolish virgins—drinking, playing cards and enjoying the courtship of sundry young males. Behind this group was a town clearly dedicated to easy living, vice and disorder.

"There are some paintings which are unambiguously didactic," Guy observed drily.

Isabel smiled. "The wise virgins look very dull," she said. "I rather suspect I should have preferred the company of their foolish sisters."

Guy turned the page, to reveal a display of three portraits. "Pieter Nason," he said, pointing to the first of the paintings. "He did some very fine portraits. There's one in the National Gallery on the Mound. And what have we here . . ."

He pointed to the painting below—a much smaller photograph, and consequently less detailed.

As Isabel gazed at the painting, she felt a sudden flutter of excitement. The face was unmistakable—that proud but ultimately rather weak face: Charles Edward Stuart, none other than Bonnie Prince Charlie.

"It's him," said Isabel quietly. "The Young Pretender." Her eye went to the description under the photograph. "Circle of Domenico Dupra, Turin, *Portrait of Charles Edward Stuart.*"

"Dupra was a reasonably well-known Italian portrait painter," said Guy. "He was first half of the eighteenth century, which would have made him a contemporary of Charlie's."

Isabel looked at the estimate. "Should we go for this, Guy? The estimate is low. Look. It starts at two thousand pounds."

Guy thought for a moment. "It would complement your portrait of James VI," he said. "We could have a tilt at it. You never know with these Stuart portraits. There might just be somebody who's very keen."

"Jacobites," said Isabel.

Guy agreed. Historical enthusiasm kept the market in portraits alive: people had their heroes, likely and unlikely, he explained. "Somebody recently offered Gandhi's spectacles at an auction in New York," he said. "They were eventually with-drawn, but had they not been, they would have brought in a tremendous sum."

Isabel thought about this. Gandhi's spectacles. She remem-bered seeing a photograph of his possessions at the time of his death: those small, oval spectacles, a pair of sandals, a dhoti; a photograph that had moved her almost to tears. That tiny patrimony spoke more powerfully of the greatness of his soul than any words could. And she reflected upon how curious it was that the people bidding for them could compete to pay thousands of dollars for things that proclaimed the ultimate unimportance of those very dollars.

She looked more closely at the picture of Bonnie Prince Charlie. She did not like him—he was vain, a chancer really, who must have shared the inflated notions of entitlement that infected all those exiled Stuarts. Yet no matter how outrageous his claims, there was an undoubted romance in his story, and it was for this reason that she was prepared to have him on her wall. Scotland had not been well treated by the English at the time; the Scottish parliament had not been consulted by West-minster in the choice of the Hanoverians, and the Stuart cause had become synonymous with the resentment of a put-upon nation. This weak and rather effete Frenchman, bedecked in tartan, had become the focal point of Scottish resistance to London's diktats, and that still resonated.

"Will you bid for me?" Isabel asked. "Let's try to get it below the estimate. Twelve hundred?"

Guy made a note in the margins. "Good as done," he said.

They finished their perusal of the catalogue and went back upstairs. Jamie arrived a few minutes later; she saw him coming up Dundas Street, with Charlie clearly asleep, tucked up in the pushchair.

"We went all the way down to Canonmills," he said as she went out to join them. "He's sleeping the sleep of the just."

Isabel bent down and looked at Charlie. The tiny features were in repose, the mouth slightly open to allow the passage of air. Such an intricate collection of cells, she thought, all miraculously put together to produce a centre of human consciousness, so fragile, so infinitely precious to those whose life was transformed by it. She straightened up. The summer sun was riding high now, gilding the hills of Fife across the Forth. A bus laboured up the hill, bound for Princes Street and the Mound, the passengers in shirtsleeves for the unaccustomed heat. For a moment, Isabel's eyes met those of someone looking out of the window, a thin-faced woman with her hair done up in a bun. The woman began a smile, but stopped, as if conscious of somehow transgressing the conventions of isolation with which as city-dwellers we immure ourselves. The bus moved on, and Isabel felt a sudden desire to run alongside it, to wave to the woman, to acknowledge the unexpected exchange of fellow feeling between them. But she did not, because she never acted on these impulses, and because it might have puzzled or even frightened the other woman.

She turned to Jamie. "Can you remind me of the words of 'King Fareweel'?" she asked. She knew that Jamie had an impressive knowledge of Scottish music, including the more arcane corners of the subject. "King Fareweel" was mainstream, the sort of thing sung by Scottish patriots in moments of enthusiastic inebriation, and by nostalgic Jacobites in cold sobriety.

The question took Jamie by surprise, but Isabel often said odd things; he was getting used to it.

"Now a young prince cam' to Edinburgh toon," he began, half singing, half speaking, *"And he wasnae a wee bit German lairdie / For a far better man than ever he was / Lay oot in the heather wi' his tartan plaidie."*

"That's it," said Isabel.

CHAPTER FOUR

THE NEXT MORNING Isabel's niece, Cat, telephoned at seven. Isabel had been awake since six and had taken Charlie on an outing in the garden. He had been late in starting to walk, but now seemed eager to make up for lost time, rushing off purposefully and quite indifferent to any falls that came his way. It was an exhausting business for her, if not for Charlie himself, as he had to be watched every moment. She had a playpen, which at least could give her time to get her breath back and do things that needed to be done in the house.

"Do people approve of those things?" Jamie had asked when the pen had been delivered. "Don't some people look on them as little prisons?"

Isabel had read about this. "Some do," she said. "But not everyone, by any means. It all depends on how long the child is in one. If they're in it for short periods of time they can enjoy playing by themselves."

"But not for hours."

"No, not for hours. And nor should children be parked in front of the television."

"Which we don't have," Jamie pointed out.

"No."

Jamie had bought something called a baby bungee, an apparatus that gripped on to the jamb of a door and allowed the child to bounce up and down on a strong elastic rope. Charlie had loved it, but on the second occasion it had been used he had bounced off one side of the jamb and then back against the other. He had been slightly bruised, even if he had not complained, but the baby bungee had been retired to a cupboard. Charlie, she had decided, was a stoic by temperament, a useful thing in this life. If this stoicism came from anywhere—rather than being an entirely random quirk of personality genes—then it must have been inherited from Jamie, who was fond of saying "It happens" when faced with any frustrating development. Stoicism and defeatism, of course, can be kissing cousins, but Isabel would never find fault in Jamie's quite exceptional ability to accept setbacks. She had never seen him angry—not once; distressed, perhaps, but not angry, and it seemed that Charlie was the same. Of course the tantrum stage still lay ahead of him, and that would be a stringent test of any stoicism he possessed; it was no use saying "It happens" to a three-year-old brewing a stamping attack.

"Sorry to phone so early," said Cat. "Crisis."

Cat was visited by crisis rather more often than others, but the difficulties these crises entailed always seemed genuine enough, even if they were clearly of her own creation. A crisis was a crisis, Isabel believed, and it was unhelpful to allocate blame. You did not ask the drowning man how he ended up in the river, nor point to the *No Swimming* notice—you rescued him; even if he happened to be Dove, Isabel thought, or Professor Lettuce. A delicious scene came into her mind: Dove and Lettuce had both fallen into a loch and were calling for help. Isabel, passing by, would not hesitate, of course, nor would she relish their evident discomfort as it dawned on them who their rescuer would be. But what if it were in her power to rescue only one of them? It was the familiar and horrific dilemma that must cross the mind of at least some imaginative or over-anxious parents: Which of my children would I save? The thought is usually too appalling to contemplate, and the question is suppressed rather than answered.

But here it arose with Dove and Lettuce, both schemers and plotters of the same stripe, and in moral terms, Isabel reluctantly concluded, both of equal merit. The deciding factor in such a case would have to be age; all other things being equal, the sole remaining basis of just discrimination would be that Professor Lettuce, being the older of the two, had less claim for a future than the relatively youthful Dove. So Dove was saved. She did not like the conclusion, but doing the right thing, even if that took the form of making the correct choice in an entirely hypothetical situation, was often uncomfortable.

Cat waited for a reply. Isabel was thinking, she decided, and was probably mentally chewing over something altogether different, as often happened.

"You need me to do the delicatessen?" Isabel asked eventually.

"Yes, if you don't mind," Cat explained. "The boiler in the flat has gone on the blink and the engineer is coming. However . . ."

Isabel was familiar with such issues: the gas people were always unwilling to commit to a time, and would give only the most general indication of when it might be.

"They said that it could be either morning or afternoon," said Cat. "And they wouldn't budge. So I have to stay in all day to let them in."

"Frustrating," said Isabel. "Of course I'll help. What about Eddie?"

Eddie was a rather vulnerable young man who lacked the confidence to look after the delicatessen on his own. Isabel believed that he was perfectly capable of doing so, and Cat did, too, but his anxiety had been acute on the few occasions on which he had been left in charge by himself.

"He'll be there," said Cat. "But you know the problem."

Isabel said that she did, and the arrangements were made. Isabel had a key to the business and would open it up at ten to nine, to be ready for Eddie's arrival. Cat promised that in the unlikely event of the gas engineer arriving early she would come straight in to work; Isabel, however, put her off. "Take a day off," she said. "That's what aunts are for."

Her own words struck her. *That's what aunts are for.* It was true, of course: aunts were for coming to the rescue, and she always tried to do just that. But were aunts for helping themselves to their nieces' discarded boyfriends? It was Cat who had got rid of Jamie—an act that betrayed appalling judgement, Isabel felt—and so she could hardly complain when Isabel took up with him. But she had complained, and had done so bitterly. Things were slightly better now, but there was still a touchiness on Cat's part that could flare up at any time—and it did.

Jamie was not yet up, and so Isabel took him a cup of tea and the copy of the *Scotsman* that came through the door early each morning. When she told him that she would be spending the day in the delicatessen, for a moment she saw a shadow cross his face. She hesitated; they did not talk about Cat because she was an unseen third person in their relationship, as a former lover sometimes can be. It was akin to a past act of unfaithfulness that can stand, a painful monument, in the history of a marriage—a forbidden memory, cauterised and sealed off, but still with the power to hurt.

"We could see whether Grace could come in," said Isabel. "She tends to be free on Saturday, so you needn't have Charlie all day."

Jamie looked at her reproachfully. "I like having Charlie all day," he said.

She was emollient. "That's fine then. He loves being with you." She bent down and kissed him on the cheek, gently tousling his hair as she did so.

"Don't do that." But he did not mean it.

She sat down on the bed. "You don't resent my helping Cat, do you?"

He looked away. "No, not really." A small rectangle of sunlight streamed in through a chink in the curtains, across Jamie's shoulder.

Isabel reached forward and placed her hand against his chest. "I think you do, you know. But I can't just . . . just cut Cat out. She's family. I can't."

He looked at her. "I never wanted you to do that." He hesitated for a moment, and then took Isabel's hand in his. "I'm the one who feels awkward about this. I know I don't need to, but I do. I feel embarrassed, I suppose, that I've . . ."

She waited, but he did not complete the sentence. "Embarrassed that you've what?"

"That I slept with her, and now I'm sleeping with you."

He spoke with transparent honesty, but the pain his words

caused him was laid quite bare. Isabel pressed his hand. "But that's . . ." She found herself at a loss as to what to say.

"Nothing?" said Jamie.

"No, of course it's not nothing."

"Then what is it?"

Isabel took a deep breath. "What I mean is that it's something you simply don't need to think about."

He sighed. "You can't just deny these things."

"I'm not saying that you should deny it. What I'm saying is that you should forget it. That's quite different." She watched him. He had a way of looking at her when something she was saying interested him profoundly—it was a sort of searching look—and she saw it now. "Do you really want me to discuss it with you?"

"Of course. Why not?"

She pressed his hand again. "Because I sound like a philosopher, and I don't always like that. Not when I'm with you. It's just the way it is."

He had not been returning the pressure of her hand; now he did so. "But that's what I like," he said. "It's like being . . . like being married to Socrates."

The analogy was so unexpected that Isabel burst into laughter. "Thank you! Socrates . . ."

Jamie grinned. "In a purely mental sense, of course. You're far more beautiful than Socrates."

"Poor Socrates—just about everybody is."

Jamie steered the conversation back to its original subject. "But what about forgetting? How can you forget on purpose?"

She acknowledged the difficulty. "All right, I know that forgetting is normally something over which you have no control.

But you can tell yourself to forget, you know. You say to yourself that you are not going to dwell on something and then the mind—the bits of the mind that are in charge of forgetting, so to speak—do the rest. The memory is suppressed, I suppose."

"So?"

"So you tell yourself that the fact that you and Cat had the relationship that you did is something you are not going to think about—that you're going to forget it. And then you will."

For a few moments Jamie said nothing. He was looking up at the ceiling now, thinking; or perhaps trying to forget.

"Maybe I don't want to," he muttered.

She gently withdrew her hand. "Then don't."

She felt a stab of disappointment, and she wished that she had not started to discuss the subject with him. Perhaps his instinct had been better: to say nothing, to leave it where it lay. The past was so powerful that sometimes when we chose to deny its potency it reminded us just who we were—its creatures.

She crossed the room and drew open the curtains, flooding the room with morning light. "Let me make you something special for breakfast," she said.

He sat up in bed, reaching for the cup of tea she had brought him. "Mushrooms," he said. "And scrambled eggs with some of that truffle oil in them—not a lot, just a few drops."

"And?"

"And a piece of very thin toast."

"And?"

"And a mug of Jamaican coffee with really hot milk. Not milk heated up in the microwave but scalded in a pan."

She smiled, and watched him get out of bed, his limbs

caught in the sunlight. I do not deserve somebody so beautiful, she thought, or so gentle; but none of us deserves good fortune, perhaps—it comes our way, dispensed at random, irrespective of what prayer flags we string across our mountain passes, what chants and imprecations we devise; it simply comes.

She stopped herself. Do I really believe that? I do not, and never have; in thinking it I have simply succumbed to a defeatist impulse. Even young children understand that often, if not always, we get what we deserve; Charlie, at his tender age, is beginning to learn that good behaviour is rewarded with a treat. And there was no reason why she should not have been given Jamie: she was attractive and she had looked after herself. Jamie himself had referred to what he called her Pre-Raphaelite beauty; "Holman Hunt might have painted you," he had said. She had protested that she found this most unlikely, but she had been flattered, and she had filed the remark away in her memory, to be taken out and reflected upon, as such compliments should be, when one was feeling one's worst, on a bad-hair day.

ISABEL HAD OPENED UP the delicatessen by the time Eddie arrived. Eddie always looked sleepy when he turned up for work. He was rarely late, but he still managed to look as if he had tumbled out of bed only a few minutes ago—which he might well have done. Isabel knew that Eddie did not eat breakfast. "I'm not hungry," he had said when she asked him. "The thought of breakfast makes me ill." But within half an hour or so she would see him pop a piece of cheese or a slice of Parma ham into his mouth.

"Breakfast?" she asked.

"It's different," said Eddie, slicing off another sliver of cheese.

"There's nothing wrong with having a snack."

When Eddie came in that morning Isabel noticed that he had a scratch on his face—a line of punctured red that ran down from the cheekbone and ended just above the edge of the jaw. Her eye went straight to it, and he noticed that, as he instinctively reached up to touch his cheek.

Isabel caught his eye. "Have you washed that?"

Eddie looked away. "Washed what?" he mumbled.

Isabel touched her own cheek, as if in sympathy. "That scratch. Let me take a look at it. Cat keeps some disinfectant in the cupboard."

She took a step towards Eddie to get a better view of the scratch, but he withdrew sharply. "I only wanted to look at it," said Isabel. "It won't hurt to put something on it. It looks a bit angry to me."

"You can't just go round putting disinfectant on people," said Eddie.

Isabel smiled. "I suppose you can't. Or at least not on people you don't know . . ." She imagined herself in the street, dabbing disinfectant on passers-by, as a religious proselyte might thrust a tract into a stranger's hand; absurd thought. But surely it was just as intrusive for people to buttonhole others with a view to converting them to a religion. She had often thought of the massive presumption of such earnest missionaries, that they should imagine that a few words from them should be able to overturn another's whole theology or philosophy of life. Did they really expect that one would say, "My goodness, so I've got it wrong all my life!" The offensive presumption here was that the one's world-view should be so shallow as to fold up in the face of the approach of the other. But that is how ideas spread, she supposed, and sooner or later if you put your proposition to total strangers you would come across one who was ready for plucking by the first person of conviction who crossed his path.

Isabel remembered the circumstances of a well-known essayist's conversion to communism. He had gone to a party and drunk too much. He had woken up in the company of a woman he did not really like. And when he went to the window to look out on to the street, he saw that the weather was freezing; subsequently he found out that the engine of the car he had borrowed from a friend had frozen and was ruined—he had forgotten to put in antifreeze. In such circumstances communism offered a fresh start—a cleaning of the old slate—and he converted.

She became aware that Eddie was looking at her resentfully. "All right," she said. "It's your own business."

"It is."

Isabel felt momentary annoyance. All she had done was to offer help, and yet he was treating her as if she had proposed some sweeping infringement of his autonomy. "As a matter of interest, Eddie," she said, "if you saw me coming in with a scratch on my face, would you ask me what happened? Would you want to help?"

He continued to stare at her.

"Well?" pressed Isabel.

"I don't know," he said. "Maybe."

Isabel felt that she had proved her point. "So you understand, then, why I offered. You'd do the same for me." She paused. "How did it happen, Eddie?"

Eddie turned away. "A branch. I was down near the canal and I walked past this bush—you know, one of those fruit ones, blackberries—and it scratched me. The council should cut those things."

"Oh well," said Isabel. "A scratch from a thorn shouldn't be too dangerous. But you should watch it. If it starts to throb, then that means that it's infected and you should go to the doctor."

Eddie seemed relieved that the interrogation was over. He went behind the counter and placed the cheese-cutting boards in position. Then, while he filled the large espresso machine with water from a jug and ran a cloth over the steam nozzle, Isabel went through to Cat's office to retrieve the cash float from the lock-up cupboard. She noticed the disinfectant on the shelf—the label showed a picture of a boy having his knee attended to by a concerned mother—*for minor day-to-day cuts and bruises.* They were innocent, those day-to-day cuts and bruises; Eddie had been scratched, and although she had initially believed his explanation of how the scratch came about, suddenly she began to doubt him. It was the same with those black eyes that people claimed were the result of walking into a door; usually they were the result of domestic violence, or of a brawl somewhere. Somebody had scratched Eddie—a girl-friend? Isabel wondered. Probably—Eddie had had that rather sinister-looking girl and although she was no longer with him, he might well have replaced her with somebody similar.

She went to the counter and put the float in the till. It was now nine o'clock, the delicatessen's official opening time, and she nodded to Eddie to take the door off the latch. It was not unusual for customers to appear within minutes of their opening—these were people who called in for a cup of coffee

on their way to work, and would spend a few minutes reading the papers at one of the small tables at the far end of the
delicatessen.

It proved to be a busy morning. Shortly after eleven Cat
telephoned to say that the gas board engineers had not come yet
and that she was sure now that they would not arrive until much
later that afternoon.

"What if we have an explosion?" she complained. "What
then?"

"We must just hope that you don't explode," said Isabel.
"That is all we can do."

"It's no laughing matter," snapped Cat.

Isabel apologised. It had not been a joke; she had meant
that she did not want the flat to explode. Cat was being unduly
literal in assuming that the reference to her home was a reference to her. She had offended Eddie, and now Cat. Yet on neither occasion did she think that the offence was warranted; they
were both too sensitive, she decided, or—and it was a worrying
thought—was she the insensitive one?

They did not stop for lunch, as the delicatessen was at its
busiest between noon and two in the afternoon. Then it slackened off, and Isabel provided cover at the counter while Eddie
ate a sandwich in Cat's office, his feet up on the table. She said
nothing about that; when Cat was away it was understandable
that mice would play.

Eddie finished his lunch and it was Isabel's turn for a break.
She poured herself a cup of coffee, telephoned Jamie to check
that Charlie was all right and then sat down with her coffee and
a cheese roll at one of the tables. A customer had left an early
copy of the *Evening News,* the local paper, on the desk, and she

paged through this. It was a parochial paper, as local papers should be, and Isabel rarely found anything of interest in it. On this occasion, though, a small headline on an inner page caught her eye: *Woman Attacked in Morningside*. She began to read the text below. A young woman, it reported, had been attacked the previous night near the Royal Edinburgh Hospital; she had fought with her assailant and he had run off. He was a slight man, she said, but that was all the description she managed. It had been dark.

Isabel read the article again and then looked up towards the counter. Eddie smiled at her.

No, this was completely inconceivable; it was ridiculous. Eddie was a gentle young man who would never attack anybody. He was more likely to be attacked himself, she thought, and indeed she believed that he had been, some time ago. Plenty of people were scratched, one way or another, and even if Eddie was making up the story of the bramble bush, and even if the scratch came from a set of fingernails, it was unthinkable that the attacker could be him. But then she remembered the expression: *someone's brother, someone's son*. Those who committed horrendous crimes were still someone's brother, someone's son; or someone's mild, inoffensive assistant at someone's delicatessen.

Isabel drained her coffee cup and rose to her feet. A woman had come in and was fingering the avocado pears, surreptitiously giving them a squeeze.

"Please don't do that," said Isabel mildly, as she came up behind the customer. "It bruises them."

The woman turned round and looked defiantly at Isabel. "How do you expect me to tell if they're ripe?"

"You can feel them very gently. Tap them if you must—use a finger. But don't squeeze them hard."

The woman's nostrils flared. "I have never been so insulted in my life," she said.

Isabel recoiled. "Oh, please! I'm not insulting you. I merely asked you not to squeeze the fruit. We have to throw out an awful lot, you know, because people have done what you've done."

The woman turned on her heel. "There are plenty of other places to buy things," she said. "Places where the assistants don't insult you quite so much." She spat out the word *assistants*.

Isabel resisted the temptation to laugh. "I'm very sorry . . . ," she began. But the woman was not listening. She looked helplessly at Eddie, who was smirking.

"What did you say to her?" Eddie asked, after the woman had left.

"I simply asked her not to squeeze the avocados," said Isabel. "And she flew off the handle."

"You must have offended her," said Eddie. "People are so touchy."

Isabel raised an eyebrow. We see the touchiness of others and not our own—obviously. Eddie watched her with the air of somebody who had seen another disgrace herself through impetuosity or sheer foolishness.

I don't have to do this, thought Isabel. I really don't have to put up with all these hypersensitive people. This was Cat's business, and Eddie and all these difficult customers were her problem and not Isabel's. She saw that Eddie was still looking at her. There was something odd about his stare, and for a moment Isabel thought: What if he knows that I know? What if he knows that I've read the report about the attack? What if he realises that now that I know, I'm a danger to him—a danger that can only be solved by . . . She brought this train of thought to an end. It was absurd, and she would not entertain any such absurd, fanciful thoughts about Eddie; she simply would not.

BY THE END OF THE DAY, Eddie had become quite talkative. His earlier surliness had disappeared, and even the scratch on his face looked as if it had calmed down. Isabel tried not to think about that, and largely succeeded: her imaginings had been ridiculous, anyway, and she felt not unlike one of those nervous women who keep phoning the police about the men they were convinced were hiding under their beds. Wishful thinking, the police might say, although they were always so tactful in such cases.

As she prepared to lock up, Eddie stood behind the counter, untying the strings of his apron.

"Cat washes that for you, does she?" asked Isabel, nodding in the direction of the apron.

"She's meant to," said Eddie. "But she always forgets. So I give it to my mum. She does all my washing."

"You're lucky," said Isabel.

"But you have somebody to do all your washing too," Eddie said. "Cat says that you have this lady who does everything."

Isabel winced. "I'm also lucky. Not that Grace does everything. But she does a lot."

"It must be great being rich," said Eddie. There was no envy in his voice; it was just an observation.

Isabel smiled to cover her embarrassment. "I'm not really rich," she said. "Again, I'm lucky. And if you have money, you know, you tend not to talk about it—or throw it around. If you've got anything approaching a conscience, you try to use it well."

"Well, I'll never be rich," said Eddie, dusting a small patch of flour off his apron. "Not that it matters."

"Exactly," said Isabel.

Eddie folded the apron and slipped it into a plastic bag. "Cat says that she has to be careful. She's got a bit of money and she doesn't want a boyfriend who's interested in the money rather than her. That's what she told me, anyway."

"She's very wise," said Isabel, realising that she had never before said that of her niece, and perhaps she should have. Wisdom came in different forms, she reminded herself. "There's nothing worse than a gold-digger." She paused, before continuing: "Is there anyone at the moment?" She intended to sound casual, but she suspected that Eddie could sense the depth of her interest.

He looked at her sideways. "Cat?"

"Yes."

"Yes. There is someone."

Isabel waited for him to expand on this. After a while she encouraged him gently. "Do you like him?"

Eddie shrugged. "Her boyfriends don't seem to last long, do they? Do I like him? Well, I haven't really seen much of him. This one has only been round here once or twice. He's too busy, I think."

Isabel probed gently. "Busy doing what?"

"You're not going to believe this," Eddie said with a smile. "He's a tightrope walker!"

Isabel said nothing. She did believe it. It was typical of Cat, even if it was somewhat original.

She picked up the keys. Eddie was ready to leave now; he

had had enough of talking about Cat, and the evening lay ahead of him. "A funambulist!" muttered Isabel.

Eddie, moving towards the door, stopped. "What's that?"

Isabel explained. "Cat's new boyfriend. A funambulist. One who walks on tightropes."

Like all of us, she thought. In the final analysis.

CHAPTER FIVE

RODERICK MᶜCAIG's second birthday party was to take place at three o'clock on Sunday afternoon, with carriages at five. Isabel smiled at the thought: *baby* carriages.

Jamie was not enthusiastic. "Do we have to go? I don't like that woman, you know. And Charlie hates Roderick. Do you really have to sit through the birthday party of somebody who tries to pull your shoes off?"

Isabel conceded that Roderick was, at present, not perhaps the friendliest company for Charlie, but pointed out that there would be other children there. "He's got to start making friends at some point. Who has he got at the moment?"

"Me," said Jamie lamely. "You. Grace."

"You can stay behind if you like," said Isabel. "I don't want to force you. I can say that you couldn't make it, which will not exactly be a lie. The truth would be that you couldn't make it because you couldn't summon up the enthusiasm. Minty won't care." It occurred to her, though, that Minty might well mind. She had looked at Jamie with undisguised interest, and she might be disappointed if he were not there. And then the further thought occurred: perhaps that was why the invitation had been issued in the first place. Perhaps it had nothing to do with Roderick and Charlie, but everything to do with Jamie.

"I'll come," said Jamie. "It may have its moments."

They dressed Charlie with care. Isabel thought that he might wear the kilt that she had recently bought for him—a small strip of Macpherson tartan, expertly pleated and complemented by a tiny sporran and ornate Celtic kilt-pin. The garment had been specially designed for a wearer who was still in nappies, thereby resolving, in a very evident way, the age-old question of what was worn under the kilt, at least in this case.

"Look at him," said Jamie. He pointed to Charlie, who was standing up unsteadily, getting the feel of his new outfit. "Aren't you proud, seeing him in his kilt?"

Isabel was. She knew that one's nationality was an accident of history and that it was difficult to justify being proud of a heritage—one never did anything to deserve being Scottish or American or whatever one was. But national pride was something that people did feel—they could not help it—and she felt it now on Charlie's behalf. And it was a form of love, she decided; loving one's country, one's culture, amounted to loving a particular group of people, and that, surely, was not something for which one had to apologise.

They set off, with Isabel at the wheel of the car, Jamie at her side and Charlie strapped into his child-seat in the back. He liked the car, and chuckled with excitement as they started the drive to Minty's house. Halfway there, with the Pentlands rising on one side of the road and the hills of Peebleshire off to the other, Charlie suddenly said "olive" again. Jamie turned round and smiled at him. Charlie stared back, as if surprised by his father's sudden attention.

"Olive?" Jamie said. "Olive, Charlie?"

Charlie said nothing, fixing Jamie with the disconcerting, utterly fearless stare that only babies and very young children are capable of.

"No olives, Charlie," said Isabel over her shoulder. "Olives all gone."

"Olives all gone," repeated Jamie. And then, turning to Isabel, he said, "That would make a lovely title for a song, you know. 'Olives All Gone.' It's very poignant."

Isabel agreed. "And the words?"

"I'll have to think," Jamie said. "I'll tell you once I've composed it." The song would come to him, he was sure; it always happened when a line struck him in this way. "Olives All Gone"—it would be about loss, of course, as so many songs were; about what we once had, but had no more.

It did not take long to reach Minty's house, which was just short of Carlops, a small village twelve miles or so out of Edinburgh. It was in a stretch of country that Isabel particularly liked. Here the land spread out to the south and east, gently rolling fields and folds, green here, ripening brown there, becoming blue in the distance. It was a landscape of mists and distances, beneath a sky that was somehow washed, attenuated, softened. It was a landscape that had been the same for a very long time, dotted with farmhouses and shepherds' cottages that were there in Robert Louis Stevenson's time, and in the time of Hume. People here did what they had always done—tending this part of Scotland, keeping it fertile, handing it on to provide for a new generation. It was a place of custom and fond usage.

Minty had given very detailed instructions, which Isabel had written down on the piece of paper she now handed to Jamie. He used these to direct her along the narrow farm track, pressed in upon by hedges, that led off the main road and past a large stand of Scots pines.

"That's it," said Isabel. "Look."

Jamie drew in his breath. "Is that her place?"

"I assume so," said Isabel. "I never imagined Minty in cramped accommodations, but all the same . . ."

The house was several hundred yards back from the farm track, which meandered off towards a low byre and a huddle of sheds in the distance. A driveway led from the track to the house; this was lined with rambling rhododendron bushes, flowering in clusters of pink and pale red. Beyond the bushes, a lawn swept up to the house itself, which was Georgian and far more imposing than the larger gentleman-farmers' houses of the area. At the time of its construction this would have been the house of a family on its way up; not quite in the league of those who aspired to a country mansion, but heading in that direction.

They turned off the farm track and made their way up the somewhat smoother driveway and to the parking place at the side of the house. There were already several prosperous-looking vehicles, which made Isabel's green Swedish car look distinctly shabby. One of these cars had evidently arrived only a few minutes before, as a woman was still in the process of unloading a small child and a basketful of supporting paraphernalia. She looked in Isabel's direction, hesitated for a moment and then gave a friendly wave as she made her way into the house.

They approached the front door, which had been left open. Minty was standing in the hall, talking to one of the other mothers. She broke off and welcomed Isabel and Jamie warmly.

"You've not been here before, have you?" she said.

Isabel shook her head. "No. But what a lovely place."

Minty looked pleased. "We searched and searched, and eventually we found this just as we were seriously thinking of going to live in Gullane. Edinburgh *sur mer,* as you know. Then this came up. It was just what we were after." She smiled at Isabel and then turned to give Jamie an even bigger smile. "Do have a look around. But it might be best later on, when I can show you. We need to get the children to the table. The masses require to be fed."

They went through to the kitchen, a vast square room floored with large stone slabs. The room was dominated by a long refectory table at which places for the party had been laid. Most of the small guests were now seated—all eight of them— with a parent beside them to feed them and to keep the food off the floor. Jamie took Charlie over to the table and sat beside him; Isabel watched from the side of the room.

As Charlie and Jamie appeared to be enjoying themselves without her, Isabel moved across to a French window to look out at the garden. The kitchen wing was at the back of the house, a Victorian addition that gave on to a small square of grass. On the other side of this lawn was a large kitchen garden, its surrounding wall built in the grey stone of eastern Scotland, several feet higher than head height. Against its outer side were espaliered apple trees and, in between them, white climbing roses, now in full bloom. Through the open doorway in the wall, she could make out what looked like fruit bushes, some of which were covered with nets against marauding birds.

Isabel became aware that somebody was standing behind her, and she turned to find Minty, holding a plate.

"I made these cheese scones for the adult palate," she said.

"Everything for the children, I'm afraid, is sweet. There are no carrots, I confess. I'm not the most modern of mothers."

Isabel laughed. "I suspect that their little hearts sink if they get carrots at a birthday party."

Minty held the plate of scones out to Isabel. "Do try one. I used Parmesan. The recipe called for Cheddar, but I find Cheddar so dull."

"I suppose it is," agreed Isabel. She felt almost guilty over her remark, which seemed to dismiss a whole tradition of cheese-making. So, as she took a scone, she added, "Some people like Cheddar, though, and they don't think it's that dull."

"Oh, but it is," said Minty.

Isabel took a bite of her scone. She was not sure if she wanted to get into an argument with Minty about the merits or otherwise of Cheddar, and so she simply said, *"A chacun son fromage."*

Minty looked at her. "And mine is definitely not Cheddar."

Isabel said nothing. The scone tasted very good, and she decided to compliment Minty on it; it would be a way of ending the debate about Cheddar. But Minty, who had now put the plate down on a nearby sideboard, suddenly took Isabel by the arm, holding her just below the elbow. Isabel felt a momentary shock; surely a disagreement about Cheddar would not lead to a *fight* about Cheddar. For a moment she imagined the headlines in the press—it would be a gift for a sensationalist sub-editor: *Edinburgh Ladies Slog It Out in Georgian Mansion over Cheese Disagreement; Shocked Kids Look On.* Minty's grip, though, was not confrontational, but conspiratorial.

"Let me show you the garden. Come."

Minty did not wait for an answer but gently propelled her guest towards the door. They went outside and crossed the lawn towards the entrance to the walled garden. A child's toy, a broken helicopter, lay sideways on the lawn, plastic rotors bent from impact; ditched on a sea of green.

"This garden was one of the things that really sold the house to us," said Minty. "There's something special about a walled garden, don't you think? And it's very useful here, of course, with the wind that comes up from Lanarkshire. Biggar, you know, is one of the coldest places in Scotland. Really freezing."

They reached the doorway into the garden and Minty gestured for Isabel to go in first. Isabel ducked, although the doorway was quite high enough to accommodate her easily, and found herself faced with the fruit bushes that she had seen from the house. There were more of them than she had imagined, though, as they occupied at least half the area of the garden, the other half being given over to salad vegetables—lettuces, red and green; kale; spring onions.

"Very functional," said Minty.

Isabel thought of her failure as a gardener. "I should grow something," she remarked. "Even a few potatoes. But we have a fox, you see, and he digs things up."

"Get rid of him," said Minty. Then she added, "We had a fox too."

For a moment Isabel imagined a fox in this domain, using one of the espaliered apple trees to get to the top of the wall, sleeking his way along the top, and then finding his way down into the garden itself. What harm would he have caused? There was plenty of room for him to dig, to make his earth, without impinging on Minty's vegetables. Four words showed that this woman, this successful banker, had no heart, Isabel thought: *Get rid of him.* Four words.

Then Minty said, "I couldn't bring myself to have him . . .

well, they don't mince their words in the country, the farmer offered to shoot him. I said no."

I have misjudged you, Isabel said to herself. Again, I have misjudged you.

"I know how it is," said Isabel. "I rather like him."

"I wasn't suggesting that you do him in," Minty explained. "But you can get somebody—there's a man in Dalkeith, I think—who will come and collect him from town and release him somewhere in the country."

"I've heard of that," said Isabel. "But I wondered whether he would really . . ."

"We have to trust people," interrupted Minty. And it seemed to Isabel that as she said this, the other woman looked at her more pointedly.

Isabel wondered what had happened to Minty's fox. Had the man from Dalkeith called?

"What . . ."

Minty seemed to have an ability to anticipate questions. "He died a natural death. I found him on the other side of the wall. At first I thought he was sleeping and then I saw that he was quite still. His grave is down by the burn over there." She pointed away from the house. Isabel looked; it would be a fine place to be buried, she felt, with those hills crouching on the horizon like great sleeping foxes, vulpine deities, perhaps, the gods to whom foxes prayed at night. A good place for a fox.

Isabel sighed. "Poor fox." It was a trite thing to say, she knew, but what else could one say about living and then dying, as we—and foxes—all must do.

Minty was silent. It was a strange moment: there was a wind, not a strong one, just a breath, and Isabel felt it against her cheek; a wind from over there, from the hills that ran towards the coast, towards the North Sea, towards the edge of Scotland. Then Minty spoke. "I don't know how to say this," she said.

Isabel looked at her enquiringly.

"I wondered whether I should raise it with you at all," Minty went on. "I decided I could. You seem . . . well, you seem so sympathetic."

Isabel was about to protest. She wanted to say "I'm not really," but when she opened her mouth all she said was, "Oh."

"Yes," said Minty. "I've got plenty of friends—close ones too. But I don't feel that I can burden any of them with this. I don't know how they would handle it."

Isabel ran over the possibilities in her mind. Matrimonial difficulties? That was the sort of matter one was usually worried about raising with friends. But what possible insight could Minty imagine that she, Isabel, could bring to the matrimonial problems of a person whom she barely knew? Financial problems? Surely not; not with this house and the private whisky label and the bank.

"You can speak to me," said Isabel. "I don't know whether I'll be much help, but you can certainly speak to me."

Minty thanked her. Then she continued, "The reason I thought that I should speak to you is because I know you have helped various people. Remember how we met—over that awful business with that young man who fell in the Usher Hall? Remember? And then somebody else told me about something you had done for another person. So I thought that you might not mind if I told you."

"Told me what?" Isabel prompted.

"Or asked you, rather. Have you ever been frightened?"

In her surprise, Isabel blurted out, "Me?"

Minty bent down to pick a small blue flower growing by the side of the path. "Wild hyacinth," she said, showing the flower to Isabel. "Uninvited."

Isabel glanced at the flower. She remembered something she had read somewhere, some generalisation about women picking flowers and men letting them be. It was Lawrence, she thought; women were always picking flowers in his novels, watched by men. "Bavarian Gentians." What a strange poem. *Not every man has gentians in his house* . . . Of course they didn't . . .

"We've all been frightened at some time or other," Isabel said. "And I'm no exception."

Minty dropped the flower, dusting her hands as if to remove its traces. "Of course. Momentarily. It's different, though, living with fear. All the time."

"I suppose it is," said Isabel. Was Minty in that position? It was difficult to imagine this competent, successful woman living with fear; it just seemed somewhat unlikely.

"Fear like that," said Minty, "is really odd. It's there with you all the time—you don't forget it. It's like . . . well, I suppose it's like a thundercloud. It's the backdrop to everything you do."

Isabel stopped walking. It was time, she thought, to find out what Minty was driving at. She was frightened—obviously—but why? Threats of legal action? Blackmail? The possibility occurred to Isabel as she looked at the house. It was respectability and success rendered in stone and mortar, but such edifices could so easily be toppled, brought down, by a few words.

"What's frightening you?" Isabel asked. "Is that what you want to talk about?"

The directness of Isabel's question seemed to irritate Minty.

"I was just trying to explain," she said. "People don't necessarily know what it's like."

"I can imagine," said Isabel quickly. "But what is it? What's making you feel that way?"

"Somebody's targeting me," said Minty.

"How?"

"Small things. Or quite big, sometimes. A sudden investigation by the tax authorities. That often means that somebody has given them a tip-off or made an allegation." She paused, looking sideways at Isabel. "Unjustified, of course. But very annoying—and expensive. Accountants' fees."

"But you can't really tell, surely," said Isabel. "They do random checks, don't they?"

Minty ignored this. "Then my PA resigned. I relied on her and she suddenly announced she was leaving. A better offer. I said that we would match whatever they—whoever they were—had offered and add five per cent on top of that. But she wouldn't even discuss it. I think she was threatened. Simple as that. Scared off."

Isabel admitted that this was rather strange. But, again, people changed jobs and had their reasons for not explaining why. Privately, the possibility crossed her mind that Minty's PA disliked her, as one might; Jamie certainly did, and Isabel had in the past.

Minty nodded. "Yes, yes, there are plenty of reasons for getting a new job. But there have been other things—quite a lot of them. The worst was last week. I came back from work in the evening and discovered that somebody had ordered flowers to be delivered to the house."

It now occurred to Isabel that Minty was not well. Paranoia

showed itself in odd ways—she had had an uncle on her father's side, a retired stockbroker, who had insisted that the postman was hiding his mail, and had eventually attacked and bitten him. The postman had been remarkably understanding and had joked about the frequency with which he and his colleagues had been bitten by dogs, suggesting that to be bitten by household- ers was really only a small escalation. That attitude—and an understanding procurator fiscal—had avoided an embarrassing prosecution. Uncle Fergus had spent his remaining days in a nursing home, quite content, it seemed, although suspicious to the end that the home's matron was intercepting his letters. She, though, had been as many matrons used to be, built like a galleon and with attitudes to match. He would never have dared bite her, Isabel's father had pointed out, and had then added the observation that deterrence and fear were major inhibitors of crime, and that criminologists might care to reflect on that.

"Flowers," said Isabel quietly.

Minty's eyes flashed with anger at the recollection. "In the shape of a wreath," she said.

Isabel was silent.

"A wreath," Minty said again. "A funeral wreath. And there were other things too. A fire in one of the greenhouses, for example. It was started deliberately. We were away at the time."

"Who might have done this?" asked Isabel. "Have you any idea?"

The question seemed to distress Minty, and it was a few moments before she answered. "I think I do."

Isabel waited. Minty was looking away from her, out towards the hills.

"Why don't you go to the police?" She realised, of course, that this question was seldom helpful. In an ordered, middle-class world there was an assumption that people could go to the police and receive the help and protection that the police are meant to provide. But that was not the world as it really was. Often there was nothing the police could do; often there was nothing that the police wanted to do. Much of the time, people simply had to look after themselves.

Minty sniffed. "What help could they offer? None. And they'd treat it as some sort of neighbourhood dispute, you know. They don't like to get involved in people's private arguments."

Isabel knew that this was true. The police liked to talk of a light touch, but that light touch could mean inaction.

She realised that Minty had not revealed the precise nature of her suspicions. So she asked again, "Who is it?"

Minty turned and looked directly at Isabel. When she spoke, her voice was lowered. "I haven't talked to anybody about this. And I don't know why I'm telling you." She stopped herself. "Well, I do, I suppose. There's something about you . . . Well, I trust you. You can keep things to yourself, can't you?"

Isabel nodded. "I hope so."

Minty added a qualification. "Of course I assume that you'll tell Jamie. That's all right. But otherwise . . ."

"I won't. I just won't."

Minty hesitated for a few seconds more. Then she made her decision. "Blackmail."

"I wondered if it would be that," said Isabel. "When you started to tell me—"

Minty interrupted her. "Not for money. Not that sort of blackmail."

"Oh?"

"It's more personal than that."

Isabel reached out to touch Minty gently on the arm. She

was not sure that she wanted to be burdened with this particular confidence. Minty, after all, was hardly more than a stranger to her. "You don't have to tell me, if you don't want to."

But Minty had clearly decided. "I know I don't have to. But I'd like to." She paused. "It's to do with Roderick."

Isabel drew in her breath. "They've threatened to harm him?"

Minty shook her head. "No. It's about him. You see, Roderick is . . . well, Roderick isn't Gordon's."

It made immediate sense. Minty may be very much the successful banker, but she was a woman, too, with a husband.

"There," continued Minty. "I've said it. I've told you something I haven't told anybody else, not a soul. Roderick is the result of an affair I had with another man. It didn't last long, but it was a full-blown affair and I became pregnant. I didn't tell Gordon—obviously—and he thinks that he's Roderick's father."

"Are you sure?"

Minty looked up sharply. "Sure? Of course I am. Why shouldn't I be?"

Isabel found it difficult to put it delicately. "Because if you were still with Gordon when you were having the affair with . . . with this other man, then might it not be possible that . . ." She left the question unfinished. It hardly needed to be spelled out further, she thought.

Minty laughed. She seemed unembarrassed by the suggestion. "Oh, I see what you mean. Well, that goes with the territory, doesn't it? If a married woman has an affair, then that could happen. All right. He could be Gordon's, too, but he isn't."

"You've had a test?"

Minty explained that she had not. The thought had crossed her mind, but she had dismissed it, initially because she did not want to know the information, and then later because she knew already. "I don't need a laboratory to tell me who Roderick takes after. You just have to look at him. Everything. Shape of head. Eyes. Everything."

Isabel knew what she meant. Charlie was Jamie's son; it was something that a mother simply could tell. "And now some-body's found out and is making demands for money?"

Minty closed her eyes. "Not found out. Knew all along."

Isabel waited for her to explain.

"The father," she said. She added, "Not money. He wants Roderick."

Isabel and Minty stared at one another for a few moments. Then Minty shrugged. "So there we are," she said. "But let's go inside and see what's going on. Did I ask you to sign the visitors' book?"

"No."

Minty took Isabel's arm. "Well then I must. Let's do it now, otherwise it gets forgotten, and I like to have a record of every-body who comes to see us here."

ONLY LATER THAT EVENING did Isabel tell Jamie about her conversation with Minty. She had wanted to speak to him about it in the car on the way home, but he had been full of what happened at the party and she did not have the opportunity. While Isabel had been out in the garden with Minty, Roderick McCaig, nominally under the control of his father, had thrown a piece of cake at Charlie. Apparently unsurprised at this behav-iour on the part of his host, Charlie had calmly picked up the crumbs of the missile and eaten them, causing an outburst of rage from Roderick, who clearly regarded the cake as still be-longing to him. The child sitting next to Roderick had then been sick over Roderick's trousers, which had not led to any improvement in the young host's mood.

"It's a jungle down there," said Jamie, smiling. "We forget what it's like to be two."

"Selvan," muttered Isabel.

Jamie raised an eyebrow. "Sylvan? As in forests?"

"No, *selvan.* It's a word that I think should exist in English, but doesn't quite. *Selva* exists in English—just—for Amazonian forest, from the Spanish word *selva.* So I think we should be able to say *selvan* for forests that are too jungly to be called sylvan."

Jamie smiled wryly. Isabel occasionally made new words when it suited her, and he found himself adopting at least the more apt of these. The pad under a toe, for instance, was a *gummer,* a neologism she had coined one day when inspecting Charlie's tiny feet. And the crook of a bassoon, that curious curved pipe that held the reed, she had called a *bahook,* a word which seemed admirably suited to its purpose, even if it had to be used carefully—and never diminutively—in order to avoid confusion with the Scots word *bahookies,* a word that bordered on the vulgar, if it did not actually tip over that border. "Well, it's certainly *selvan* down amongst the two-year-olds," he said.

"And up here too, amongst the . . ." She almost said *forty-year-olds,* but stopped herself, and said, instead, "adults."

"Meaning?" he asked.

She was about to explain about her conversation with Minty, when Charlie started to cry in the back of the car and Jamie had to turn round to attend to him. So it was not until later, over dinner, that she told him of Minty's unexpected frankness in the walled garden. Jamie listened attentively, sipping on the glass of New Zealand wine Isabel had poured him.

She was trying the products of new vineyards and had chanced upon one they both liked.

When she finished, Jamie asked her whether she had believed Minty. "I'm not sure about her," he said. "Even if you believe what she says—and it sounds rather unlikely, I would have thought—you still have to wonder why she's telling you all this. What's it got to do with you?"

He asked the question but almost immediately realised that he knew the answer. Isabel was about to interfere in matters that did not concern her. She did it all the time, as a moth will approach the flame, unable to stop herself. She had to help; it was just the way she was.

Isabel sensed what he was thinking. "I didn't commit myself," she protested. "But it was a real *cri de coeur*. She was frightened—she really was."

"But what are you meant to do?" asked Jamie. "Why doesn't she hire somebody? A close-security guard or whatever they call themselves. She's got the cash."

"It was difficult for her to speak about it," said Isabel. "I don't think that she would find it easy to open up to a total stranger."

Jamie sighed. "Isabel, you're a lovely, helpful person. Everybody knows that, and it means that anybody could take advantage of you. Minty's as sharp as all get-out—she knows that you're a soft touch."

Isabel looked into her glass. "All I said was that I'd look into it. I gave no promises."

Jamie shrugged. "Well, all that I would say is be careful. Don't get in too deep. That woman's dangerous."

"Come on!" said Isabel. "She's ambitious and a bit pleased with herself, but she's not dangerous."

"Well, her son is," countered Jamie, and then laughed. "Just don't get sucked in."

"If I'm sucked in, I'm sure I'll be spat out," said Isabel.

Jamie was not sure what she meant by this, and neither, in fact, was she. So he drained his glass and stood up.

"Let's go and sing something. Or rather, you accompany me and I'll sing. What would you like to hear?"

Isabel thought for a moment. " 'King Fareweel'?" she asked.

Jamie agreed. She had enquired about the words a couple of days earlier, on Dundas Street, outside the Scottish Gallery. Why was she thinking about Jacobite songs?

"Because I saw a picture of Charles Edward Stuart," Isabel explained. "The song came into my mind. That's all."

She sat down at the piano and played; Jamie sang. And when he got to the lines about Prestonpans, she faltered and stopped, her hands unmoving on the keyboard.

> At Prestonpans they laid their plans,
> And the Heilan lads they were lyin' ready,
> Like the wind frae Skye they bid them fly,
> And monie's the braw laddie lost his daddy.

"I'm sorry," she said. "I don't find this song very easy." It was too painful to think of those boys deprived of their fathers, and these simple words made her think of how Jamie was so relishing being Charlie's father. Charlie, her braw laddie, and his daddy.

"All right," said Jamie. "Let me sit down there." He gestured to the piano stool, which was wide enough for two. Isabel shifted over, and he sat beside her. He reached forward and played a chord, and then moved to another. "That's it," he said.

"That's what?"

He repeated the chords. "That's the tune I was going to compose," he said. " 'Olives All Gone.' Listen."

He played a simple, rather sad melody; she thought it beautiful.

> *Olives all gone, olives all gone,*
> *The olives I loved, now they are gone,*
> *Summer will bring more, you say,*
> *The trees will bear fruit;*
> *That may be true, my dear,*
> *But the olives are gone.*

Isabel listened, solemnly, then burst out laughing, to be joined by Jamie. She kissed him lightly on the cheek, and he kissed her back, not lightly, but with passion.

She said, "Oh," and he said, "Isabel Dalhousie, please marry me."

CHAPTER SIX

THAT SHE SAID YES, and then yes, again, changed everything, but also changed nothing. There was no change in her
world the next morning when she got out of bed to attend to
Charlie; she was still Isabel Dalhousie, mother, with a child to
look after and a house and philosophical review to run. She was
still responsible for her somewhat unruly garden, with its atten-
dant fox and rhododendron bushes; she was still the owner of a
green Swedish car; she was still the aunt of the rather unpredictable and sometimes moody Cat; she remained a patron of
Scottish Opera—to whom she reminded herself to send a
cheque; all of that was the same. But now she was Jamie's
fiancée it seemed to her that her future—that bit of ourselves in
which to a greater or lesser degree we live our lives—had
changed utterly. Now the future was no longer a vague,
uncharted territory; following Jamie's proposal on the piano
stool after the singing of his new song, "Olives All Gone," it had
acquired a shape.

Of course he had proposed once before. It was a year or so
earlier, when they had come out of Lyon & Turnbull's auction

rooms and made their way to the Portrait Gallery restaurant. He had told her that he wanted to marry her; she had been reluctant and had put him off, not because she had any doubts about him, or his seriousness, but because she was concerned—overly concerned, perhaps—about his freedom. That was when she was more sensitive than she now was about the difference in their ages. But now she barely thought about it. *So what?* people had said. And the liberating effect of those two, sometimes immensely dangerous words, had eventually been felt. So what if Jamie was a bit younger than she was; so what?

She had regretted her refusal and had hoped that he would mention marriage again, but he had not. Subsequently she considered broaching the subject herself, and on one or two occasions had come close to doing so, only to be inhibited by a vague sense of embarrassment. The problem was this: a woman did not ask a man to marry her, at least conventionally. There was no reason for it, of course, other than social custom, and Isabel knew that this was changing. People said that plenty of women were proposing to men—a third of all women, she had read— but prepared as she was to accept this figure, she could not think of anybody she actually knew who had proposed to their husbands. That did not mean that they had not done so, of course; there are some things that a large number of people do but few will admit to.

Entertaining subversive thoughts, for example, in a society in the grip of a political hegemony is not something that people will readily admit to, such is the power of intellectual intimidation; and yet people do have such thoughts. And when it comes to something that reflects on a person's desirability or popularity, then the tendency to reticence may be particularly marked.

Not everyone would care to admit to finding a spouse through an advertisement—or to be the subject of an advertisement; where is the romance in finding somebody through a lonely hearts column, cheek by jowl with Cars For Sale and Miscellaneous Bargains? Therein lay an admission of personal failure: the glamorous, the attractive, the sought-after, they had no need to advertise, whereas the inadequate and the unwanted did.

This thought crossed her mind—only to be quickly dismissed. It was not like that at all: there were plenty of perfectly eligible people who resorted to the services of an introduction agency or who advertised, and the results were often very successful. And there were plenty of women—there must be—who even if they proposed to a man might just as easily have received proposals themselves. No, the male monopoly of proposals, such as it was, was untenable and should be abandoned. And yet, and yet . . . the fact of the matter was that she had lacked the courage to propose to Jamie.

It did not matter. She could now say *my fiancé,* and they could exchange rings. She wanted to give him one too and had already seen one she liked in a jeweller's window in Bruntsfield. It was a discreet band made of rose-coloured gold; a lovely thing which it had never occurred to her she would eventually purchase. And when it came to a ring for her, when Jamie had mentioned it she had suggested something modest; she did not want him to spend too much. Of course, now that they were engaged the whole issue of the disparity in their respective means could disappear. Her possessions would be his by virtue of the marriage, and vice versa, of course; Jamie was about to become well-off.

There were other things to think about that were considerably less attractive than rings. Prominent amongst these was the question of what, if anything, to say to Cat. Isabel's niece had grudgingly accepted her aunt's relationship with Jamie, her former boyfriend, but both of them, by unspoken agreement, kept off the subject when in one another's company. Now Isabel had to decide whether to mention the engagement to Cat, or whether, in fear of her ire, to say nothing, leaving her to hear of it from somebody else. Eddie could be the messenger, perhaps, or even the personal announcements column of the *Scotsman* could break the news, not the bravest way out, but one that might make it easier for Cat to deal with news that almost certainly would not be welcome.

Even if she was still feeling euphoric—almost light-headed—after the evening's events, Isabel had several things to do that morning. Jamie had hinted that breakfast in bed would not go amiss—for the second time, she observed, in three days, but she agreed, none the less, to make it for him.

"When we're married," she said, "I take it that you won't expect breakfast in bed every day. Or will you?" She would make him breakfast in bed every day if that was what he wanted; of course she would. She would do anything for him.

"Of course not," he said. "This will be the very last time. I promise."

It sounded so strange to utter the words *when we are married*. As a moral philosopher, and arbiter, in that role, of hypothetical private lives, she was used to talking about the marriages of others. Now it was her—Isabel Dalhousie—whose future was being referred to. *Married*: the word had a delicious flavour to it; like the name of some exotic place—Dar-es-Salaam, Timbuktu, Popocatépetl. Marriage was a whole territory, a citizenship, to be adopted and inhabited, as the neophyte takes on the ways and thinking of a new religion. She had been married before, of course, but it had been something false, something quite different.

When she took the breakfast tray up to Jamie, she found that he had taken Charlie into bed with him and was reading to him, a story of a fox and his family who defeat a trio of unpleasant farmers. The story had been translated into Scots as *The Sleekit Mr. Tod,* and it was this version that Jamie was reading to Charlie. It was well beyond his understanding, of course, but the little boy was listening intently.

"I want him to understand Scots," said Jamie. "It's our language, after all."

Isabel smiled. "Of course. But he probably has to understand English first."

Jamie looked doubtful, and returned to the story. "A tod is a fox in Scots," he explained to Charlie. "That's why he's called Mr. Tod."

Charlie stared at his father with grave incomprehension.

Jamie began to read again. " 'And so the wee tod askit his faither, *Will there be dugs?* ' "

Isabel left the room, a smile lingering on her lips. *Will there be dugs?* Will there be dogs? That might be the dread question that every fox thinks when contemplating his end—if foxes are aware of mortality. *Will there be dugs, or will it be easy?*

LEAVING THE HOUSE shortly after ten, Isabel set off across the Meadows for George Square and the University Library. It was one of her favourite walks, as it afforded a good view of the skyline of the Old Town, a serrated line of chimney pots and spires that followed the ridge stretching down from the Castle to Holyrood. Behind that line was the Fife sky, across which scudded clouds blown in from the North Sea: wisps of grey, banks of darkening purple, splashes of white. Edinburgh could experience within a few minutes all four seasons, and the skies characteristic of each.

The University Library occupied the south side of a square that had been largely destroyed by the architectural vandalism of the sixties. One side of the square survived though, and this was bounded by a cobbled street running south to north. The buildings on this side, a perfect row of Georgian houses three storeys high, were now occupied by university offices and chaplaincies, by small academic departments and the University Press. Here too was a chapel for students of Orthodox faith, a basement transformed by icons and the chanting of priests; here, Isabel remembered, was the office of the Dictionary of the Older Scottish Tongue, a language that had words for this little bit of a small island, this land of rain and clouds and shafts of poetry.

Everywhere in this city, everywhere Isabel went, there were memories. As an eighteen-year-old she had come to a poetry reading on this side of the square, in the School of Scottish Studies; it was given by a Gaelic poet, who read in both his own language and English. Isabel had been unable to understand his Gaelic, but had followed it on a crib sheet thoughtfully provided by the organisers; it had sounded like the wind and waves breaking on the shore; the words of a language that suited its landscape. And then, in English, he had read a poem about the death of his mother, whose breath, he said, had run out, like the tide draining out of a sea loch; now he ached, he confessed, for the star that had been extinguished. To be the mother of a poet, she thought, must be a fine thing.

She went into the library, which, as a former member of the philosophy department—although a low-paid and junior one—she was still entitled to use. It was unusually quiet, as the undergraduate students were away for the summer, leaving the library to those studying for higher degrees, the pursuers of masters' degrees and doctorates. She saw one of the librarians whom she knew slightly, a young man from the Isle of Skye who always looked vaguely apologetic, as if the service that they were offering was somehow unsatisfactory. She imagined his saying, *We don't have that book, I'm so sorry, but there are other books, you know, and we might have those* . . . But that was not what he said as he scurried past Isabel on some errand. Instead he said, "Dr. Henderson has gone. Did you know that? He was such a nice man." Isabel, who had no idea who Dr. Henderson was, expressed regret. *What a shame.* And it was, she said to herself; if this librarian considered him a nice man, then that was what he probably was. And he would be regretted, as nice men were when they left. But gone where?

"Where?" she asked.

The librarian frowned. "Where?"

"Where has he gone?"

The librarian looked askance at her; surely she knew. "He died. He was run over."

Isabel gasped. "I'm so sorry."

The librarian gave her a slightly reproving look and excused himself to continue his errand. That misunderstanding was not my fault, Isabel told herself. One does not say of a person who has been run over that he has *gone*. *Gone before,* perhaps, if one is both religious and euphemistic—not to say distinctly old-fashioned—but one did not simply say *gone*.

She made her way up to what she called the philosophy floor, where the philosophical journals were shelved. There were very few people around at this level of the library, and she experienced the somewhat disconcerting feeling that can accompany being alone, or almost alone, in a large room. Here it was intensified by the long rows of books, marching off to the vanishing point. Books are not mute, she thought; they have things to whisper, and here in this open-plan library there are no walls to mute their whispers.

She made her way slowly down one of the passages between the stacks. There were so many journals, and these groaning shelves housed only those with a physical existence. Behind them, somewhere in the ether, were the electronic journals that never ended up on paper—a whole virtual world in which the exchanges of opinion were every bit as real as those that resided in print. And yet that virtual world seemed so shadowy by comparison with these squat volumes, and perilous too: Isabel had browsed a philosophical bibliography recently and come across a reference to a journal called *Injustice Studies*. The title had intrigued her, and all the more so because the list's compiler had written underneath the title: "Seems to have disappeared." She imagined the editor of *Injustice Studies* complaining: *It's so unfair, it really is. Our journal was really important, and then . . .*

But there was no danger of the journals around her disappearing. *Proceedings of the Aristotelian Society,* the *American Philosophical Quarterly, Ancient Philosophy:* these were names which were set for the long run. And the titles were so familiar, although some of them she had never looked at and these reproached her now. The bound volumes of *Ancient Philosophy* were important to somebody, and one of them contained a slip of paper where a reader had bookmarked an article. She would understand the issues if she chose to open one of the volumes, but she knew that there were conversations within which she would never have the time to participate in. And that, of course, was the problem with any large collection of books, whether in a library or a bookshop: one might feel intimidated by the fact that there were simply too many to read and not know where to start.

Isabel sighed. At the end of the book stacks there was a window looking over the trees below. It was a bright morning, and the foliage was painted gold by the sun; I might be out there, she thought, sitting on the grass, gazing up at the sky, enjoying the warmth, rather than immured in here, with these dead voices and the sheer weight of old paper. For a moment she was tempted. She did not have to do this. She did not have to edit the *Review* and add to this great mountain of argumentative scholarship. Why did she? Did it change the world one iota? Did it make the faintest difference to anything? People acted as they did, made their decisions, treated one another well or badly according to the tides of their heart, and whatever little debates she hosted in her journal would have no effect on how they did any of this.

She put the thought out of her mind: it was simply wrong, as undermining doubts so often are. Everything, every human activity that went beyond the purely functional, could be challenged in this way: painting, music, drama. And yet all of these made a difference—a major difference in many cases. The readers of Isabel's journal were affected by the conversation within its covers—if nothing else, the living room of their moral imagi-

nation became bigger. And this must surely have some bearing
on the way they dealt with the world, even in the small transactions of life: awareness of the pain of others here, a word of
comfort there. Of course, the admission of kindness to one's life
did not spring from any contemplation of the views of Hobbes
(selfish Hobbes) and Hume (the good, generous Davey), but it
did no harm to know about all that. And that was where philosophy really did count: it set out the major choices behind all
those practical day-to-day questions of charity and understanding and simple decency; it was the weather, the backdrop
against which those practical matters were debated.

The thought cheered her. All these volumes, passive and
unmoving, rarely opened, it seemed; all of them were building
blocks in the edifice of ideas that made for a humane and
civilised society. And her own journal, shelved in this very room,
was part of that. Well worth doing, whatever hours of sitting in
the sun it precluded; books cost that. She remembered reading a
poem that somebody had written about Walter Scott and his
Herculean writing labours. What hours of love that great literary
effort had deprived him of, the poet wrote. Yet Isabel thought
that this observation might be misleading. Hours of love left little behind, unless the love was directed at mankind in general;
Walter Scott's years of exile at his desk created a voluminous
legacy.

Her eye ran down the titles of the journals on the shelves,
and she stopped. Reaching into a pocket, she extracted the slip
of paper on which she had written the reference: the name of
the journal, the volume year and the page number. And the
author's name, of course: *Dove, Christopher.*

She bent down. The journal in question was stored on the

bottom shelf, and its volumes as a consequence were dustier. She ran her finger along the spines, and stopped at the year she had written down. She eased the book from its shelf, a tight fit, and then took it to one of the tables at the window. From the dim semi-darkness of the book stacks to the light of the window table—the contrast was sharp, and she shut her eyes for a moment. But then she turned and looked out through the great sheet of glass, out to the rooftops of Marchmont across the Meadows; and beyond that, just visible in the distance, the inner slopes of the Pentlands. She had climbed there with Jamie on a bright day in January when the hills had been covered in snow right down to the burns below. The wind had come in from the west—a knife-like wind in spite of the broad sunlight and the high cloudless sky. Off the tops of the hills powdered snow had streamed in thin white veils from the ridges, blown by the whistling wind, white against blue, like smoke from the top of a volcano. Now, in the summer, the hills were nothing to do with January; green, blue, gentle.

She opened the volume and found the page she was looking for: "Reflections on Free Riding," *by Christopher Dove, M.A., D. Phil., senior lecturer in philosophy, University of Durham.* It had been written before Dove was appointed to his chair at the newly minted university in London where he now professed, a university that Isabel thought sounded more like the destination of a bus rather than a place of learning. The lack of charity behind that thought jarred, and she reminded herself that Dove's institution would be doing good and useful work, even if it was unglamorous, and pedestrian, and staffed by self-important people like Dove: education, however administered, was a good in itself, and not everyone could receive it in a *grove.* More than that, it might well be all the more precious when passed from teacher to pupil in a prison cell, or in a tumble-down classroom, or by the flickering light of a candle. No, it was mean-spirited to tar Dove's university with the brush that should be reserved for him, and she would not think like that. Or she would try not to. Yet how could any academic institution worthy of the name not see through a man like Christopher Dove . . .

She began to read Dove's article. Free riding, he explained, involved taking the benefit of collective action without contributing in return. I know that already, thought Isabel. The free rider might not vote, then, because it might be irrational to expend the energy involved in seeking out a polling station when he knows that his vote will make no difference to the outcome. How ridiculous! Isabel read on, her irritation increasing with each page. Dove, it seemed, was pinning his colours to the mast of the free rider, endorsing the argument made by a small group of philosophers who had supported this thoroughly dubious position. It was unadulterated selfishness, she thought; an example of the individualistic posturing that had once been so fashionable and had encouraged both greed and economic disaster. It was *not* rational to look after oneself at the expense of others, for the simple reason that we sank or swam together. But of course Dove would have thought this a clever position to affect: to take out a pin and prick long-established notions of civic duty. Cast a vote? Why bother if it takes one away from something more individually enriching. Did he really believe that?

Isabel struggled to contain her irritation. She had a job to do and she began to tackle it, making her way through Dove's footnotes and writing down the cited references. The literature on the subject was surprisingly large and Dove was not one to hide his learning under a bushel. Isabel wrote down each citation, noticing that one article, in particular, seemed to have caught Dove's attention. "Self and Community" had been published in an American review ten years earlier and was the work of one Herbert Ponder, adjunct professor of philosophy at a Southern California university. "Ponder's defence of the enlightened self-interest position is masterly," wrote Dove. "Indeed, it is widely regarded as the *locus classicus* of the argument against pointless involvement in joint action." It is *not* enlightened, she said to herself. It is the opposite of everything that the Enlightenment stood for.

Isabel wrote down the reference and returned to the stacks. Professor Ponder's article had been published in the *American Philosophical Quarterly,* and she quickly located the relevant volume. Taking it back to her seat at the window, she went straight to the article. Again there were footnotes, though fewer than in Dove's own piece—four in all, only one of which had a reference to another paper. She noted down the reference, this time to the *Canadian Journal of Philosophy,* and to an article by a professor from the University of Toronto. Armed with her note, she made her way back to the stacks, replacing the *American Philosophical Quarterly* in its place as she went past. A, B and then C: the *Canadian Journal of Philosophy,* special symposium on "Reasons for Action." She opened the volume and began to read as she walked back to her table. She stopped. It met her eye, leapt from the page, the result of an absurdly long shot. But some long shots come home to roost, just as some metaphors are destined to be mixed. Dove, she thought, you shouldn't have done this. But you have. And now it is with your own petard that you are hoist.

CHAPTER SEVEN

THERE WAS AN ISSUE that had now become pressing. She had put it off, as one postpones a difficult encounter, a confession or an apology, but she now had to confront it. How would she break the news to Cat that she and Jamie were planning to marry? In the usual run of events, that issue presents itself the other way round, and if anybody worries about announcing a potentially awkward engagement, then it is the niece who worries about the reaction of the aunt. But this was a rather unusual situation, as the aunt does not normally become engaged to the niece's former boyfriend.

But before Cat was informed, Grace would have to be told. There was no real reason why this should be difficult, but Isabel still found herself feeling anxious about how her housekeeper would react. She had time to think about it, though, as the day following the proposal was Grace's day off and it was not until a day later that she was able to broach the subject.

"I have something to tell you," she said to Grace as she came into the kitchen on Tuesday morning.

Grace hung up the lightweight raincoat that she wore

throughout the summer, irrespective of the weather; she appeared not to have heard Isabel. "That bus," she said.

"What bus?"

"My bus. The one I waited twenty minutes for this morning. Twenty minutes!"

Isabel made a sympathetic sound. Grace had strong views on public transport and what she considered its egregious failings.

"I had a word with the driver as I got on," Grace continued. "I said to him: 'Do you know how long I've been waiting?' I spoke perfectly politely. I didn't shout. I didn't even raise my voice. I simply said, 'Do you know how long I've been waiting?' "

Isabel looked interested. "And did he?"

Grace tucked her scarf into the sleeve of her coat. Few people wore scarves in summer, but she did. This is Scotland, she had once explained to Isabel, and we must be prepared for every eventuality. At all times.

"Some people have no manners," she said.

Isabel said nothing.

The indignation in Grace's voice rose. "You'd think that if you have a perfectly civil remark addressed to you, then you'd respond accordingly."

"It might be hard to drive and talk," said Isabel mildly. "I'm sure that he wasn't being deliberately rude."

Grace glared at her. "He said, 'Would you kindly address your concerns, in writing, and in duplicate, to the relevant office of Lothian Regional Transport, the address of which may be obtained from the telephone book.' Those were his exact words. Can you credit it?"

Isabel suppressed the urge to laugh. She could picture the

encounter: the outraged Grace and the phlegmatic driver, trying to drive a bus along Grange Road while being berated by his passenger.

"Ridiculous," she said.

It was a comment that covered all aspects of the situation, but Grace interpreted it as referring to the driver's response. Mollified, she nodded, and then, remembering what Isabel had said, she asked what it was that she had to tell her.

"Jamie and I are engaged."

Grace smiled broadly. It was an immediate, spontaneous reaction, and it set Isabel at her ease. "About time," she said, and she stepped forward and put her arms about her employer. "It's great news. Great."

Isabel was astonished. Grace had never given her even a token kiss—birthdays had been marked with no more than a handshake—and now this warm, enthusiastic embrace.

"I'm very glad you're pleased," Isabel muttered.

Grace disengaged herself. "But of course I'm pleased." She looked at Isabel as if any other reaction were inconceivable. "Of course I'm pleased. Do you think that I liked it—your . . ." She paused and avoided Isabel's eye. "Your living in sin?"

Isabel gasped.

"I'm sorry," said Grace quickly. "I didn't mean to say that. But it's what I felt."

Isabel made a gesture of hopelessness. "What do you expect me to say? How do you think I feel about that? Living in sin? What exactly do you mean?"

Grace was now becoming slightly flustered. "It's an expression. That's all. An expression. It's what people say."

"Used to say," snapped Isabel, her growing anger now showing itself in her tone of voice. "Twenty, thirty years ago. It's a dreadful expression."

Grace shook her head vehemently. "I didn't mean it like that. It's not sin. Not really."

Isabel stared at her. She forgave Grace a great deal—her outbursts, her possessiveness of Charlie, the implied criticism in many of her remarks, but she found it difficult to accept this. "My relationship with Jamie may not be entirely conventional," she said, "but one thing I am very clear about, and that is that it is not in any remote sense of the word sinful."

"No. Of course not."

"Then what did you mean?"

Grace looked down at the floor. Suddenly she started to cry. She started to say something, but the sobs obstructed her words. Isabel immediately felt guilty. She should not have reacted so sharply; it was only an expression. It had nothing to do with sin.

She reached out and touched Grace's sleeve. "I'm sorry," she said. "I overreacted. I know what you mean."

Grace did not look up. "I only want you to be happy," she said. "I really do. I wanted him to marry you. All along I wanted him to marry you, rather than to live . . ."

"Together," supplied Isabel quickly. She was sure that Grace had been about to refer to sin again, and she helped her avoid it.

"Yes," said Grace. "And now that he's asked you, I really am happy."

Isabel comforted her. Grace's shoulder was bony—surprisingly so—and it was hard to pat it reassuringly; but she did, even though the thought came into her mind that it felt like patting an old horse, where blades of bone lay only just below the surface of the skin and felt like . . . felt like this.

"You must understand," Isabel began, "that sometimes I feel a bit sensitive about the fact that Jamie is younger than I am. That's probably why I bit your head off just then. I don't mean it."

Grace wiped at her cheek with a small handkerchief. Isabel noticed that it had been embroidered in one corner with an elaborate letter G. It was a small thing, but the sight of this made her feel a sudden rush of sympathy for the other woman. Our small possessions, she thought, can say so much about vulnerability.

"You shouldn't feel like that," Grace said. "Not these days."

"Oh, I know that," said Isabel. "Everybody says that it's absolutely fine. They keep saying it, and I suppose I know that they're right. But every so often, just every so often, you see an expression on somebody's face that tells you that's not the way they're thinking."

"A look of disapproval?"

"Exactly. Nothing too obvious, but it's there. People can't hide their feelings, you know."

"Ignore them. It's none of their business."

Isabel sighed. "Oh, I do ignore them. But I don't think they see it as being none of their business. We are great interferers, you know. We're an inherently moral species. If we see something we disapprove of, we experience reactive feelings, even when we know it's none of our business. And maybe it's just as well that we do."

Grace was puzzled, and Isabel explained. "If we didn't react to the behaviour of others when we're not directly affected, then people would get away with murder. Literally. We wouldn't intervene over genocide if it was happening in somebody else's country. We wouldn't have done anything about Hitler. Tyrants could act with impunity."

"They do, anyway," said Grace.

"I suppose so. We're selective in our moral outrage. We're very ready to vent it on the weaker tyrants but not so much on the strong ones. Who did anything about Stalin?"

"They didn't want a nuclear war."

Isabel had to agree. "No, they didn't. I suppose that demonstrates that moral philosophy has to be practical. It has to take into account who has a big fist. It also has to bear in mind who we are, our human limitations. It's not just something that one does in armchairs." As she spoke, she thought of her own armchair. The last time she had sat in it, she had drifted off to sleep while watching the news. For a moral philosopher's armchair, she thought, it's somewhat under-used.

GRACE WAS ONLY TOO PLEASED to be left in charge of Charlie that morning while Isabel went into Bruntsfield. She would take him down to the canal, she said, to look at the boats. And then there was her friend who lived in Harrison Gardens and who always welcomed a visit from Charlie. After that he could have his sleep.

With these arrangements in place, Isabel made her way along Merchiston Crescent to the post office at Boroughmuirhead. The streets were quiet; students from Napier University had been discouraged from parking in the area since the introduction of a permit system that restricted parking to the local residents. This uncluttered the streets, except on occasions when a student was late for a class and decided to feed the meter. It was also, she thought, an example of how people might be forced to be good. If we were not prepared to walk—

the environmentally responsible thing to do—or to wear crash helmets—the personally responsible thing to do—then those in power over us might force us to do these very things. The difficulty with this, of course, was squaring such an approach with human freedom. Isabel had not been much of a skier, but on her relatively few ventures on to the slopes she had enjoyed the feeling of the wind in her hair. Having to wear a helmet to ski—as some people were proposing—would spoil that sensation. And where would such enthusiasm end? Walking itself had some dangers—as the late Dr. Henderson had unfortunately found out—and there must be figures somewhere for the risk of falling over and cracking one's skull even when walking a short distance, as she was now doing.

Would anyone seriously propose that it should be compulsory to don a helmet to walk? The question was absurd, and yet even as she asked it she realised that even such an absurdity could not be ruled out. If a society could ban the throwing of sweets into the audience during a pantomime, or insist that people holding a church barbecue should attend a course to teach them how to fry sausages safely, then it was capable of anything. Yes, she thought, our very ordinary freedoms were being rapidly eroded by the nanny state, but it was difficult to make the point without sounding strident, or like an opponent of motherhood and apple pie. So she had done nothing to defend these freedoms, which made her . . . the realisation was a shocking one: it made her one of Christopher Dove's free riders.

The purchase of stamps at the post office at least took her mind off issues of civic duty and freedom. Then, crossing the road, she made her way towards the delicatessen. She had decided to tell Cat directly about the engagement and to breeze her way through any hostile reaction. She should not be intimidated by her niece; the worst thing one could do with a moody person was to pander to her moods. If Cat chose to go into a sulk, then she could do so, and Isabel would simply bide her time until she was ready to come out of it. She always did get over things, even if it took a little while.

Five or six doors from the delicatessen was the small jewellery shop, run by two young women, where Isabel had seen the ring that she thought she would buy for Jamie. She had imagined that she might go there with him and have his ring finger measured, but now, on impulse, she went in. One of the jewellers was at her workbench at the back of the room, peering through a large magnifying lens at some intricate piece of jewellery. She looked up when Isabel came in and smiled; they knew one another slightly, as Isabel occasionally took in items from the collection of jewellery she had inherited from her mother. There had been a pearl necklace that needed restringing. It had belonged to a great-aunt in Mobile, Alabama. "Particularly fine pearls," the jeweller had said. "Look at their lustre." Isabel had looked and had seen why it was that pearls needed their own adjective: pearlescent. There was no other word for their colour, their sheen, their very texture.

"Pearls?" the jeweller said.

"No, a ring this time," said Isabel. "I saw a ring in the window—a man's ring. Gold."

The jeweller set aside the necklace she had been examining and switched off the workbench light. "Was it rose gold?"

Isabel said that it was. "It was a lovely colour. That's why I noticed it."

"We still have it," said the jeweller, standing up and reaching for a bunch of keys. "I made it myself. I thought that a man might walk past the window and buy it as a signet ring. But none has. Perhaps there aren't enough men."

Isabel laughed. "There never are, are there?" And she thought: that's absolutely true—the demographers confirm it. Yet one of these increasingly rare men has asked me to marry him.

The jeweller extracted the ring from a display case and handed it to Isabel; it felt heavy in her hand, as it should, and warm too. She held it in her palm and knew. This was the ring she would give Jamie.

"Could you have it engraved?" she asked.

The jeweller nodded. She was looking at Isabel with interest, as if she was aware that this was an important moment. "Of course. I could do it myself. It's broad enough. Sometimes it's tricky with very delicate rings, but there'll be no problem with this one. Just write down what you want."

The jeweller handed Isabel a small piece of paper and a pen. Isabel gave her back the ring and took the paper. But then she realised that she had no idea what she wanted engraved. Jamie's initials? The initials of both of them? A date? The problem for Isabel was that she found herself in this realm of personal, emotional gesture, and she was unsure of the territory. There were people, she felt, who were much better at this sort of thing than she was. There were people who were unembarrassed by writing *Eternal Love* or *I'll love you always,* or such messages; people who thought nothing of putting the most intimate Valentine Day's messages in the newspapers, or proposing to somebody on the scoreboard at sporting events. That was not really her style. Perhaps she could have *Amor omnia vincit—*

Love conquers all things; but then that was masking sentiment in Latin, and it also raised issues of truth. Did love indeed conquer everything, or did we merely hope that it did? She did not want to engrave something that was *debatable*.

She picked up the pen and wrote out a few words. Then she handed the piece of paper to the jeweller.

The jeweller read the message. "Isabel Dalhousie gave this ring." She smiled. "That's nice wording. I was worried that you were going to write *Eternal Love*."

"I couldn't," said Isabel. "Because it isn't. Nothing's eternal."

The jeweller put the piece of paper down on her desk. "You should see some of the things that engravers are asked to do," she said.

"People are odd," said Isabel, adding, "but generally they mean well."

The jeweller seemed intrigued by this. "Do you really think so?"

"Yes," said Isabel. "Most people know what's right. Most people understand the needs of others. They know what we should do."

"Maybe," said the jeweller as she looked for a suitable ring box. "May I congratulate you, anyway? I assume that the ring is for somebody special."

"My husband-to-be," said Isabel.

The jeweller smiled. "Congratulations. May I ask: Who is he?"

Isabel had been looking out of the window. There was a small knot of pedestrians on the other side of the road waiting for the crossing light to turn green. One of them was Jamie.

"As it happens," she said, "that's him over there, on the other side of the street."

The jeweller came round to the front of the desk. "Him? The one in the red sweater?"

Isabel noticed that it was an older man. "No," she said. "The one next to him."

The jeweller said nothing for a moment. She watched Jamie waiting to cross the road. "He's lovely."

"Thank you," said Isabel. "He is." She hesitated. "May I bring the ring back for engraving later? I want to give it to him now. Since he's there."

"Of course."

The jeweller passed over the ring. Isabel could come back later and pay, she said. She knew her; that would be all right. "I shouldn't watch," she said. "I promise I won't."

"But you can," said Isabel.

She went out into the street. Jamie had crossed the road now and was heading towards her. Seeing her, his face broke into a broad smile.

"I was going to Hughes'," he said when he reached her. Hughes' was the old-fashioned fish shop on Holy Corner, the intersection so-named for the three churches overlooking it. "I decided to make kedgeree tonight. I was reading about it and it made me want to make it. Is that all right with you?"

"I love kedgeree," she said. And then added, "And you."

He looked taken aback, but he was clearly pleased. "Thank you. And I love you too."

She was holding the ring in her hand, holding it tight. Now she opened her fist and he looked down. He raised his eyes to hers; surprise yielded to a tender look of enquiry. "For me?"

"Yes."

He took the ring from her and slipped it on his finger.

Now Isabel looked at him questioningly. "Does it fit?"

"Yes. A tiny bit loose, maybe. But it fits."

"They can adjust it." She tossed her head in the direction of the jeweller's window; there was a slight movement within, nothing noticeable from outside.

"You've beaten me to it," he said. "That's where I was going." He paused. "Should we go there right away?"

She nodded. "They're open."

He looked at the ring, holding up his hand to admire it. "Thank you," he said. "Thank you, Isabel."

He had to stoop slightly to kiss her. She raised her face to his. She saw behind his head, above the rooftops of Bruntsfield, a gull riding a current of air, briefly dipping and then disappearing behind the stone chimney stacks.

ONCE THEY HAD FINISHED their business in the jeweller's, Jamie would brook no opposition from Isabel. "I'm coming with you," he said.

"Is it wise?"

He shrugged his shoulders. "Maybe. Maybe not. But we can't creep round the issue, can we?"

She thought about this for a moment. She was not sure she had the stomach for this, but she decided he was right. Cat's attitude was a boil that needed to be lanced rather than dressed. If she proved to be incapable of accepting the fact that Isabel and Jamie were together and would remain so—a strikingly dog-in-the-manger attitude—then there would just have to be one of those family ruptures that sometimes cannot be avoided. Cat would have to choose.

They approached the delicatessen in silence. Jamie hesitated briefly at the door. "You know," he began, "it makes all the difference to me, the fact that we're engaged. It's put everything else—everything with Cat—into the past, the real past."

Isabel said nothing, but reached out to take his hand.

"So I really don't mind about this," he went on. "I'm going to look her in the eye. I'm not going to let her bully us."

"Good for you," whispered Isabel.

"She's one of those people who uses psychological power over others," Jamie replied.

Isabel nodded her agreement. "She has her faults," she said. "But I don't want her to be unhappy."

Jamie swallowed. "Of course not."

"Here goes."

There were a couple of customers in the delicatessen, but they were engrossed in an examination of the shelves, scrutinising the list of contents of a packet of pasta. Pasta, thought Isabel; it was simple enough, but for some there was much to be said about the ingredients, sodium, potassium, trace minerals, fats and so on.

Eddie greeted them from behind the counter. "She's in there," he said, nodding towards Cat's office.

Isabel took the lead, knocking gently. "Cat?"

She pushed the door open. Cat was seated at her desk; in front of her was a fridge manufacturer's brochure. She greeted Isabel warmly enough, and then, seeing Jamie behind, gave him a greeting too, although less enthusiastically, thought Isabel.

"You aren't busy, are you?" Isabel began.

Cat shook her head. "Not specially. One of the fridges is on the blink though, and I'm going to have to replace it."

"Can't it be fixed?" asked Jamie.

Cat glanced at him, as if he had asked an unnecessary question. "No, not economically. These days everything is so expensive to fix that it's cheaper just to replace it."

Like your men, thought Isabel, irresponsibly. But what she said was quite different. "I wanted you to know that . . ."

"I was thinking of a red one next," Cat went on.

A red man?

"Is something funny?" asked Cat.

"No," said Isabel. "I'm sure that a red fridge would do the trick very well. But what I wanted to tell you was that Jamie and I are engaged."

Cat stared fixedly at the fridge catalogue. For a few moments nothing was said, and Isabel glanced nervously at Jamie. He smiled back, and then looked at Cat.

"We're really pleased," he said.

Cat pulled herself together. "Of course. Well, that's very nice." Her voice was flat; it was *not* very nice. It was *certainly* not very nice. "Actually, it's rather a coincidence. So am I."

CHAPTER EIGHT

ENGAGED TO a tightrope walker!" Jamie exclaimed as he and Isabel walked back to the house.

"So it would seem," said Isabel. "I hope that . . . well, I hope that he's all right."

"We'll see when she brings him round for a drink this evening," Jamie continued. "What do you think tightrope walkers drink?"

"Very little, I'd hope," said Isabel. "One wouldn't want to be under the influence of anything while on a tightrope. One has to be able to walk absolutely straight."

They both laughed. But Isabel was concerned: Cat had been engaged before, although not so soon after meeting the man in question. She was not sure how long Cat had known this new fiancé, but it could not have been very long.

"So he's called Bruno," she mused. "It seems quite suitable, doesn't it? It's a bit exotic. One wouldn't expect a tightrope walker to be called something like Eric, or Jeff."

Jamie grinned. "I'm sure that he's very nice," he said.

Isabel looked at him sharply. "Are you?"

"Sure that he's nice? Yes."

"But look at her recent boyfriends," she said, mentally adding, *not you.* "The bouncer from that club. That other one whose name I can't even remember. Toby—who was a cheat. No, I'm afraid I have less faith in Cat than you do."

"She said that he's really a stunt man," Jamie reminded her. "Remember. Tightrope walking is only part of what he does."

"We all have to diversify," observed Isabel. She paused. "And I suppose that applies to funambulists as much as anybody else. What worries me in all this is that she may not be telling the whole truth."

Jamie seemed shocked. "I don't think Cat's a liar. She's not exactly straightforward, but she's not a liar, surely?"

Isabel reassured him. No, she did not think that Cat was lying, but she wondered whether this announcement of her engagement to Bruno was not perhaps just a little bit in advance of the event. She might have been thinking of becoming engaged to Bruno but he might not yet have proposed, or he might have proposed but not yet been accepted. And then, hearing the news of Isabel's engagement, Cat might have felt that she could not let her aunt get engaged before she did. And so this might have been a defensive engagement rather than one which had been entered into after due deliberation.

Jamie listened to this, but it struck him as fundamentally unlikely, given that Cat had suggested bringing Bruno round for drinks that evening. "She'd realise that we'd talk about it," he said. "And she would hardly have time to set it up by tonight."

"No. Probably not. It's just that I feel a bit uneasy about it."

Jamie said that he knew what she meant. "We'll just have to

see," he said. "The important thing is that she didn't seem too fazed by our getting engaged. That's a relief, at least."

Isabel was cautious. "Give her time," she said. "Sometimes things take a bit of time to sink in." She gave Jamie a look of caution. "One thing about Cat that we have to remember is that she's unpredictable." There was, of course, an inherent contradiction in that, she told herself. An unpredictable person could not be predicted to be unpredictable.

"The liar paradox," she said.

Jamie, who was thinking of Cat's unpredictability, looked perplexed. "What?"

"A Greek philosopher named Eubulides," said Isabel. "He had a Cretan say, *All Cretans are liars.* If what he said was true, then the statement itself could not be true. You see?"

Jamie looked bemused. "If I'm going to be married to a philosopher, I suppose I should start reading up on some philosophy."

Isabel did not think this necessary. A couple did not have to know the same things; if she knew more about philosophy than Jamie did, then he knew more than she about history, and music, and a lot of other subjects. They were, she thought, just about equal.

"You don't have to start reading philosophy," said Isabel. "And I can't see where you'd find the time. Remember what Wittgenstein said: one lesson in philosophy is about as useful as one lesson in playing the piano."

"No use at all?"

"Well . . . ," Isabel mused. "Wittgenstein knew about playing the piano, of course. His brother was a very accomplished pianist—a one-armed pianist, as it happens. Composers wrote special one-handed pieces for him, but he could manage ordinary pieces too. Don't you find that extraordinary?"

Jamie looked thoughtful. He was wondering how the bassoon might be adapted for a one-armed bassoonist—it would be difficult, if not impossible. It was hard enough to play the bassoon with two hands and if one could only use five fingers at any one time, then that would require foot-operated keys, perhaps, or levers that could be squeezed by knee pressure. No.

"You're looking defeated," said Isabel. "Was it the thought of a one-handed system for the bassoon?"

He gave her the look that he sometimes gave her when he felt she was reading his mind. "As it happens, yes."

"Perhaps one will evolve," said Isabel. "But talking of evolution, did you know that Charles Darwin mentioned the bassoon? He was fascinated with earthworms, who he said were indifferent to shouts and tobacco smoke and could not hear the bassoon."

Jamie smiled, and filed the information away in his memory. One of his pupils, a particularly grubby small boy, might like to hear that. Now, though, he wanted to get back to the discussion of Cat's tightrope walker, and Isabel was leading them into something quite different—as she often did. "But what's the liar paradox got to do with Cat's tightrope walker?"

"Nothing to do with him," said Isabel. "But everything to do with her. I said that the one predictable thing about Cat is that she is unpredictable. But if that statement is true, then what I said about her unpredictability is untrue."

"Oh."

Isabel took Jamie's arm. "You don't have to bury yourself in philosophy. I can do enough philosophy for both of us."

"And I can play enough music for two," he said.

"Exactly."

They walked on in silence, content with one another, each aware that this moment, like a number of others that they had experienced since the engagement, had a noumenal feel to it: there was a mystery to it, a sense of the sacred. For his part, Jamie felt that he was looking at the world differently, that quotidian and unexceptional surroundings now seemed charged with an excitement and a feeling of possibility. *Through lover's eyes:* that was how he was seeing the world again, and that would be the first line of a song that he felt was already coming to him, right there in Merchiston Crescent, halfway home.

> *Through lover's eyes*
> *I see your face;*
> *Through lover's eyes*
> *I gently trace*
> *The contours . . .*

No. That was not going to work. He muttered the words again, with Isabel listening; she loved these impromptu songs Jamie seemed to be able to summon up from somewhere within him, so effortlessly.

> *Through lover's eyes,*
> *Through lover's ears,*
> *I see and hold*
> *The wondrous world*
> *My lover sees, my lover hears.*

"That's beautiful," she said. "And the tune?"

He hummed it first, without its words, and then sang it,

softly, as they turned the corner into their road. Further down the pavement, a woman they both knew slightly, a neighbour from a few streets away, was walking her dog, a brindle greyhound. The dog looked up sharply, sniffing at the air, and Isabel knew at once that with its sharp hearing it had picked up Jamie's song.

Jamie stopped. "I need to work on it a bit," he said. "The trouble about writing songs is this: Who's going to sing them?"

"You and I," said Isabel. "And little Charlie when he's a bit bigger. He'll love that song about olives."

"He'll have forgotten about olives by then. He'll want songs about trains and bears and so on," said Jamie.

"You can write those too."

Jamie smiled. "He likes music. I sang him 'Dance to your Daddy' the other night, and he cooed with pleasure. I need to sing him 'The Train to Glasgow' some day, if I can find the words. All about a fortunate boy getting the train to Glasgow."

"Children like simple tales," said Isabel.

"And we don't?"

Isabel thought about this. It was just too easy to say that adults did not like stories that were simple, and perhaps that was wrong. Perhaps that was what adults really wanted, searched for and rarely found: a simple story in which good triumphs against cynicism and despair. That was what she wanted, but she was aware of the fact that one did not publicise the fact too widely, certainly not in sophisticated circles. Such circles wanted complexity, dysfunction and irony: there was no room for joy, celebration or pathos. But where was the *fun* in that?

She answered his question. "We probably do. We want resolution and an ending that shows us that the world is a just place. We've always wanted that. We want human flourishing, as Philippa Foot would put it."

"One of your philosophers?"

"Yes, Professor Philippa Foot. She wrote a book called *Natural Goodness*. I would offer to show it to you had I not just agreed not to burden you with philosophy."

"I like the sound of her," said Jamie. "Professor Foot. Is she naturally good?"

"I think she is," said Isabel. "Though usually people who are naturally good have to work at it. The goodness may be there, but they have to cultivate it, work to bring it out." She paused. "She's the granddaughter of an American president, Grover Cleveland. One does not necessarily expect an Oxford philosopher to be the granddaughter of anybody like that."

Jamie was lost in thought. "If you're not naturally good—let's say that your inclinations are, in fact, distinctly on the bad side, then can you become naturally good? Or will it just be superficial?"

They were almost at the gate. "I think you can," said Isabel. "Change your nature, that is. I suppose it depends on what sort of faults you're talking about."

"What if you only have one?" asked Jamie.

"That would be a rather short list," said Isabel. "Have you only got one fault? Most of us have rather more." She frowned. "I have, for example . . ."

Jamie cut her off. "None."

"Oh, I do." She wondered whether he truly thought that.

Jamie pushed the gate open. "Is this really the sort of thing you spend your time thinking about?" He smiled at her as he ushered her through.

"I am a moral philosopher," said Isabel.

Jamie was still thinking about faults. "What are the really difficult ones?"

"Addictions," said Isabel. "Faults that aren't necessarily people's fault."

Jamie stopped. "Drinking too much? Alcoholism?"

"Yes," said Isabel. "I don't think that people choose to be alcoholics, or heroin addicts for that matter. And if they don't choose, then how can it be their fault?" We are responsible, she explained, only for those things that we choose; everything else *happened* to us—we did not do it.

Jamie objected. "Maybe they should have shown more self-control to begin with?"

"But if they don't *have* that capacity for self-control?" Isabel said. "If they're weak? You don't choose your character, you know."

"Don't you?"

They resumed their walk down the path. Jamie reached for his key. "What if you know that you have to practise certain things? As musicians have to? We aren't born being able to play the piano."

"That's precisely what I'm saying: in order to become better people, we must practise," Isabel said. Jamie had a nose for philosophy, she thought, but she was not sure that this was what she wanted. The best sort of relationship, she thought, was where each person had a private area, a place of mental retreat. She did not necessarily want to talk to him about these things; he did not belong here. He lived in a world of music, and beauty, to which she was readily admitted but in which she did not really have a right of abode. We live where we belong, she thought; that is where we really live. But although she understood this, she did not think she could spell this out to him, as it would sound condescending, which it certainly was not, or unfriendly, which it even more certainly was not. There was a time when men had said to women, *Don't you worry your pretty little head about that;* what outrageous, patronising condescension. And women, or so many of them, had suffered it meekly, because they had been trapped.

They heard a squeak from within. Grace must have returned early from the walk by the canal and had now brought her charge into the hall. Held up by Grace, Charlie was able to look at them through the letter box while Jamie fumbled with his keys. Isabel bent down and stared into the bright eyes that watched her, jubilant at her return, brimming with delight. Dogs, she had read somewhere, think each time their owners leave the house that they have lost them for ever. Did small children think the same, she wondered; for if they did, each parting must seem like the beginning of a lifetime apart, each return a reunion with those one thought one would never see again. Or was it exactly the opposite with children? Did they think that we were always there, that we would never go away, and that our occasional absences were no more than a temporary interruption of our attention, as in a hotel when room service is for some reason suspended?

THERE WERE TWO TELEPHONE CALLS before Cat came round with Bruno, both of them important, but only one of them welcomed. The one that Isabel was pleased to receive was from Guy Peploe, who telephoned her shortly after lunch with the simple message, "We got it."

Isabel, whose mind had been on her editing, asked what they had got.

"Charles Edward Stuart."

She remembered that this was the day of the auction in London. "Oh. Well, that's very good news."

"It is. And there's something else."

"Oh yes?"

"We got it cheaply. One other person in the room was after it. And another phone bidder, apart from us." He paused. "But that's not what makes me feel rather excited."

Isabel reached across her desk to the catalogue. The relevant page had been turned down at the corner and she went straight to it. Charles Edward Stuart, Bonnie Prince Charlie, last real hope of the Stuart dynasty, looked out at her from a feigned oval. A very weak face, she thought; pretty, but weak. How could those tough Highlanders have fallen for such a foppish-looking pretender?

Isabel asked whether there was anything special about the painting.

"Have you seen that Nicholson book?" asked Guy. "The one on the iconography of Bonnie Prince Charlie?"

Isabel knew the book. There was a copy somewhere in her library.

"Go and take a look at the engraving of the Toqué portrait of Charlie," said Guy. "The one that was lost."

Isabel was puzzled. "The engraving was lost?"

"No, the original painting. It was engraved by somebody before the painting was lost. So the only way we know what it looked like is through that engraving."

"Oh."

"Yes. Take a look at it. Then tell me what you think."

"Now? It'll take some time to find Nicholson." She looked at her shelves, her overstocked bookshelves. She imagined Nicholson himself lost in the piles and confusion of books. She imagined calling him, *Professor Nicholson! Professor Nicholson!* And a faint answering cry coming from somewhere in the midst of all those books.

"Not now," said Guy. "Some time soon, though. Take a look. He has a picture of the engraving in his book."

"And?"

"And it's identical to our painting," said Guy. "The one we've just bought."

Isabel took a moment to digest this. She was not sure about the implications; she had bought the portrait with a view to putting it in a spare bedroom where her mother's picture of Mary Queen of Scots had always hung. She had known that portrait all her life, and she knew that it was a special favourite of her mother, her sainted American mother. She was not sainted—not in the conventional sense; indeed Isabel had discovered that her mother had conducted an affair, but that did not change her view of her. Her mother had represented love, as most mothers do to most people; not that this love was always helpful. Boys, she knew, could be smothered by it, could feel that they had to escape, but she had never felt that. She wondered about Jamie's mother, whom he rarely mentioned. His parents had separated and his father had moved to Spain. His mother had remarried, to a surgeon, when Jamie was at music college, and they had gone off to live in London.

Jamie had said that they wanted to come and meet Charlie,

but they never had, which had secretly appalled Isabel. And hurt her too: she had decided that they must disapprove of her—why else would they not come and meet their only grandchild? Well, she would not force it, if that was how they felt. They might meet Charlie at the wedding—if there was a wedding in the formal sense. She realised that not only had they not talked about that, she had not even *thought* about it. She would like something quiet and understated, and she imagined that Jamie would too: a ceremony in St. Mary's Episcopal Cathedral, perhaps, with a full choir and her friend Peter Backhouse on the organ playing Parry's "I Was Glad." She smiled. On the other hand, there was always the Register Office in Victoria Street, which presumably had no arrangements for music, not even a tape recorder. She imagined that the Register Office would be fairly similar to Warriston Crematorium, both being functional places run for the convenience of citizens by well-meaning bureaucrats; both with no time for too much fuss; both dedicated, in the final analysis, to changing the status of those whom they served. Surely Jamie would not like that.

Guy's voice came down the line: "Are you still there, Isabel?"

"Yes. I was just thinking."

"About Toqué?"

She looked up at the ceiling. "And other things."

The conversation wound to a close. Guy would make further enquiries. In the meantime, Isabel should not raise her hopes too much, as there were always disappointments in the art world—so many pictures were not what their owners wanted them to be, and this might be no exception. "I think it's likely to be exactly what it says in the catalogue. Dupra's circle, not Toqué. But I'll have a closer look, just in case."

She wondered how important one had to be before one was given a circle. She had no circle, she thought: just Jamie and Charlie and Grace . . . and Brother Fox, of course. Or she was in his circle: *Circle of Brother Fox, Scottish, early twenty-first century.*

"I am naturally cautious," Isabel said, before Guy hung up. But even as she said this, she wondered whether it was true. And if it was, was it something to be pleased about, or something to regret? Was natural caution found in people who did something with their lives, or was it a quality of those whose lives ran narrowly and correctly to the grave? The question depressed her. She did not want to be naturally cautious, she decided; she wanted to throw caution to the winds and . . . and what?

Grace appeared at the door of her study, a duster in hand. This was unusual: Grace did not like dusting, and only rarely did so. "We're almost out of dishwasher detergent," she said. "I'm worried that we'll run out. Could you get some more?"

Isabel looked up. "Let's just risk it," she said. If one was going to throw caution to the winds, one had to start somewhere.

Grace looked at her in astonishment. "Risk it?"

Isabel shrugged. "I thought that perhaps . . ." She did not finish her sentence. "No, what I meant was, yes, I'll get some more. One would not want to risk anything."

"Of course," said Grace. She gave Isabel a curious sideways look and left the room. That, thought Isabel, is the trouble: I live a life in which caution simply cannot be thrown to the winds; the winds in Edinburgh would throw it right back in one's face. It was just that sort of place, and that is what its winds were like.

THE SECOND TELEPHONE CALL, the less welcome one, came an hour or so after Guy Peploe's. This was from Minty Auchterlonie, or rather from her assistant, who asked, in rather cold tones, whether Isabel was available to take a call from her employer. Isabel said that she was, and there followed a brief pause before Minty came on the line. There were voices in the background during this pause, and she heard a man saying, "Due diligence? Have they done it yet?" The expression intrigued her—due diligence sounded rather like natural caution; perhaps it was the same thing. And she imagined one could not throw due diligence to the winds either.

Minty sounded anxious. "I'm sorry to bother you," she said. "But I really needed to speak to you. Can we talk freely?"

Isabel said they could. What listening ears did Minty imagine? Unsympathetic, hostile people, crowded about Isabel's desk eager to hear something compromising, some scandalous morsel?

"Good," said Minty. "I'm afraid that I've had another call from Jock, Roderick's father. He wants me to bring Roderick to see him tomorrow. He insists. He says that he wants me to come to the Botanical Gardens."

"Why? Why there?"

"God knows. He likes to see him in places where he can play with him, I think."

Isabel waited for her to continue.

"And I can't," said Minty. "We're going over to Skye for a few days. We're taking some American clients of Gordon's to Kinloch Lodge. It's important. What would I say to Gordon? That I can't go? That I have to meet my . . . my former lover?"

"Awkward," said Isabel.

"More than awkward. Distinctly more than."

Isabel cleared her throat. "I don't really know what to suggest." She thought: this is what happens when one has affairs. This is what happens.

"And I just don't trust Jock," Minty said.

Isabel tried to sound politely interested. "Oh?"

"He could so easily become a loose cannon," Minty continued. "I'm terrified that he'll phone the house."

Isabel shrugged. "I suppose that's always a danger."

"And if he spoke to Gordon, then . . . well, he might say something."

Isabel made a noncommittal remark. What she wanted to say was that this was a risk of having a clandestine affair—the best-known and most obvious risk.

Suddenly Minty became businesslike. "Can you go?"

"Me?"

"Yes. I don't like to ask you, but I'm at my wits' end. Please go and talk to him. Tell him that I just can't do this. Offer him money."

Isabel drew in her breath. Danegeld—the money that the Anglo-Saxons, and others, paid the Vikings to stay away. But the problem with Danegeld was that the Danes came back for more.

Minty continued. "Fifty thousand pounds. Tell him that if he drops all claims to Roderick I'll give him fifty thousand pounds. Sixty. Go up to sixty."

"No, I'm sorry. I really don't think—"

Minty cut Isabel short. "Just this one thing. That's all I ask. Just go and meet him. Keep him from doing anything stupid."

For a moment Isabel said nothing. She had her reservations

when it came to Minty Auchterlonie, but there was no doubting the anguish behind her words; the voice on the other end of the line, she thought, was that of a trapped woman. And with that assessment, Isabel realised that she could not turn Minty down. This was a cry for help, and one could not—and certainly *she* could not—leave such a cry unanswered.

"I'll go," she said. "But I don't know what I'll be able to do. Surely it's better for you to try to speak to this man. Reason with him. Reach some sort of compromise."

"I can't," said Minty. "I'm scared of him. I'm scared of what he'll do."

Isabel wanted to say that she did not think of Minty as being a type to be scared, but she could not.

"I just can't face him," Minty went on. "Do you think I'm a coward?"

Isabel said that she did not. "You're in a very difficult position," she said.

"I can't face him," Minty repeated. "I'm afraid of what I might do. I want to kill him. I really do."

Isabel tried to calm her down. "You feel angry, that's all. And a bit frightened. Understandably."

"Angry."

"Well, I understand," said Isabel. "But this offer of payment—I don't think that we should mention money just yet. I think that I should see whether I can reason with him first. I want to talk to him about what he's been doing. This campaign against you. People can sometimes be shamed into stopping what they're doing if you confront them. Shame is a powerful thing, you know."

The silence at the other end of the line made Isabel wonder

whether Minty really understood about shame. But of course she did; Isabel had been wrong about her. Minty was quite normal; she was not a psychopath, as Isabel had once thought her to be, and that meant that she would have a normal understanding of shame, and guilt, and all the other emotions and feelings forming the emotional backdrop to our lives.

"You go over to Skye," said Isabel. "And I'll go to the Botanical Gardens."

As she said this, Isabel suddenly realised that Minty was sobbing. "You're really kind," the other woman said. "I can't believe that you're doing this for me. We hardly know one another, and yet you're doing this for me."

"I'm very happy to do it," said Isabel. She said so, but she was not happy to do it; she was not. She resented Minty, who had intuitively understood that Isabel would help her even though she had no right to make this claim on Isabel's time and charity. But although she resented her, Isabel knew—and Minty knew too—that she would have no alternative but to act. If she had never studied philosophy and never wrestled with issues of our moral obligation to others, she would not have had to act at all. But she *had* done, and she could not unlearn everything she had acquired in Cambridge and Georgetown; nor could she forget that she was a citizen of Edinburgh, of the city of David Hume. I am obliged to act, she thought; by geographical propinquity, and by the mere fact of being human, I am obliged to act.

They discussed the details. Minty told Isabel a little more about Jock, where she should meet him and how she would recognise him. Then came the note of caution. "It would be best not to phone me," said Minty. "Gordon might wonder."

Isabel assented, but reluctantly. She did not like subterfuge

in any form, and she felt uncomfortable about contacting Minty
as if they were fellow conspirators. She was not in collusion
with Minty Auchterlonie; she was helping her, out of charity,
that was all. Sometimes, she thought, the barricades in this life
are in the wrong place; but they are still barricades, and they
have to be womanned.

CHAPTER NINE

ISABEL HAD DECIDED that the last thing one should do when one met a funambulist was to ask about tightrope walking. This exercise of tact was not particular to tightrope walkers; there were numerous situations, many of them much more mundane, in which one refrained from talking to people about what they did. One did not ask judges about how they felt when they sent people to prison; one did not enquire of airline pilots whether they had ever had a near miss; and one did not ask overweight chefs whether they found it difficult to keep from sampling their creations. In all of these examples such questions would stray into sensitive territory, and it was the same with tightrope walkers, who must feel, Isabel thought, the inherent absurdity of their profession.

"He may be proud of it, of course," Jamie pointed out. "It may be exactly what he wants to talk about."

Isabel suspected that even if Bruno were proud of being a tightrope walker, Cat would be cagey about it. "He's in the theatre," her niece had said opaquely, which gave the game away, in Isabel's view.

"Let's just not mention it," she said to Jamie. "If he mentions it himself, then we can ask. Otherwise, let's not say anything about it." She paused. "Of course, there's nothing wrong in being a tightrope walker. We need them."

Jamie looked at her in amazement. "Do we?"

Isabel shrugged. "Perhaps not. But what I'm saying is that we must respect the dignity of all labour."

Jamie shook his head. "But is it labour?"

"Oh, I don't know. But let's not raise it, anyway. Just don't mention it unless she does."

Jamie agreed, although reluctantly. "But I'm really interested," he said. "I'd like to know how he trained for the job. I'd like to know what was the highest rope he's ever walked on. Do you think he's one of these people who walks across the Niagara Falls?"

"Nobody walks across the Niagara Falls any more," said Isabel. "Waterfalls are very tightly regulated these days."

Jamie burst out laughing. "That sounds very funny."

"Or sad," said Isabel, becoming thoughtful. She remembered reading about the visit of Pius XII to the Niagara Falls when he was a papal envoy to the United States. He had been taken to Niagara and had gazed out over the river. Then, presumably feeling that something was expected of him, he had proceeded to *bless the falls.* That had tickled her. What was the point of blessing a natural feature? Did he expect that the falls would behave better if blessed? Or would they just bring more pleasure to visitors if they had the benign disposition of blessed falls rather than unblessed falls? The irreverent thoughts gave way to more sober reflection. We all wished for places to be made special somehow; people had holy rivers, after all: the

Ganges, the Brahmaputra. And Isabel was sure that there were others, even if she could not name them. *Thousands have lived without love, not one without water.* Auden again—he came back to her, at these odd moments; she could not help it.

When Cat rang the bell, Isabel was with Charlie in the sitting room, reading to him from a battered copy of *Now We Are Six.* A poem about the changing of the guard at Buckingham Palace might not have been the most intellectual of fare, but for Charlie, not yet two, it was as metaphysically challenging as the most obscure lines of John Donne or Andrew Marvell. But whereas Donne and Marvell did not go *tiddly-om-pom-pom* in metrical terms, Milne did, and that was what Charlie liked. So it did not matter that Charlie had no idea why one of the sergeants should look after the guards' socks or why Alice was about to marry one of the guards. Nor did it matter when Isabel read *Hiawatha* to him that he had no inkling as to what a wigwam or the shining Big-Sea-Water was; what counted was Longfellow's use of metre, a monstrously repetitive business, which Charlie loved, and which could be counted upon to send him into a state of somnolence after fifty lines. Noticing this, Isabel had toyed with the idea of suggesting to some far-sighted publishers that they publish a book specifically targeted at insomniacs. This volume would not offer advice on how to tackle sleeplessness (there were far too many people advising us about *everything,* she thought); it would simply contain passages the reading of which could be relied upon to send the insomniac reader to sleep. *Hiawatha* would be there, but so would, for quite different reasons, excerpts from Caesar's *De Bello Gallico,* and from one or two modern political memoirs.

Isabel put down the Milne and announced to Charlie that

she would have to leave him for a moment to answer the door. She laid him down gently in his playpen, and then said, "Your cousin's at the door, Charlie."

Charlie looked up at her expectantly. "Olive," he muttered.

"Not now," said Isabel. "But well done."

She went through to the front hall and opened the door. Cat was there, and immediately behind her was a man whom Isabel took to be Bruno. The evening sun, slanting in from the west, was in Cat's hair, creating a halo effect.

Isabel stepped forward and gave the younger woman a light kiss. "And this, I assume, is Bruno."

"Yes," said Cat, moving aside to let Isabel reach out to shake hands with her new fiancé.

Bruno inclined his head. His expression was one of be-musement shading into condescension. It was the look of some-body who would rather be somewhere else but was there anyway and was prepared to be tolerant.

When he spoke, Bruno did so with a curiously high-pitched voice. "Pleased to meet you."

It was entirely involuntary, but Isabel felt the muscles about her mouth tighten. She knew she should not feel that way, but she did. She did not like the tone in which Bruno said *Pleased to meet you*. There was a jauntiness to it, almost an irony, as if he were saying that he was pleased but was not, or was indifferent. He is here on sufferance, she thought; he has come here only because Cat has insisted. She disliked that intensely. It was like one of those occasions at a cocktail party when you find yourself conversing with somebody who is looking over your shoulder to see if there is anybody more important to engage in conversation.

She looked at Bruno, being struck by the fact that he was short; he was like a jockey—short and wiry. Every previous boyfriend of Cat's had been tall, and here was Bruno, half a head shorter than Cat herself, and even that, she noticed as her eyes ran down his legs to his feet, was in his elevator shoes.

They went inside. Jamie appeared from the kitchen, wiping his hands on a tea cloth. He embraced Cat quite easily, kissing her lightly on each cheek before shaking hands with Bruno.

"I've heard a lot about you," Bruno said.

Again Isabel experienced an involuntary reaction, this time a slight wince. It was an ill-chosen remark—immediately embarrassing for the one to whom it was addressed. The knowledge that one is being talked about is not always welcome; it makes one wonder just what has been said, particularly in a case like this where relations between Jamie and Cat had not been especially easy.

Isabel could see that Bruno's comment made Jamie feel uncomfortable, and she was on the point of making some anodyne remark on the weather when Jamie spoke.

"Oh yes?" he said. "And I've heard a lot about you."

Bruno glanced at Cat. He was clearly annoyed. "Can't imagine there's much to be said about me," he said. "Apart from my film credits, of course."

Isabel seized the opportunity. "Now that's something I didn't hear. Nobody mentioned films."

Bruno turned from Jamie to Isabel. "You've never seen me on the screen?"

"I watch so little," Isabel said, waving a hand in the air. "I'd like to see more of . . . more of everything, but where's the time?"

"I was in *Oil*," said Bruno. "That was the last one. You know it?" This last question was addressed more to Jamie than to Isabel, since Bruno had obviously decided she knew nothing about films.

"*Oil*?"

"Yes. It was set on an offshore oil rig up near Shetland—or most of it was. Joe Beazley directed. You know him?"

Isabel looked thoughtful, as if trying to remember Joe Beazley amongst the many film directors of her acquaintance. "Joe Beazley? No, I can't say that I know him."

"What were you in *Oil*?" Jamie asked.

"Stunts," said Bruno. "That's what I do. I'm a stunt man."

"I thought that you were a tightrope walker," said Jamie.

Bruno laughed. It was a rather unpleasant sound, Isabel thought; more of a snigger really. "I do that as well," he said. "It goes with doing stunt work. Know what I mean?"

"Sort of," said Jamie.

They were still standing in the hall, and Isabel now gestured for them to move into the sitting room, where Charlie was enjoying his last few minutes before bedtime. Bruno bent down to tickle Charlie under the chin, calling him "mate" as he did so. "You fed up, mate? I don't blame you. Tell you what: I'll teach you to escape from that thing."

Charlie looked at Bruno with distaste. He had not enjoyed having his chin tickled and his brow knitted into a frown. Isabel wanted to laugh: Cat had done it again. Bruno was worse, far worse, than she had imagined.

"Are you an escapologist as well?" she asked.

Bruno looked up at her. "Escape-how-much?" he asked.

"An escapologist. I wondered whether you were both a funambulist and an escapologist."

Now Cat decided to intervene. Throwing a sideways glance at Isabel, she said, "Isabel can talk English. It's just that sometimes she forgets."

"Forgets what?" asked Bruno.

Jamie cleared his throat. "What stunts did you do in *Oil*?" he asked.

Bruno seemed pleased with the question. "I was covered in oil in one scene," he said. "They used molasses, actually. It looks just like crude, but it's easier to get off."

"You must get yourself into some sticky situations," interjected Isabel.

Cat threw Isabel a warning glance.

"And then, in another scene," Bruno continued, "I had to do a fire job. Asbestos clothing, flames, the works. They had me toppling over and ending up in the drink. I almost hit the rescue boat when I went in, but it didn't show up in the shot so the director didn't make me do it again."

Cat smiled appreciatively. "Bruno says that filming is very dull work. He says that they do the same thing over and over again, just to get it right."

Bruno nodded in agreement. "It's a tough business, even if you aren't a stunt man. You work for the dough, you really do. Except for the body doubles. That's easy money."

Jamie was intrigued. "Body doubles?"

Bruno grinned. "They're the people who stand in for actors' body parts—an arm, maybe, or a foot—depending." He hesitated, looking at Cat as if for a signal. She smiled encouragingly, and he was emboldened. "And nude scenes. You know, bedroom stuff. When they want to show a bit of flesh. You don't have to show the face, and so they use the body double rather than the actor." He turned to Isabel and winked. "Know what I mean?"

It occurred to Isabel that she should wink back, and she did. Jamie saw this, and his mouth opened as if he was about to say something. Then Bruno winked at Isabel again.

THEY BOTH HAD DIFFICULTY getting to sleep. Isabel knew that Jamie was still awake by the sound of his breathing; once he was asleep he breathed so quietly that it was as if nobody was there.

"Oh well," she muttered.

Jamie turned. He put an arm gently about her shoulder, pushing the sheet and blanket aside. "You behaved," he said. "In fact, I thought you behaved very nicely."

She was relieved. She had made a supreme effort—for the sake of her relationship with Cat—and it was a relief to know that at least Jamie had been impressed. "That wink," she said.

He chuckled. "Yes. I saw it. What did it mean?"

"A wink is usually a sign of complicity," said Isabel. "It says, 'We're on the same side, aren't we?' "

Jamie sighed. "It's not going to work, is it? And do you know what? I feel rather sorry for him. He may be pretty keen on her."

Isabel feared that he was right. "He's rougher trade than her usual boyfriends," she said. "I hope that when it comes unstuck he won't be difficult."

Jamie confessed that this had been worrying him too. "There's something about him," he said. "Something rather odd. You know how it is with some people, there's a sense of their being on the edge. Wound up like a spring."

Isabel knew what he meant. She had sensed it too, and it had worried her. "Do you think we should warn her?" She felt the weight of his forearm on her shoulder; it was a reassuring feeling

Jamie was silent for a moment. Then he spoke. "No. We mustn't. She won't take well to any interference. She'll have to discover it by herself."

Isabel knew that he was right. The decision not to interfere was counterintuitive though, and she knew that it was going to be hard. The arrival of Bruno was potentially disastrous; even saying his name was proving difficult now, so strongly negative were the associations.

"At least we won't have to wait long. It probably won't last," she said, drowsily.

"Or *he* won't," muttered Jamie.

Jamie's remark jolted Isabel back to wakefulness. "What?"

Jamie explained. "His job is pretty dangerous, isn't it? Flaming jackets, oil, molasses . . . tightropes. All very dangerous. High life insurance rates, I would have thought. Poor chap."

The last two words, thought Isabel, were vital. They converted a heartless remark into a sympathetic one, showing the power of small words to do big things.

CHAPTER TEN

Jᴏᴄᴋ sᴀɪᴅ he would be at the entrance to the Old Greenhouses at eleven o'clock," Minty had said to Isabel over the telephone. "He's very punctual. He'll be there."

Isabel had asked Minty to describe him. "There may be other people there," she said. "I don't want to sidle up to the wrong man. Not that I'd really *know* how to sidle."

Minty did not find this amusing. "What does he look like? Tall," she said. "Very good-looking. The sort of man whom married women fall for." She waited for a reaction, but Isabel said nothing. "Which is why I did," she added lamely. "I know, I know . . ."

"Anybody can succumb to temptation," said Isabel. "It's easy enough."

"I can't see you giving in to temptation," said Minty. "I really can't."

Isabel was not sure what to make of this remark. It could be complimentary or otherwise; Minty might be suggesting that she was too strong—which would be complimentary—or too unlikely to attract temptation, which would hardly be flattering.

"You don't know me all that well," said Isabel. There was mild reproach in her response, but Minty did not appear to pick up on it, instead asking Isabel to contact her at the office once she and Gordon were back from Skye. "I may not be able to talk freely," she said. "For obvious reasons. But please tell me what happened."

Isabel reached the Botanical Gardens slightly early. It was a warm morning, the air still and the sky unclouded. Edinburgh could not count on many days of that sort, even in a good summer, and people were quick to respond. The bus down to Stockbridge was full of men in tee-shirts or with their sleeves rolled up, the women in thin cotton blouses. The person sitting beside Isabel faced out of the window, the sun on her face, her eyes closed, and muttered, "Gorgeous sun! Gorgeous sun!" Her words were like the words of a prayer, offered up that the sun should not change its mind and disappear.

"It's great, isn't it?" murmured Isabel.

The woman half turned to her. "I miss it so much," she said.

"Perhaps we live in the wrong country," Isabel remarked.

The woman laughed, and returned to her sun worship. "No choice," she said. "Like the rest of life. No choice."

No choice. She was right, thought Isabel—most of us had no choice as to where we lived. Once again, she had cause to reflect on the fact that the big lottery was the very first one, the one that determined what we were: French, American, Sudanese, Scottish. And with that, there came a mountain of baggage—a culture, a language, a set of genes determining complexion, height, susceptibility to disease and so on. And for most people that was their fate: later changes, if they could be made at all, would be accidental or hard-fought-for. The woman on the bus would like to live in Spain or Portugal, she imagined,

closer to the sun, but could not do so because she had a job, a
husband and a past that tied her to Scotland and its weather.

What was the solution? To bemoan the fact, or to love
where you were? To love where you were—obviously. And that,
by and large, was what people did. They accepted, and the
acceptance became love. Is that why I love Scotland, she asked
herself, because it is simply the place that I *have* to love? No. It
was not the reason.

She followed the winding road that led along the side of the
Water of Leith before meandering up the brae to the Botanical
Gardens. Turning round here, one was afforded an unusual
view of the city skyline, of the Castle, of the spiky churches and
the crouching lion of Arthur's Seat, mantled gold in the sunlight. She took this in briefly, and then looked down at the river
below her, its surface half silver, half peaty brown. It rarely
became very deep: one could wade across and never wet one's
knees in most places. Only after heavy rains in the Pentlands
did it seem at all impressive, but she felt a strong affection for it
as the river of her childhood. They had picnicked beside it up in
Colinton Dell, where it tumbled over a weir, her father demon-
strating to her how to make flat stones skip over the surface,
something she never achieved. And her mother lay back on their
tartan picnic rug and drew on a cigarette, sending tiny clouds of
smoke skywards. "You look like a volcano, Mummy. A volcano."
She remembered her words, after all this time, just as she
remembered how her mother had not appreciated the remark.
Isabel had felt hurt and surprised, because she had never been
able to take parental anger or disappointment.

She took the path that led round the back of Inverleith
House, which stood surrounded by trees in the middle of the
gardens. Again there were memories—this time of being

brought to see an exhibition in the days when the building was used by the Scottish National Gallery of Modern Art. She had been brought with her class from school and they had been taken round an Anne Redpath exhibition. Miss McLaren, their art teacher, who believed that every twentieth-century artist of any note had been influenced by Cézanne, had duly found signs of this in the Redpath paintings. "Cézanne again," she had said. "And Matisse. She was influenced by both, of course, as so many were. Look at the colours in this painting, girls. The hillside. The path. Does that not make you think of Cézanne?"

She had not thought of Miss McLaren for years. That outing to the gallery had until now been absent from her memory, and although she could remember the art teacher and what she said, she could not recall which of her classmates had been with her. It was a blank. Twenty years from now, would she have forgotten why she was here today, and what was about to happen? She imagined so. And then went on to think: twenty years on, Charlie would be coming to the end of his university days— a young man about to embark on a career. She could not picture it, nor could she imagine how she would feel, although it would be the same as everybody else feels in similar circumstances. That at least was a consolation: separation and loss were something that we all experienced; the pain was shared, and was perhaps easier for that.

She was approaching the hothouses. She looked at her watch: three minutes to eleven. There was nobody there, and for a moment she wondered whether Minty was playing with her, sending her off on a wild goose chase, wasting her time; there were unbalanced people who did that sort of thing. She looked behind her along the path that she had followed from the back of Inverleith House. In the distance a woman wearing a bright red jacket was pushing a small child in a pushchair. The child seemed to be wearing a bonnet of some sort and the woman had a large sunhat on her head. If Jock Dundas came now, he might think that the woman was Minty and that the child was Roderick; he could easily think that.

She turned round again and saw that the door of one of the hothouses was being opened from the inside. A man came out and closed the door behind him. He was not far away and Isabel saw that he was a tall man with a head of dark hair. He looked at her briefly and then up towards the woman on the path behind her. He screwed up his eyes, as the sun was bright, and stared at the other woman, momentarily uncertain.

Isabel was sure now, and was close enough to the man to address him. "No, that's not her."

She had approached him from the side, and he spun round sharply.

Isabel smiled. "That woman over there is not Minty."

The man threw a puzzled glance in the woman's direction and then looked back at Isabel. "I'm sorry, you are . . . ?"

Isabel was struck by Jock's profile. Of course Minty had fallen for him. "I'm Isabel Dalhousie," she said. "I'm a . . . a friend of Minty's."

Jock did not react for a moment. Then he frowned. "Is there something wrong? Is Roderick all right?"

Isabel reassured him. "He's fine. I've come instead of Minty, that's all."

At first Jock had been impassive, but now he began to look irritated. "Look, I don't want to be rude, but I was due to meet Minty. I don't really see why—"

Isabel cut him short. "Minty is very upset," she said. "And I want to talk to you about that."

He shook his head. "I don't see what any of this has got to do with you."

"She asked me to speak to you. She wants me to ask you to stop."

He looked up at the sky. "Sorry, but this really is none of your business."

You're quite right, thought Isabel. It's absolutely none of my business. But she did not say so. She did not like Jock's attitude. It was the attitude of a bully, and bullies never liked others to become involved in their programmes of intimidation.

She took a deep breath. "Listen, Mr. Dundas. You are treading on very dangerous ground, you know."

Her remark clearly took him by surprise. He opened his mouth to say something, but no sound emerged. Isabel decided to press her advantage; she felt more confident now.

"You have no right," she began. "You have no right to do what you're doing. You should count yourself fortunate that Minty hasn't contacted the police by now."

Jock's surprised expression now turned to one of astonishment. "The police? What on earth are you talking about? What have the police got to do with my efforts to see my son?"

He stopped himself, as if he had given away something he had no intention of revealing.

"I know he's your son," Isabel said quietly. "I know that."

"Well then, I have a right to see him, I'd have thought." There was a note of petulance in his voice.

"But no right to intimidate Minty," Isabel countered. "Threatening phone calls. Sending a wreath to the house."

Jock's look of astonishment returned. "What?" His voice rose. "What are you saying?"

Isabel could tell immediately that his surprise was genuine, and she was entirely thrown by the realisation. Immediately she reached a conclusion: Jock had not been intimidating Minty—that was clear. Either that, or he was a most accomplished actor.

"Come on," he said angrily. "Tell me what you're talking about."

The woman who had been coming down the path was now not far away, and Isabel thought that she could probably hear what was being said. She nodded in the direction of the hothouse door. "Look, can we go inside?"

Jock, still angry, muttered his agreement and they went into the greenhouse. The warmth of the day meant that the air inside was uncomfortably hot, in spite of the automatic windows having opened to their maximum extent. The air was heavy, too, with the scent of a flowering plant, a thick, rather sickly smell.

"Let's walk to the other side," said Isabel. "We can talk."

"And you can explain to me exactly what you meant just then." The anger in Jock's voice had not abated.

Isabel told him about Minty's belief that he was trying to put pressure on her to surrender custody of Roderick. "Is that true?" she asked. "Are you?" She imagined what the answer would be.

The accusation appeared to surprise Jock. "Of course not. Of course I'm not doing anything of the sort. My God, what do you take me for? I'm a lawyer, for heaven's sake."

Again, Isabel was in no doubt about the genuineness of his indignation. "I'm sorry," she said. "I've been misled. I'm not accusing you of anything."

Jock brushed aside the apology. "All I want is to see him. That's all. And I don't want to break up her marriage or anything like that. That's why I'm trying to see him discreetly—so that her husband doesn't realise."

Isabel shook her head. "All right. But surely you realise that you can't go on doing that. Sooner or later he's going to mention something to his father . . ." She corrected herself quickly. "Mention something to Gordon about seeing a man with his mother. Can't you see that? And then what?"

"I've thought of that," said Jock. "I've told Minty that these meetings can be described as business ones. I'm a lawyer. I could easily be doing business with her bank."

It seemed rather unlikely to Isabel, and she gave him a searching look. "Really? Do you really think that would be credible? And what's the point? What's the point of getting to know this little boy when you know that in the long run nothing can come of it? He's never going to treat you as his father."

Jock was silent. The confident, rather arrogant expression of a few moments ago had yielded to something rather different. Now there was a look of defeat—a look of sadness.

"I hoped," he said quietly.

"Hoped? What for?"

He did not answer.

Isabel decided to probe. "Why can't you just accept it? Why can't you say to yourself that Roderick may be your son but in reality he's hers—and Gordon's? Find somebody else. Have a proper son. One you can bring up yourself, not see furtively, like some sort of criminal."

They were standing still now, next to a tropical creeper that had sent out elongated tendrils and strange cup-like blossoms. Isabel did not like the scent of the flowers, which was vaguely meaty, with a whiff of carrion.

Jock looked into her eyes, and she saw pain. "Has it occurred to you that you don't know what you're talking about? Sorry to be blunt, but has that possibility occurred?"

Isabel lowered her gaze; she was in no mood to argue. She would telephone Minty when she got home and remonstrate with her for involving her in the whole business. She had assumed that Minty was telling the truth when she spoke of Jock's difficult behaviour, but now she thought that Minty had exaggerated—at best—or even lied.

"I can't have another child," Jock said suddenly. "Last year I had orchitis. You know what that is?"

She was taken by surprise. She did know. It was becoming clear to her now.

"People talk lightly of mumps," he said. "Even the name sounds a bit jokey. But it's deadly serious—at least in some cases. And I'm one of those cases. I can't have children now. Or ever."

Isabel looked down. She had been ten minutes or so with Jock and her entire understanding of the situation had been completely called into question. Not only did she suspect that the campaign that Minty referred to was an imagined one but she had also come to understand why Jock might be so desperate to have some relationship with Roderick—sufficiently desperate to concoct a ridiculous and unrealistic scheme to see something of the boy. She felt confused, as if she had tumbled into a place where things were not quite what they purported to be. It was easy to feel that, of course, and it was unsettling; it was why people clung so fervently to their beliefs about the world.

She took Jock's arm. "I'm sorry," she said. "Perhaps I've misunderstood the situation. I'm very sorry."

They began to walk back towards the hothouse door.

"What are you going to do?" asked Jock.

"I'll contact Minty and tell her that I can't do anything to help her," she said. "In other words, I'll withdraw."

Jock shook his head in frustration. "Can't you do something? Can you persuade her to see it from my point of view?"

Isabel was not sure how to answer him. It seemed to her that the situation simply could not be resolved in a way that would allow for compromise. If Jock came out into the open and took legal action for access to Roderick, it could result in the end of Minty's marriage to Gordon, which would hardly predispose her to sharing Roderick with him. If Gordon forgave Minty her unfaithfulness, it might help Minty but would not help Jock's claim to see the boy, as it was difficult to imagine his agreeing to let another man develop a relationship with Roderick, even if that other man was the boy's real father. Why should he? And if it went to court, a judge would almost certainly take the view that Roderick's best interests would be served by his remaining with Minty and the man whom he had been brought up to believe was his father. In any event, Jock stood to lose.

It would have been simplest to disengage altogether, to wash her hands of them both. And she almost did; but not quite. It was moral proximity again: this man standing before her was not a moral stranger to her—he was asking her for help and she could not turn him away. She simply could not. "All right, I'll talk to her," she said. "But I really don't see any solution that'll help you." She broke off as they went through the door. Now, out in the sunlight, feeling cooler and more comfortable than in the artificial warmth of the hothouse, she said, "Mr. Dundas, I think that you may just have to accept that Roderick can never be yours."

He stared at her. There was nothing firm or confident in his manner now. He was like a man facing sentence. And this made Isabel all the more certain: this was not a man who had been threatening anybody.

"Do you know how I feel?" he asked. His voice was low and unsteady.

"I think I do," said Isabel.

"It's like being dead," he said.

He spoke quietly, each word chiselled out with complete clarity. Of course he was right—that is what such a loss felt like. *Stop all the clocks,* as WHA had said in that harrowing poem of his. Yes, that is how she herself would feel if somebody came to her and said, "You may never see Charlie again."

She could not think of anything to say to that, and indeed she did not want to; any gloss on his remark was unnecessary. The feeling behind the death analogy was perfectly vivid. This poor man had made a terrible mistake in becoming involved with Minty Auchterlonie in the first place, probably an ill-thought-out, regretted fling. And then it had brought these dreadful, painful consequences. But who had seduced whom? She him, Isabel imagined; he would have been an entertainment for Minty, as men can be for predatory women, a bit of variety to relieve her of the tedium of the worthy—but wealthy—Gordon. And now she had the result of that, a little boy who very clearly was loved to distraction by his natural father, who, through him, had been given a vision of fatherhood, only to see it abruptly snatched away.

Most problems, Isabel had always believed, could be solved by the telling of the truth. This, though, was not one of them. She saw no solution here other than the denial of the love that

Jock had for his son. She wished that she could have found some words of comfort for him, but she could not. There were none.

Minty was the one who was responsible for this, she felt. She had brought this anguish to this man because she had thoughtlessly engaged in an extramarital affair. She paused. Of course Jock might have been responsible too: an affair, after all, always involves two—only complete narcissists are capable of having an affair with themselves. Here, though, it was easy to imagine Minty as Siren, luring Jock on to the rocks. So she was to blame for that, and, while one was about it, she had had no right to bring Isabel into the situation with those invented stories of threats and danger.

Isabel would speak to her and decisively wash her hands of the whole business. Jamie was right—again. She should not get involved in the affairs of others, especially when the other person reveals herself as manipulative and ruthless, ready to use people where and when it suited her. Jamie was also right in another respect. He did not like Minty; how astute he was, how acute his judgement. Minty Auchterlonie, she now decided, was in that category of people who did nothing but bring trouble into the lives of others, whatever they did. The only way of dealing with them was to keep out of their way, to isolate them as bearers of a dangerous infection who must be stopped from going out into a city with their burden of germs. But who was there to stop Minty Auchterlonie? Isabel?

She made to take her leave of Jock.

"You'll talk to her?" There was anxiety in his voice.

She nodded. "Yes. But, as I've said, I don't see it making the slightest bit of difference to anything."

"But please do it anyway. Please."

"I shall. I said I shall." She paused. Minty had told her to offer him money; now it seemed quite unnecessary, and quite inappropriate. And yet, it was there in the background, and might just move the situation on; one never knew.

"There's something else," she said. "I don't know whether I should even mention this. You may feel very insulted. I suspect you will."

"What?"

"Money. She told me that she would . . . would compensate you for dropping your claim on Roderick."

He was quite still; he did not move. But she saw that something was going on in his mind. He turned his head away.

"I'm sorry even to have raised this," she said.

He shrugged. "You were an emissary. I'm a lawyer and I know that you have to say unpalatable things when you're acting for somebody else."

She was relieved that he did not appear to be angry. But if he was not angry, then what had he been thinking when she made the offer?

"Minty mentioned a figure of fifty thousand pounds," she continued.

He did not meet her gaze. He was looking at a bee orchid, now in flower: a blaze of gold. So are we all reduced by money, thought Isabel; so are we all corrupted.

CHAPTER ELEVEN

ISABEL HAD TRIED not to think about Christopher Dove, ignoring him as one studiously avoids looking at an ominous rain-cloud spotted on a country walk. But such acts of self-delusion provide only temporary relief, and she knew that sooner or later she would have to answer his letter and the charge it contained. She was not a prevaricator by nature and she would get round to it, but it seemed at the time that there were just rather too many unpleasant or delicate duties waiting to be performed.

She would have to write to Christopher Dove; she would have to speak to Minty Auchterlonie; she would have to buy Cat an engagement present and make a further effort to like Bruno; she would even have to bring herself to watch *Oil* so that she could tell him that she had seen him on the screen. He would like that, Isabel thought, and it might be a way of building a relationship between them, which she knew she had to do. She had to do so many things, and most of them, it seemed to her, were things that she did not really want to do. That, though, was what life was like for most of us: doing things that we would probably not do if we really had any choice in the matter.

She thought about this as she sat at her desk the following day. Jamie had caught an early train from Haymarket to Glasgow, to play in a recording session—lucrative work that came his way occasionally and that he enjoyed. Grace had taken Charlie for a walk down Morningside Road, where there was household shopping to be done, and that left her with the time to get through the mail that had piled up again on her desk. But no sooner had she started than the telephone rang.

For a moment she toyed with the idea of not answering. It was a delicious feeling, ignoring the phone, a feeling of freedom almost wicked in its intensity. Why, she asked herself, should we be so enslaved by such instruments?

She looked at the telephone on her desk, struggling with the temptation to let it ring itself out. How many rings would that be? If it was Jamie on the line he would let it ring and ring because he would know that she was somewhere in the house. But if it was a stranger it might ring only five or six times before the caller gave up.

After eight rings she reached forward and lifted the receiver. "Miss Dalhousie?"

The man's voice was one that she had heard before, but not for some time and she could not place it.

"Lettuce speaking."

Her hand tightened about the receiver. Of course, that was it; those precise, rather pedantic tones were familiar because it was Professor Lettuce, former chairman of the editorial board of the *Review,* professor of moral philosophy, author of *Living Strenuously* and, most significantly, friend and mentor of Christopher Dove.

"How nice to hear from you, Professor Lettuce." The words

came out before she could stop them. It was a lie, and she should not have uttered them. It was not nice to hear from Professor Lettuce—it never had been. Lettuce: what a ridiculous name, she thought. Poor Lettuce: his salad days were over. She smiled; a secret joke, even such a weak and childish one, made it so much easier.

"And I am pleased to be talking to you, Miss Dalhousie."

Are you really?

"I happen to be in Edinburgh, you see," Lettuce went on.

Isabel tried to sound enthusiastic. "Well, what a pleasant surprise. Shall we meet up?"

She did not want to meet him but felt that she had to say it.

"That would be a great pleasure," said Lettuce. "I'm giving a paper this afternoon. The philosophy department at the university is running a series of seminars and they very kindly invited me up to say something about my new book on Hutcheson."

Isabel caught her breath. "Hutcheson?" Realising that she sounded surprised, she corrected herself. "I didn't know you were working on him. I knew of your interest in Hume, of course."

Professor Lettuce chuckled. "Yes. It would be more logical, of course, to move on from Hutcheson to Hume. I have done things the wrong way round. But there we are. The point is this: Would you by any chance be free to meet me for lunch? I know it's no notice at all, but I wondered."

Isabel looked at her watch. It was almost eleven and she had accomplished virtually nothing that morning. If she went off for lunch now, then she would probably not get back to her desk until well after two, when Charlie would wake up after his afternoon sleep and she would want to spend time with him.

The next issue of the *Review* would have to be ready for the printer in six weeks' time and that meant . . .

"I do hope you can make it," urged Lettuce. "I have something fairly important I'd like to discuss with you."

Isabel tensed. It would be difficult now to decline Lettuce's invitation as she knew that he would not talk about anything important on the telephone. He had always been like that when he had chaired the editorial board, alluding to information which he was party to but nobody else knew, or could be admitted to. "He's talking as if he were the head of Secret Intelligence," she had once whispered to a colleague at the annual meeting of the *Review*'s board.

"Perhaps we should call him C," came the reply. "Or M, or whatever it is that these people call themselves."

"L," whispered Isabel. L suited Lettuce so well, just as one would have thought that D might have fitted Dove—but did not. Christopher Dove was a perfect name, in Isabel's view; it had the ring of Trollope to it, every bit as suited to its bearer as was Obadiah Slope. She had always felt that people could grow into their names, just as we brought about self-fulfilling prophecies once we realised they applied to us. Obadiah Slope might have become a schemer because his childhood companions expected him to be one. Professor Lettuce must have gone through his childhood being the butt of mockery from other boys—fortunate boys not named after vegetables—simply because of his unusual name, and perhaps for this reason his character had developed in the way it had. There was always a reason for wickedness, she was convinced—a reason to be found in the classroom or the playground, or even earlier, in the crib, when the mother failed to love, or the father withheld his approval, or something else dark and unhappy occurred. There was inevitably an explanation for the coldness of the heart that years later could be so damaging in its effect. Let that never happen to Charlie, she thought. Let him never be loved too little . . . or too much.

"Are you still there?" asked Lettuce, somewhat peevishly.

"Yes, I am. And yes, I'll be happy to meet you for lunch."

"Good," said Lettuce. "Something light, I think, if I'm to do Hutcheson justice this afternoon. A salad perhaps."

Isabel could not resist the temptation. "That would be very appropriate," she said.

Lettuce did not notice. "Good," he said quite evenly, and, once they had agreed where to meet, they brought the call to an end.

The telephone rang again almost immediately. This time it was Jamie, who was on a coffee break halfway through the recording session and wanted to chat. "This conductor is a slave-driver," he said sotto voce. "We're being given an eight-minute break. Eight minutes!"

Isabel made sympathetic noises and then told him about the call she had just taken. "You'll never guess who's just been on the phone," she said. "Professor Lettuce. He's invited me to lunch."

Jamie laughed. "Perhaps he's turned over a new leaf."

Isabel smiled. There was something very reassuring about weak humour; it took the tension out of a situation, made children of us once more. But such humour was only possible when shared with the closest of friends and with those whom one loved; they always knew that you were capable of better.

"Poor Professor Lettuce," she said.

"Don't give him a dressing-down," said Jamie.

"Surely your eight minutes is up by now," Isabel retorted.

THEY MET in the Tower Restaurant, a rather expensive place perched on top of the Royal Scottish Museum. Isabel had suggested the venue because she appreciated the view it afforded of the rooftops of the Grassmarket and the Castle beyond. And, as she had once said to Jamie, "When meeting for lunch somebody one's uncomfortable with, it's important to have somewhere to *look,* don't you agree?"

"I agree with almost everything you say." Jamie paused before adding, "Within reason. And sometimes even with strange remarks like that."

"But I'm serious," protested Isabel. "When you sit down with somebody and make eye contact, you're drawn into each other's *sphere.* Unless you can think of a better word for it."

"For *sphere?*"

"Yes. Essence? Soul? Being?"

Jamie thought. "I suppose *sphere* expresses it."

"So," Isabel went on, "you need to be able to escape. And that's why a table with a view is important."

She looked at Jamie as she said this, and he returned her gaze. She noticed that his eyes, which were hazel, had small flecks of another colour in them: green. His eyes were kind. Somebody—a friend of Isabel's—had once described Jamie's eyes as being Scottish. But of course they are, Isabel had said; Jamie's Scottish, all of him. That's not what I meant, the friend had responded. I meant that there's a certain sort of look that you get a lot of in Scotland, in which the eyes are, well, almost translucent. You look through the eyes and you see something else—you see a whole country, light made thin by Scotland. You know our light, how thin it is; you know our colours.

She looked up from the table. She had been the first to arrive, and now here was Professor Lettuce coming in, standing at the door, looking myopically across the restaurant. She raised a hand to wave but he did not see her; the waiter at Lettuce's side did, though, and pointed to where Isabel was sitting.

"What a fine choice," said Lettuce, as he took his seat. "I didn't know about this place." He said this almost accusingly, as if he should know about restaurants and Isabel should not.

"Yes, it is rather nice, isn't it? I like the view. Have you looked at it?"

Lettuce twisted round in his seat and looked out over Chambers Street. "Roofs," he said.

Isabel did not know what to say to that. She handed him the menu and he adjusted his glasses to read. "My stomach is not what it was," he said. "I find that I take very little at lunch."

She thought of the word he used: *take*. Most people *ate*; one had to be terribly grand to *take*.

"It's best not to overeat," she said. She might have said *overtake*, she mused, but that would have made a very odd statement, more about driving than eating.

"You're smiling."

Lettuce was staring at her. She noticed his slightly prissy expression, one that some large men have; an expression of fastidiousness that for some reason seems at odds with their size.

"A passing thought," she said. "I have a tendency to think about wordplay. Don't you find yourself drifting off from time to time—some odd little notion?"

He wrinkled his nose. "No. I can't say I find that at all."

"Well, maybe it's a thing that women do."

Lettuce smiled. "It's as well that you said that, not me. These days it seems impermissible for men to make general remarks about the minds of women. Not the other way round, of course. You women can say what you like about men."

Isabel had to admit that this was true, although she did not like hearing it from Professor Lettuce. She had noticed that the constraints on such remarks seemed to apply only to men. Women could say, quite freely, that men could not multi-task, for instance, but men could not say that women could not reverse cars as well as males could. Or if they said that they would inevitably be accused of condescension, or sexism, or some other unforgivable -ism. It was contextual, she realised; it is not just what is said that is judged, it is what was said before. So what men say now is taken in the context of what they used to say—and what they used to do, too, which as often as not was to put women down and make jokes about how women reversed cars. Whereas the words of women, who rarely put men down— except in some Amazonian fantasy—were free of this contextual baggage. So the motives behind a man's words were now evaluated in the light of what men *used* commonly to think. Yet that, surely, was as wrong as saying that a person with a criminal record is likely to have committed the offence with which he is now charged. There were rules of evidence that were designed to stop exactly that conclusion, in the name of simple justice. So Professor Lettuce was right about this; it *was* unfair, but she was not sure that she wanted to concede the point, to Lettuce at least.

"Well, you can, can't you?" challenged Lettuce. "You can say what you like and we can't. I can't, for example, say that science has demonstrated real differences between the male and female brain, and this makes for differences in the way in which men and women respond to distress or view art. Or even for differences in the way they reverse cars." He laughed at his last example; he laughed.

She realised that Lettuce was talking for men here—for the whole class of men. It was a major assumption. And did the generality of men, she wondered, want people like Lettuce to speak for them?

"Oh, I don't know. I think that there's a time after a period of unfair treatment—or even oppression—when the tables are turned, so to speak. The victims of past injustice are given a bit more leeway, I think."

Lettuce's lips were pursed in disapproval. "Two wrongs do not make a right, Miss Dalhousie. A simple adage, but applicable, would you not say, to many contemporary forms of social engineering?" He had always called her Miss Dalhousie, and the formality, it seemed to Isabel, was meant to exclude. She was not a colleague, in his eyes; she was not a man, with whom he would feel comfortable. It was as simple as that. And, of course, he resented her purchase of the *Review* and the restructuring of the editorial board; his exclusion at the hands of a woman must have cut deep.

Isabel chose her words carefully. "Men have treated women badly in the past, Professor Lettuce. In many parts of the world, they continue to do so. They put women down. They try to stop them being educated, being given any opportunities."

Lettuce listened impatiently. Now he interrupted her. "Not in this country, Miss Dalhousie. Not in this country."

"Oh? Are you sure about that?"

Professor Lettuce's head shook slightly with irritation. "Such treatment is illegal. And nobody is stopping women being educated here. Look at university admissions. When I look out over my classes of undergraduates these days, all I see is women's faces. The occasional man. But mostly women."

"Girls are doing better in the school-leaving examinations," said Isabel mildly. "They appear to have better qualifications."

Lettuce's irritation increased. "That is because boys are now at a disadvantage," he said. "They are the ones who are being made to feel inferior."

The waiter appeared at the table. Isabel was relieved; she did not want to argue with Professor Lettuce, much as she disliked him. I must try to like him, she told herself; I must try to like this man, even if only a little.

"I'm sure you're right about boys," she said. "We must do something for them. No, you're quite right."

Her remarks seemed to assuage Lettuce's tetchiness. "Yes, I really believe that we must. Not that this should in any way diminish our efforts on behalf of girls. But we must do something for the boys."

With this common ground identified, they ordered lunch. "I shall have this salad," said Lettuce, pointing at an item on the menu. "What's in it?"

The waiter leaned forward to see which salad had been chosen. "Lettuce," he said. "Tomatoes, olives and avocado."

"Perfect," said Lettuce.

Isabel made her choice and the waiter moved off. For a few moments there was silence. Then Isabel spoke. "You said that there was something you wanted to discuss with me."

Lettuce looked out of the window. Isabel could tell that he was avoiding meeting her gaze.

"It's a somewhat unfortunate matter," said Lettuce. "Not something which I would have wished to become involved in."

Isabel waited for him to continue. He was still looking out of the window. Now he cleared his throat. "Christopher Dove has drawn my attention to a most unfortunate matter," he said. "I had not been aware of it myself, but he, quite rightly, I must say, brought it up."

Isabel sat quite still. She knew exactly what it was. So Dove had involved Lettuce; she should have guessed that from the start.

"You're referring to an apparent case of plagiarism," she said.

Lettuce transferred his gaze back into the restaurant. Now he looked directly at her and she was able to see his eyes with their small folds of flesh above and below.

"Precisely."

"I received a letter from Christopher Dove about that," she said. "I have been attending to it."

"Attending to it?"

Isabel took a deep breath. She could feel the tension within her rising. This was a fight.

"Yes. As is appropriate in such a case, I wrote to the author and asked for an explanation as to why the passage in question appeared to be lifted from somebody else's article."

"So you wrote to this . . . what was his name?"

"Dr. Jones."

"You wrote to Dr. Jones."

Isabel felt her resentment mounting. What business was it of Lettuce's how she handled this issue? There were established ways of dealing with accusations of plagiarism, or accusations of anything, for that matter, and Lettuce knew this full well. He had been chairman of the editorial board for years, and during that time they had been obliged to deal with more than one allegation of plagiarism.

"I followed the usual procedures," she said testily. "You'll remember yourself how things work. I wrote and asked the author to comment."

"And?"

Isabel bit her lip; this was not a courtroom and she was not a witness. "He wrote back to me and explained that it was entirely accidental. He admitted that he had read the other person's article and said that he had taken notes from it. He said that he must have inadvertently transcribed a paragraph or two into his own text." She paused. Lettuce was watching her with a look that was almost triumphant. "It's easily done, you know. You make notes and then you forget that a few sentences are word-for-word transcriptions. You've probably done it yourself, you know."

Lettuce snorted. "Highly unlikely."

"Really?"

"Yes. I'm extremely careful about that sort of thing—as one should be."

Isabel rested her hands on the table. The gesture calmed her. "I've accepted what Dr. Jones said. And I'm going to put a small note in the next issue—in the corrections column— saying that his article inadvertently included material without acknowledgement, and that this acknowledgement is now made. *Cadit quaestio.*"

"*Cadit quaestio!*" Lettuce exclaimed. "The question certainly does not fall, Miss Dalhousie. *Cadit nihil!* Nothing falls."

Isabel remained cool. "I really don't see what else I can do, Professor Lettuce. I believe that I've acted fairly."

Lettuce reached into the inner pocket of his jacket and took out a folded piece of paper. "Oh really? Well, I'm afraid I must disagree with you on that, Miss Dalhousie."

Isabel stared at the piece of paper. "It's Dr. Dalhousie, actually. I do have a doctorate, you know. Of course you know that."

Lettuce ignored this. "I'm afraid that I am going to have to ask you to resign," he said. "I know that you now own the *Review,* but the *Review* is also its readers and you have a duty towards them and towards the wider philosophical community, and frankly I don't see how you can possibly continue in office."

He unfolded the paper and handed it to Isabel. "This is a photocopy of a letter from the man who wrote the original article—the one that Jones plagiarised. It is the letter that he wrote to you before—*before*—you published the Jones article. You will see that he warns you that he believes that Jones has plagiarised him and asks you not to publish. But you know the contents, of course, even if you chose to ignore it."

Isabel looked at the letter in amazement. It was addressed to her, she saw, and it said what Lettuce claimed it did. But she had never seen this letter before; she was sure of that.

"This letter may be addressed to me," she said. "But I never saw it. Never."

Lettuce smirked. "Really?"

She looked up from the letter. "Yes. Really. Let me repeat myself, in case you did not hear. I have never seen this letter before."

Lettuce spread his hands in a gesture of puzzlement. "Or you chose to ignore it? Do you not think that that is the conclusion people will reach?"

Isabel closed her eyes. She was aware that the waiter had returned to the table and was laying plates before them. She kept her eyes shut. The waiter moved away and she looked down at her plate. She could not possibly eat, although Lettuce had now started to tackle his salad.

"Either this letter is a forgery," Isabel said quietly, "or, more likely, it simply failed to reach me. Many letters go missing, and I notice from the address that this person wrote to me from abroad. Letters from abroad are even more likely to get lost in the post, you know."

Lettuce dabbed at his mouth with his table napkin. "I wish I could share your certainty," he said. "At any rate, I fear that the matter will look very embarrassing when Christopher Dove makes it public."

There was now a silence that lasted several minutes. Isabel sat quite still; Lettuce lifted up his napkin again and wiped his mouth, fussily, fastidiously. She saw a small speck of salad dressing on his cheek, missed by the napkin. At last she spoke.

"I have nothing to reproach myself for," she said. "I have acted quite properly, and I am telling you the truth when I say that I did not receive that letter. But you obviously do not believe me. That is very clear."

Lettuce shrugged. "It is not a question of whether *I* believe you, Miss Dalhousie—it's a question of whether the readers of the *Review* and the general . . ."

Isabel supplied his term. "Community of philosophers."

"Exactly, whether the general community of philosophers will believe you. That's the question."

Isabel took a deep breath. "I shall tell you what I am going to do, Professor Lettuce."

Lettuce smiled. He was enjoying his triumph. "Please do."

"I am going to write to this person . . ." She gestured to the letter. "I shall write to him and explain that I never received his letter. I shall, further, tell him that I have received assurances and an apology from Dr. Jones and that I have accepted those assurances and that apology—"

Lettuce interrupted her. "No good," he said. "Not enough. You—"

Isabel cut him short. "No, certainly not enough. I agree. I shall also be writing to your friend Christopher Dove, and will tell him that I have recently discovered a startling instance of plagiarism in his own work. It occurs in an article that he published some years ago. A piece he wrote on self-interest, in fact. I am sure that it was unintentional. I have noted the chapter and verse and will send them to you immediately when I return after this lunch. Perhaps you might discuss this with Professor Dove."

She watched Lettuce's expression. She saw the small eyes open more widely in astonishment; she saw the chin sag suddenly. Her eye was drawn to the speck of salad oil—still there.

"You have some oil on your cheek, Professor Lettuce," she said. "Just there."

While Lettuce, flustered, reached for his table napkin, Isabel lifted her fork and began to tackle the small helping of fettuccine she had ordered. "Now, perhaps we should discuss your friend for a moment, Professor Lettuce."

"My friend?"

"Christopher Dove. You know, I've always found it odd that you and he are so close, bearing in mind his reputation."

Lettuce appeared to have recovered his composure. "He

enjoys an excellent reputation, Miss Dalhousie. He is highly thought of by . . ."

"You," interjected Isabel. "Yes, but not by many others. Perhaps you're not aware of his controversial friendship with a young woman who was a doctoral candidate of his. You may not have heard that the external examiner of that particular thesis lodged a note of reservation with the university. He said that Dove had interfered with the report on the thesis, slightly changing the tenor of some of his remarks."

"I cannot believe that," said Lettuce. "A typographical error or two, at the most."

"That's what the university chose to believe," said Isabel. "But then I knew one of his colleagues, who said that the departmental secretary had told him that Dove had told her to do it. She was too worried about her job to complain."

"Nonsense," said Lettuce. "Vulgar rumours." He wrinkled his nose. "And I'm surprised to hear you spreading them, Miss Dalhousie, though perhaps I shouldn't be." He tried to affect a look of disapproval but failed. He looks dyspeptic, thought Isabel. He's wilting.

Isabel twirled a piece of pasta on to her fork. "I must say that I'm disappointed that you don't seem to be ready to accept the very obvious truth about Christopher Dove," she said casually. "Especially when Cambridge University Press has asked my advice about finding somebody of sound judgement to edit their new edition of Hume papers. I know the commissioning editor there, as it happens."

Lettuce stopped eating. "Hume papers?"

"A very important new publishing project," said Isabel. "Five volumes over ten years. And there's to be a major conference to mark each new volume. Bloomington, Indiana. Tel Aviv. Helsinki. Siena. Sydney."

She watched him. He was quite still. "Starting off in Bloomington," she went on. "Have you been there, Professor Lettuce?"

Lettuce shook his head. He had coloured slightly, she noticed.

"I had a wonderful visit there," Isabel said. "A few years ago—in the spring. The blossom was out and it was just perfect. I was very well looked after. They took me to the Lilly Library. They have the most remarkable collection there—literary papers from all sorts of people, all neatly boxed away. And an astonishing collection of miniature books. Tiny ones. Smaller than that plum tomato you're trying to eat. You should impale it on your fork, you know."

It took Professor Lettuce some time to marshal his thoughts. As she waited for him, Isabel, toying with her pasta, found herself feeling some sympathy for her now-deflated adversary, caught between ambition and loyalty to his dubious ally. He was like one of those lettuces that, when you squeeze them, are all air between the leaves and reduce to more or less nothing, just a few thin green leaves. Although Lettuce was older than Dove by at least a decade, if not more, he was not the ringleader; it was dawning on her that it was Christopher Dove who was the prime mover in whatever plans the two of them had hatched. Lettuce was the mere messenger here, and he had seen the ground completely cut from beneath his feet with this countercharge against Dove. Now, watching him try to recover, she felt sorry for him; he was like a great beached whale struggling to get back into the water. To be pitied rather than despised.

"I'm most interested in Hume . . . ," Lettuce began. Then he stopped.

Isabel reached out across the table and placed her hand on his wrist. "I have no desire to fight with you, you know. I bear you no ill will over what happened."

He opened his mouth to speak. "Christopher said—"

"Christopher Dove does not like me. He tried, quite wrongly, to get me out as editor of the *Review*. I fought back. But I am quite prepared to regard all of that as past business. I really am. And I hope you are too."

Lettuce's eyes were on her as she spoke. He looked down at her hand upon his wrist, as if trying to make sense of it, but he did not try to shrug it off.

"I fear that Christopher may have misled me," he said. "And if that is so, I believe that I owe you an apology."

"Which I am happy to accept," said Isabel quickly. "So let's forget all about it and talk about your new book on Hutcheson. Isn't it extraordinary how the influence of the Scottish Enlightenment is still felt so strongly?"

She moved her hand, and Lettuce went back to his salad. "You're quite right," he said. "And Hutcheson has not had adequate attention paid to him, I feel. His insights into morality and our sense of beauty seem so fresh, even today. I pay quite a lot of attention to those in my new work."

"Good," said Isabel. "I very much look forward to reading it."

Lettuce now smiled. "I've been a rather foolish Lettuce," he said.

The strange turn of phrase caught her by surprise; referring to oneself in the third person always made Isabel feel uneasy, conveying, as it did, a slight sense of dissociation from self.

Here it seemed almost comical—sounding like a childish refer-ence to oneself as a vegetable; mind you, the French, she remembered, called one another *chou,* in affection. She reached out again and patted his wrist. "You've been human—that's all. We all make mistakes."

He looked at her in gratitude. "Thank you."

She inclined her head. She had not expected him to thank her; indeed she rarely expected anybody to thank her for any-thing. Gratitude was a lost art, she felt. People accepted things, took them as their right, and had forgotten how to give proper thanks. Professor Lettuce, for all his faults, had at least said thank you and she, in turn, was grateful for that.

CHAPTER TWELVE

JAMIE ANNOUNCED that he would cook dinner that evening—scallops, with green beans and dauphinois potatoes. Isabel, who had taught him how to make the potato dish, was pleased—and he was proud. "Nobody else in the orchestra can make potatoes dauphinois," he said, adding, "as far as I know."

With his preternaturally sophisticated palate, Charlie liked potatoes done this way, turning up his nose at ordinary boiled potatoes.

"Where did he get these sophisticated tastes from?" asked Jamie, looking firmly at Isabel.

It was not from her, claimed Isabel. Boiled potatoes were fine with her; but so were scallops and truffle oil and smoked wild salmon. "His grandfather, of course, my father, had a liking for savouries—potted shrimps, angels on horseback—that sort of thing. Maybe it's from him."

"We had mince and tatties when I was a boy," said Jamie. "And rice pudding." Mince and tatties were standard Scottish fare, as ordinary as could be.

"But you were lucky to have the mince," said Isabel. "Remember that there were those who had only the potatoes? A tatty and a pass? When the children's potatoes were passed over the meat—just passed—to get a whiff of the flavour on them? Then the father ate all the meat."

"All right," said Jamie. "We had mince. But when I was a music student we didn't have a fridge in the flat."

Isabel was politely interested. "Really?"

"Yes. And the hot water in the bathroom came from a tiny gas geyser."

"Such hardship."

"You may laugh. Today everybody has everything, right from the word go."

Isabel looked at Charlie, who had been playing in his playpen during this conversation. "He'll never remember mince and tatties," she mused. "Because he refuses to eat them. Or haggis. And he will assume that people have always had mobile phones and the web to give the answer to anything you want to know at the touch of a key. And invisible mp3s instead of CDs."

"Who remembers vinyl?" asked Jamie. "Do you?"

Isabel did; there was vinyl in the attic. One day she would mount an electronic rescue and save it, but she had been putting it off. In its vinyl form the music seemed somehow more tangible, more real. As a series of ones and zeros it seemed to her that something was being lost, in the same way that books might be lost when their contents are rendered digital. And bookshelves, and libraries, and printing presses, and binderies; if people spoke of books as friends—which they so often were— then could they say the same of an electronic file?

Jamie added, "And he'll probably find it remarkable that there was a time when we thought that we would have water and fuel and food indefinitely."

Isabel thought this was true. "I suspect he will."

"And he'll find it hard to believe that there really was ice at the poles and Amazonian jungles and creatures like polar bears and elephants." Jamie paused. "His world is going to be very different, isn't it?"

"Yes. It already is."

He looked at her. This was a shared moment of loss, of the sort that lovers may experience when they realise they are to part, or when a parent helps a child pack on leaving the family home; a moment made poignant by impending separation. None of us, she thought, wants the world we know to come to an end; we do not want familiar things to be taken from us.

Charlie was dispatched to bed. He was tired, and settled well—almost immediately. Isabel kissed him and passed him the stuffed animal he liked to cuddle, although he was too sleepy even for that. I never imagined such happiness, she thought. And then she remembered Jock Dundas and his efforts, misguided and unrealistic though they were, to get to know his son, and it made her realise how fortunate she was, and in so many respects. She turned out Charlie's lamp, leaving only the slight glow of his night-light to keep at bay the terrors of the night, whatever they were for him—*ghaists* and *bogles,* to use the Scots words. She had been frightened of these when she was a child, although her parents had reassured her that darkness was just an absence of light, nothing more. One does not believe one's parents, of course, who would be so easily lulled into complacency by those self-same *ghaists* and *bogles.* Ghosts haunted not only houses, but hearts too. Isabel was going through the door, and stopped as the lines came back to her. *Some ghaists haunt hooses, this ane haunts my hert / An' aye I hearken for its lichtlie step.* She went downstairs and into the kitchen, where Jamie was laying out slivers of smoked salmon on freshly buttered slices of brown bread. He looked up, and she crossed the floor to him. She put her arms around his shoulders and kissed him.

He was surprised; his fingers were fishy and he could not touch her. "Why?"

"Why not? I was thinking of a poem I once read, about a ghost that haunts the heart. I felt frightened."

He smiled. "You shouldn't. Not with me here."

"I know."

He reached for a kitchen towel to wipe his hands. She released him.

"The woman in the poem looks forward to her encounter with the ghost that haunts her heart. She's not frightened at all."

He looked away. Was she talking about Cat? Cat did *not* haunt him any more. And Isabel was no longer haunted by John Liamor, surely. He reached for the bottle of wine that he had opened and put into an ice-cooled sleeve. He poured two glasses and handed one to her.

"Are you ever frightened?" she asked.

He thought for a moment. He had been frightened, but it was a long time ago. At school there had been a boy who delighted in picking on him, twisting his arm behind his back until he screamed for mercy; it was something sexual, he later realised, but he was too innocent to know that then. The older boy wanted him but could not have him, so love became hate, as it so readily could. He had been frightened because he did not understand.

"I used to be frightened," he said. "Of rather odd things. Not now, though. Not for a long time." He looked at her. "And you?"

"I'm frightened of losing things," she said. "I'm frightened that something's going to happen to you—or to Charlie."

His face showed his concern. "What parent doesn't feel that? You think that something awful will happen if you don't do something or other. You bargain with fate."

She took a sip of her wine. "You have to put it out of your mind. Otherwise . . ."

"Exactly."

"Minty Auchterlonie. There's something about her that frightens me. I'm not *really* frightened, I suppose. But she makes me feel . . ."

"Anxious?" Jamie prompted.

"More than that. I get the impression that if you crossed her she'd think nothing of doing something really vindictive."

Jamie shrugged. "She might, I suppose. But sometimes . . ." He broke off. "I saw Peter Stevenson today, you know. In Bruntsfield. When I was getting the scallops from Hughes' fish shop. He was buying kippers."

Isabel laughed. "How reassuring."

"Your mentioning Minty reminded me," Jamie went on. "We got chatting. I was walking back up to Church Hill as I had to go to the supermarket. I mentioned to him that we'd recently met up with Minty again. Remember, he helped you first time round with her."

"Oh, yes."

"Yes. He still doesn't trust her, you know. He's convinced that Minty pulled the wool over your eyes over that insider-dealing matter a few years ago. He said that although she's the head of that bank there are quite a few people in Edinburgh who don't approve of her."

Isabel was interested, but only moderately so; there was nothing surprising in what Jamie had said. To get to the top of anything, and particularly finance, she imagined that one would have to be prepared to step on a lot of people. Minty must have done that—and made enemies in the process.

"But then he said something that made me wonder. I meant to tell you when I got back, but I forgot to. Sorry."

Isabel waited. Jamie had now started to slice the potatoes for his potatoes dauphinois. "Why is this dish called dauphinois?" he asked.

Isabel was not sure. "It may be because it's from the Dauphinois Alps," she said. "That's probably the reason. On the other hand, there may be a more romantic explanation. Did the Dauphin like his potatoes done that way?" It was unlikely, but it brought the Dauphin to mind, and his brief marriage to Mary Queen of Scots. For a moment she pictured them sitting together at a table in the French court, Mary with her teenage groom, offering him potatoes dauphinois.

"It was very tragic," she said.

Jamie sliced another potato and laid the slices on their bed of cream and garlic. "What was very tragic?"

"The Dauphin. Francis. Mary loved him, you know, although they were betrothed when they were terribly young. She loved him. And then he went and caught an ear infection that led to an abscess in the brain. Imagine how painful his death must have been: screaming agony because pain in the ear is so close to *where you are*. Perhaps they had some painkillers in those days—various plants. I hope they did. Opium, maybe. Otherwise, just imagine it."

Jamie brought her back to the subject. "Minty," he said. "Peter said that she was in trouble—or could be. He wasn't very specific."

Isabel was immediately intrigued. Peter Stevenson was one of the best informed of her friends; he knew things others did not, but rarely spoke about them—which was one of the reasons, she thought, why he knew things in the first place. Could Peter Stevenson be aware of Jock Dundas and the issue of Roderick's paternity? Surely not. Minty would hardly have talked about that, not if she wanted to keep it secret from Gordon. Edinburgh was a village: a word in the wrong place travelled every bit as quickly as a word in the right place.

She asked Jamie what Peter had said, and he told her, "Just that. Minty's in a bit of trouble, and he was not surprised. He said something about her sailing too close to the wind."

It was a metaphor that Isabel liked, and used herself. It conveyed very well the notion of taking full advantage of something and then being just a little bit too greedy and suffering the consequences. It fitted Minty perfectly, except that it seemed that she always got away with it. There she was, head of an investment bank, living a life of comfort in her Georgian house with the view of the Lammermuir Hills, and she had ended up in that position by . . . by sailing too close to the wind—there was no better expression for it. And Christopher Dove too? Had he sailed too close to the wind? No, in his case another meteorological metaphor was appropriate perhaps: he had reaped whirlwinds—or at least what he had sown.

She looked at her watch. It was not too late to phone Peter. If he was in, she could walk round to his house in ten minutes or so, talk to him and then be back within the hour. How long would the potatoes dauphinois take?

"I know this sounds impetuous," she said, "but I want to see Peter. Could I go round there while your potatoes are dauphinoising?"

Jamie looked at her in astonishment. "Why? Can't it wait?"

It could wait, of course, but Isabel herself could not. If she did not see Peter now she would spend the night pondering the implications of what he had said to Jamie. And if she did that, then the next day she would be too tired to work, would get behind with the *Review*, and that would prey on her mind sufficiently to ruin her sleep the following night. No, she had to talk to Peter now.

Jamie tried to be gracious. "All right. But please don't be too late—potatoes dauphinois get soggy if you leave them."

She kissed him lightly on the cheek and went to the telephone. Susie, Peter's wife, answered and said that Peter was in the garden with the dog. Of course he would be happy to see Isabel; they had no plans for the evening and she was not yet even thinking about supper. "We had a late lunch today," she said.

Isabel put on a light coat; the day itself had been warm, but evenings in Edinburgh could be chilly, particularly when the sky was empty of clouds, as it was this evening. Deciding to add a scarf to the coat, she went out of the house and set off for the Stevensons' house in the Grange. It was not a long walk, but it was an interesting one for Isabel, as wherever she walked in Edinburgh she passed places with particular associations for her. So now, by taking a shortcut, she found herself walking past the house of Alex Philip, the architect whom she had consulted about possible alterations to her house, and then past the house of Haflidi Hallgrimsson, the composer whose latest piece she had listened to a few days previously. And round the corner from that she saw the road that led to the house of a well-known politician, and past the house of another of whom she had heard a most cutting remark passed—ten years ago, but still clear in her mind. She knew that she should not find it amusing, but she did: somebody had said of that person, with devastating accuracy, "He always does the right thing. It just so happens that the right thing is always in his best interests." It was a remark devoid of charity, and she wondered whether there was a duty not to bring such words to mind but rather to let them fade. It would be an act of memory-housekeeping of the sort that perhaps we all needed to undertake from time to time. In this way might one rid the heart of ghosts, she thought.

Could we remember, though, only those things we wanted to? Could there be acts of forgetting, just as there could be acts of remembrance? Human memory was frequently difficult and unruly, but it was not beyond telling. And it was possible, she thought, to say to another who wanted one to forget something, an embarrassing or shameful incident perhaps, *Yes, I have forgotten it.* That was a lesson that one of her school friends could take to heart; whenever Isabel saw her now she delighted in remembering how as twelve-year-olds they had teased a vulnerable teacher, imitating her voice when she turned to write something on the blackboard, unaware of her lack of sureness of herself, her crippling inadequacy in the face of taunting schoolgirls. *Don't remind me of that,* Isabel wanted to say, but did not because it sounded like an abrogation of responsibility for what she, like the other girls, had been. And yet that twelve-year-old *was* a different person in the moral sense; she, the mature Isabel Dalhousie, would never do what that near-teenage girl had done. It was not her; it simply was not her any more.

She crossed the road at Church Hill and made her way along the road to the gateway of West Grange House. Peter was in the garden, bending over to examine something in a flower bed, and was alerted to the arrival of Isabel by the barking of his dog.

"I know it's an odd time to come and see you," said Isabel. "But there's something I need to talk to you about."

Peter smiled. "And it couldn't wait?" he said. "Your impatience has always been one of your most charming qualities." He gestured to a bench to the side of the front door. "We can sit there. It's still warm enough to be outside. And light enough. The one consolation of our poor Scottish summers is the light, don't you think?"

Isabel agreed. Then there was a silence, during which Peter looked at her expectantly. Eventually he said, "Minty Auchterlonie?"

She nodded.

"I thought it might be," said Peter. "Did Jamie tell you that I met him at Hughes'?"

"Yes. And you said that you thought that she was in trouble."

Peter nodded. "I did. And she is."

She waited for him to expand on this, but when he spoke again it was to question her. "Are you . . . Well, I was about to say *interfering* again, but I realise that's not exactly tactful. And I realise, too, that you can't help yourself."

From someone else she might have resented this remark, but not from an old friend. "I don't know if it's interfering to respond to a clear request from somebody," she said. "She sought me out. She asked me."

Peter conceded. "All right. I take it back. No interference."

"And I *can* help myself," Isabel added.

Peter was gracious. "Of course you can. Anyway, Minty: Do you want me to tell you what I know?"

She wondered if he was teasing her. "Will you?"

Peter looked at her as if weighing her up. "Well, I'm not sure if I can say much."

Isabel reassured him. "I won't repeat what you tell me. I'm quite discreet, you know."

"Oh, I know that," said Peter. "But I'm afraid I can't give you all that much to be discreet about. I have my suspicions, though."

"About her honesty."

Peter thought for a moment. "Yes, you could say that. The definition of business honesty is a tricky thing, but it certainly covers what you don't say just as much as what you do say."

Isabel knew what he meant. There were many situations where failing to say something one should say could seriously harm somebody else; the difficulty, though, was judging just when there was a duty to say something in the first place.

"My understanding," Peter continued, "is that Minty Auchterlonie has been accused of withholding information from an investor in her bank, a man called George Finesk. He's furious as a result and is muttering about suing her. Nothing's happened yet. But people have heard about it and that can't be doing her much good."

"And did she do this?" asked Isabel.

Peter hesitated before replying.

"Perhaps," he began. "She's not a crook. I suspect that she's far too clever to break the law. But she is what I call flaky. She bends the rules to suit her own interests. She's got to the top in a man's world at a very young age, and she has an extraordinary record of bringing home the bacon. So people have been prepared to give her the benefit of the doubt, as you did, wrongly in my view, over that insider-dealing affair, when she managed to push the blame on to a largely innocent colleague of her fiancé. And I am aware of several other occasions when she has taken unprincipled shortcuts."

Isabel absorbed this. Peter was careful in his judgements, and if he had reached this view of Minty there would be good grounds for it. "And this George Finesk?" she asked. "What about him?"

Peter leaned back on the bench. "As it happens I know him reasonably well. He used to own a large tea estate in Darjeeling—the Finesks had stayed on in India after Independence, through difficult times politically and financially, and eventually George inherited the estate from his father in the late nineteen-eighties. He ran it for a while before he sold out to some big Bengali investment company. George loved India but his wife had an aged mother in the Borders, and for one reason and another he thought it better to come home.

"They had money in Scotland too—they used to be shipping people from Glasgow, on his mother's side. George used this to set up a family investment company—quite a successful one. Minty would know this, of course, and so when she was looking for a new investor in the bank, he was an obvious person to approach. George proved amenable and came up with one and a half million. That's quite a bit of money, even for him."

Peter stopped, and they sat in silence while Isabel thought over what he had said. She wondered whether there was a connection between the threats that Minty had been receiving and this argument between her and George Finesk. Could George Finesk have been so outraged that he might have started some sort of campaign against Minty, fighting underhand dealings with underhand methods? It seemed improbable, and yet the whole issue was unlikely if one stopped to think about it. It was unlikely that Minty would have an affair, and let herself become pregnant, and yet she had. It was unlikely that the father of that child would suddenly develop a burning interest in getting to know his son, and yet Jock Dundas had done exactly that. It was unlikely that she, a total stranger to these issues, should be enlisted as an intermediary—at the child's birthday party, no less—and yet she had. It was all unlikely.

"So what's going to happen?" asked Isabel. Peter had explained it clearly enough, but she still felt a bit out of her depth. In particular, she felt that she was no match for Minty Auchterlonie and her machinations. The world of finance was not Isabel's world, yet it was the very air that Minty breathed.

Peter shrugged. "It depends on whether George continues to make a fuss. He may give up. Or he may not. I suppose that Minty and her co-directors are hoping to keep a lid on the whole thing—but I imagine they'll still be frightened that George may be so angry that he'll expose the matter regardless of the consequences to his investment."

They sat on the bench for a little while longer, joined after a few minutes by Susie, who brought out glasses of diluted elderflower cordial. "From the garden," she said. "We have an elder at the back that never fails us."

"I have one too," said Isabel. "Each year I say this will be the year I make elderflower cordial, and each year I forget, or put it off, or think of an excuse. I suppose I'm just weak."

Susie shook her head. "You're not. You've got a journal to run, as well as a child and a fiancé. You've got more than enough in your life."

"But I could do something about elderflower cordial. It's not a big thing."

"Well, you have to draw the line somewhere," said Susie.

"The problem, though, is where to draw that line," observed Isabel. "Don't you think?"

Peter looked at her. "Yes, that's right. And it seems to me that you have difficulty with that. Hence your getting involved in other people's problems." He paused. "Are you doing that right now? Are you getting mixed up in Minty's affairs?"

She knew that she could not conceal anything from Peter; he would know immediately. And yet she could not tell him about Minty's approach to her, as she had promised that she would pass that secret on to nobody but Jamie.

"A bit," she said. "Unfortunately, I can't talk about it. I hope you'll understand."

Peter did. "But I really feel I should warn you," he went on. "Be careful. That woman is dangerous. Just be careful."

Susie looked anxious. "I've never liked her," she said quietly. "She's . . ." She looked around for the right word. Susie was charitable.

"Wicked," said Peter. "Susie's too kind to say it."

Isabel looked over the lawn at the monkey-puzzle tree that grew in front of the Victorian greenhouse. There was something ruthless about Minty—that was clear enough—but was she wicked? There were plenty of people who were excessively ambitious and self-seeking, who would think nothing of tramping over others to get what they wanted, but were such people *wicked*? Wickedness was surely something very extreme: an attitude of utter and callous disregard for the feelings of others, coupled with a desire to hurt them; it was a deliberate, chilling perversity. She had no evidence that Minty showed such a cast of mind, even if she was selfish and greedy. No, she would have to reserve judgement on that just a bit longer.

"Wicked," repeated Peter. He looked intently at Isabel as he spoke, as if to make certain that she understood exactly what he meant.

SHE ARRIVED back at the house slightly later than she had anticipated. She went into the kitchen to find Jamie leaning against the sink, looking disconsolately at a red Le Creuset oven dish on the draining board. He looked up when she came in, but then his gaze fell.

"Your potatoes dauphinois?" she asked.

He nodded. "Burned," he said. "Ruined. I put them in and went off to play the piano. I forgot about them."

"And I was late," she said. "It's my fault. I'm very sorry."

"It wasn't your fault," he said. "It was mine."

She walked across the room and put her arms around him. "Darling Jamie."

It seemed to her as if he was somehow resisting her. His body felt taut, wound up like a spring. She touched his cheek with the back of her hand, gently, as if to take his temperature. His skin was smooth. His eyes had been closed; now they opened. She saw the flecks of colour.

"I don't love you just because you can cook potatoes dauphinois," she said.

His eyes widened. "You don't?"

They both laughed.

"Nor because you play the bassoon," Isabel went on. "Nor because your hair goes like that at the front and you can make up funny little songs out of nowhere."

"Stop."

"Why?"

"Because you're making me laugh when I don't want to laugh. I want to feel cross."

She disengaged from him, smiling with pleasure. "Look," she said. "Take off the top layer—like that—and, see, everything is fine underneath. We can have potatoes dauphinois after all."

He did as she instructed, laying each burned slice on a plate beside the oven dish.

"Somebody phoned," he said as he tipped the contents of the plate into the bin.

Isabel licked a piece of creamy potato off the tip of her finger. "Who?"

"He wouldn't say," Jamie replied. "He asked for you and then just more or less slammed the phone down when I said that you weren't here. Rude."

Isabel felt a sudden twinge of concern. "Not a voice you recognised?"

"No."

"Scottish?"

Jamie looked thoughtful. "Maybe. Yes, probably. Not very broad. In fact, not broad at all."

Isabel wondered. "A lawyer's voice?"

Jamie looked bemused. "How does one tell that?" But then he nodded. "Yes, maybe."

CHAPTER THIRTEEN

SHE WOULD HAVE CALLED Jock Dundas at nine o'clock the next morning, which was the earliest she thought that his office switchboard would answer, had it not been for the fact that Jamie suddenly shouted from the garden. She immediately feared that something was wrong—he had taken Charlie out on to the lawn to pull him about on the small, red-wheeled cart that he loved so much. Charlie had fallen out of the cart; Charlie had cut himself; Charlie had swallowed something and stopped breathing—the possibilities ran through her mind as she ran for the back door and pushed it open.

Jamie was standing in the middle of the lawn and Charlie—oh, relief—was sitting securely in his cart, looking up at his father, wondering why the ride had ended so abruptly. Adults could be relied upon, generally, but not always; there were puzzling interruptions of service.

Jamie, looking over his shoulder, beckoned to Isabel to join him.

"There," he said. "Over there by that big . . ."

"Azalea?"

"Yes. That bush with all the red flowers."

She strained her eyes. "What?"

"Brother Fox. Underneath."

She stared at the shadowy undergrowth. Was that red shape him, or leaves?

"We were standing right here," said Jamie. "And he went right past. Limping. He's injured. I think quite badly."

Isabel now thought that she could just make the fox out; and then, yes, his tail moved, and she saw the shape of a haunch. She took a few steps forward; the fox was not far away and he must have seen her coming. There was a sudden parting of leaves and he emerged, his head lowered, his body strangely twisted. She saw the patch of black on his side—a mat of hair and dried blood.

Brother Fox paused; he looked at Isabel, his head still held low, and then he moved away, going back into the undergrowth, heading for the back wall. She stood quite still. She wanted to go to him and tend him, but she knew that it was impossible; he would bite, and she would only make things worse.

She went back to stand next to Jamie. He had picked Charlie up out of his cart, and the small boy was watching his mother intently as she approached.

"Did you see that wound?" she asked.

Jamie winced; he was more squeamish than Isabel, who could look at blood dispassionately. "Think of it as tomato sauce," she had once said to him. But that had not helped, and had made him think of blood when he saw tomato sauce, which was hardly the desired result. "It looks nasty," he said.

"Has somebody shot him?"

Jamie shook his head. Brother Fox had his enemies in the neighbourhood, for sure, but he doubted if they were armed. "Maybe a dog." *Will there be dugs?*

Isabel shivered; she did not like the thought of fox hunting. Why dress up, she wondered, to kill something? If foxes had sometimes to be killed—and farmers had to protect their lambs—she felt that it should be done with regret rather than delight. "His balance seems affected. When he came out he was . . . well, it was like a lurch."

It seemed to Isabel that this was no different from any other situation where somebody needed her help. "We have to do something."

"Yes."

They walked back towards the house. She remembered the man in Dalkeith with his traps; she had never thought that she would have occasion to contact him, but now perhaps she did. They would never be able to catch Brother Fox unless they could get him into a trap. If they did that, then they could call the vet and the wound could be cleaned out. If they did not do this, then Brother Fox would either get better himself, as happened in the wild, or die a slow and painful death, as also happened in the wild. It seemed to Isabel that the second possibility was the more likely.

"I'm going to phone the man from Dalkeith," she said. "His number must be in the yellow pages. Under *Pest and Vermin Consultants*."

"Rat catcher," said Jamie.

They went inside. Charlie was beginning to niggle, which meant that he was ready for his morning nap; he had been up since six that morning. While Jamie took him to his room, Isabel went into her study and took out the heavy volume of yellow pages from the drawer in which she kept it. She paged through it: *Painters and Decorators—Quality Work Since 2001*. And before that? *Potato Merchants, Pipers*—who would pay them? she wondered. Finally she found it. *Pest and Vermin Consultants.* She saw the distinctive advertisement, with its picture of a small army of cockroaches, wasps and moles in panic-stricken retreat. Moles? She did not think of them as pests, but then she had none burrowing under her lawn; her attitude might change if moles were actively *undermining* her. So William McClarty of Peebles Street, Dalkeith, was a mowdie man as well. The mowdie man was the mole-catcher in Scots, the subject of a poem she had once known by heart. The mowdie man came on to the land a figure of vengeance, and stalked the mole, the mowdie, whose velvet coat and tiny paws would break the heart of anyone, the poet said—except the mowdie man's.

There were two numbers—one with *(house)* beside it; the other with *(all other times)*. She telephoned the house first but there was no reply. She imagined the phone ringing in the empty corridor of the mowdie man's house; a dog barking perhaps at the insistent ring, but the mowdie man himself out, stalking the land, driving off those armies of pests. She dialled the other number and the mowdie man answered immediately, or so she thought. But it was not him. "It's his brither," came a voice. "You wanting Billy?" She explained that she was, and she was asked to hold the line. So the mowdie man had a brother, she thought, who . . .

"Billy McClarty speaking."

She told him who she was. Then: "I have a fox."

"There's a lot of them in Edinburgh. They've been breeding like Cath . . ." He stopped himself. "Like nobody's business."

Isabel was astonished. She had heard that a long time ago, but nobody said it these days, she thought. . . . And yet, his name was Billy McClarty and the Billy could be a giveaway. An Orangeman: Billy McClarty was an Orangeman.

"Like rabbits, you mean," she said.

Billy McClarty was silent for a moment. Then he continued, "You want him away?"

She caught her breath. She felt as if she were a conspirator, contacting a hit man with a view to a contract killing—which it was, in a way. Their victim was a sentient being, with memory, plans, a family—with some sense of who he was. For a moment an intrusive, unwanted thought crossed her mind: one might invite Billy McClarty to take Minty away; to set a large trap in her walled garden, baited with . . . What would one bait a Minty trap with? The answer came to Isabel almost immediately: money.

"No, I don't want him away."

Billy McClarty continued. "Cannae kill him there," he said. "I get into trouble with neighbours. Where are you, by the way?"

She told him, and there was a grunt of recognition at the other end of the line. "There are lots of folk there who encourage foxes," he said. "I've heard of a daft wumman there who gies chicken to the fox. Those dafties wouldnae like it if I killed him, ken?"

Isabel said nothing. She was that daft woman. So one of the neighbours had considered trapping Brother Fox, for how else would Billy McClarty know about her? It was a very uncomfortable feeling; Brother Fox *belonged* to her.

She decided to explain. "I like him," she said. "I know you won't sympathise, but I actually like this fox. And yes, I do give him chicken. He has as much right to exist as you do, Mr. McClarty."

Billy McClarty sounded unsurprised. "Oh, aye?"

"Aye," said Isabel. "So we understand one another now."

"I think we do." He paused. "Nobody's asked me to trap that fox."

"Well, I'm asking you now," said Isabel. "He's been injured and I want to get the vet to take a look at him."

"Hundred pounds," said Billy.

Isabel had no idea what the going rate for the trapping of a fox was. One hundred pounds sounded rather a lot—fifty? He was sure to be overcharging her.

"How about fifty?" she ventured.

"That would get you only hauf a fox," said Billy. "You choose. Fifty for hauf a fox. One hundred for a whole fox."

She agreed, and they arranged a time. Billy would try to get into town by four in the afternoon; he had work to do until then. She would need to have a roast chicken available—or, if possible, a pheasant. "He cannae resist a pheasant. Mind you," he warned, "a sick fox sometimes doesnae eat. Even pheasant. We'll see."

Before she rang off, Isabel had a last shot to fire. "And a final thing, Mr. McClarty: I'm not daft."

Billy McClarty laughed. "I wasnae meaning to be rude."

"Well, in general people don't like to be referred to in those terms . . ." She did not complete the sentence. It would not help to lecture Billy McClarty on this; it would merely confirm his view. And she needed him now; or, rather, Brother Fox needed him. The contradiction struck her forcibly—this agent of Nemesis for foxes was about to become his rescuer.

SHE DECIDED that it would be better to see Jock Dundas in person. A telephone conversation was sufficient for ordinary transactions, but not for those circumstances in which one needed to assess the other person's reaction. Minty had mentioned the name of his firm, and it was simple work to arrange with his secretary an appointment for later that morning. Isabel looked at her watch; if she left now and walked to the lawyers' offices in the West End she would arrive with a few minutes in hand.

She chose to walk down to the bridge at Harrison Gardens and to follow the canal towpath to the basin at Fountainbridge. There were few people about—a handful of dog owners taking their dogs for a walk, a couple of runners glistening with sweat and engaged in an earnest discussion between their exhausted pantings, a teenager on a bicycle—the youth wore a leather jacket on which the words *Attack Squad* were embroidered in red. Who was being attacked, she asked herself, and why? He looked pallid, not unlike Eddie, and certainly not the type to attack anybody, Isabel thought, which was probably why he wore the jacket in the first place. Real members of an attack squad presumably never advertised themselves.

The towpath afforded an unusual view of the city—the backs of tenement buildings with their rough stone walls making for a crazy-paving effect, pinched back greens on which drying washing was pegged on laundry lines, arched stone bridges, a disused brewery. And in the basin itself, where the canal came to an abrupt end, brightly painted barges were tethered against the side of the canal, smoke coming from their tin-can chimneys, bicycles and other day-to-day paraphernalia stacked on narrow decks. The corners of a city, she thought, are where the

sense of place was strongest. The world saw the official Edinburgh, the elegant Georgian squares, the lines of fluttering flags
in Princes Street Gardens, the bands and the spectacles. It did
not see the back greens, the closes, the streets where people led
ordinary lives. It was possible, she reminded herself, to love
both equally—the Scotland of the romantic tourist posters and
this unadorned, workaday Scotland—and she was, in fact, fond
of both of them and not ashamed, as some were, of the romanti-
cised vision. Myth could be as sustaining as reality—sometimes
even more so.

She left the canal basin and made her way towards Lothian
Road. Like all cities, Edinburgh changed quickly: a block or two
could bring one to a different world. Lothian Road was traffic
and bustle; all cheap Italian restaurants where spaghetti bolog-
nese would count as the day's special and low-life bars outside
which black-suited pugilists served as bouncers, their broken
noses bearing stark witness to their profession. Isabel did not
like this street and wished it was not there, but knew that it had
its role. Soldiers came here at night, down from the barracks at
Redford, ready for hard drinking and picking up girls. If there
was blood on Scottish pavements it was because of old wounds,
not new; things that had happened a long time ago, old hard-
ships, old cruelties, old exploitation and old injustice.

And then, quite abruptly, the surly atmosphere of Lothian
Road gave way to the Edinburgh of law and finance, and,
amongst other discreet entrances, to the doorway of Messrs
McGregor, Fraser & Co., Solicitors and Notaries Public, Writ-
ers to Her Majesty's Signet. Isabel went in that door, just on the
edge of Charlotte Square, and found herself in a waiting room
not unlike the drawing room of one of the Georgian flats that

graced the square just a few hundred yards away. A sofa and several armchairs surrounded a low table on which a selection of the day's papers were arranged alongside *Scottish Field, Homes & Interiors Scotland* and *The Economist*. There was an air of calm to this room that belied what the business of McGregor, Fraser was all about: conflict and holding on to what one had. In the back offices somewhere in the building, there would be people in their shirtsleeves watching turbulent markets and planning litigation; but out here, in the front, there was no sign of that.

The receptionist who had greeted Isabel smiled and spoke quietly into her telephone. Then she invited Isabel to wait. "Mr. Dundas will only be a moment."

He was not much more than that. "Ms. Dalhousie?"

Isabel looked up from the magazine she was perusing. She had started on an article about a man and his friend who had transformed a run-down Glasgow flat into an elegant venue for entertaining. George (*left*) and Alice (*right*) had met at art college where they had both studied design. "We both liked red," said George. "It was a bond between us," explained Alice. "Reds brought us together." And now the Glasgow flat which had been "the most ghastly beige colour when we saw it first—we were almost sick on the spot"—was largely red. "George knew a guy who made really good bespoke furniture. He had trained with Lord Linley and his work was all over London . . ."

She put the magazine down with some reluctance. She would never be able to find out more about George and Alice, but she was not worried about them—reds would hold them together, she had no doubt about that.

She stood up and looked at Jock Dundas, who was standing

in the doorway. He looked grave, and she knew immediately that her instinct had been right.

"This way, please," he said, indicating a short corridor. At the end, behind a half-ajar door, was a small interview room furnished in dark mahogany.

"Please sit down."

"Thank you."

He closed the door behind him and returned to take a seat at the table.

Isabel studied him. He was frightened; behind the air of professional competence and suave self-assurance, there was fear.

Jock Dundas spoke first. "Why have you come to see me?"

"Because I believe you telephoned me yesterday."

He looked down at the table. "I didn't leave a message. Perhaps I should have."

She wanted him to look at her, but he would not meet her eyes.

"Are you afraid of something, Mr. Dundas?"

He looked up sharply. "Yes, of course."

"May I ask what is it that you're afraid of?"

He dropped his gaze. "You," he muttered.

Isabel's surprise prevented her from saying anything for a few moments. Jock Dundas spoke again. "You didn't expect me to say something like that?"

Isabel recovered her composure. "Of course not." She paused. "Why on earth would you be frightened of me?" Then she added, "It's ridiculous."

Again the lawyer's reactions made it apparent that he meant what he said. "Is it? Is it ridiculous? Or is that just part of your technique of intimidation?"

Isabel's voice rose. "Of what?"

He articulated the word carefully. "Intimidation."

Isabel leaned forward. "I am at a loss, Mr. Dundas. An utter loss."

If Isabel had been able to read Jock Dundas earlier, now he could do the same to her; and he, too, realised that Isabel was not dissembling. She was indeed at a loss, and this conclusion led to a sudden change in his demeanour. "You aren't . . . you aren't what Margaret Wilson said you are?"

Isabel spread her hands in a gesture of puzzlement. "I have no idea what Margaret Wilson said I was." Margaret Wilson? The name was vaguely familiar, but possibly only because its two elements were. Isabel knew plenty of Margarets and plenty of Wilsons; she could not place Margaret Wilson, though.

Jock Dundas sat up. His earlier air of defeat had vanished and he was once again the confident lawyer, safe on his own ground.

"And I'm afraid I don't know who Margaret Wilson is. Or I don't think I do."

"Margaret Wilson," he said, "is one of Minty's colleagues. They're also quite close friends."

"I see. And?"

"She came to see me after you and I met in the Botanics. She said that she had to warn me about something."

Jock Dundas had taken a pen out of his pocket and was fingering it, slipping the cap on and off. Isabel watched his fingers; they were tanned and the nails were carefully manicured. He was an elegant man; Minty would never have consorted with anybody crude.

Jock continued with his explanation. "Margaret said that

she had found out that Minty had approached a woman enforcer. That's the word she used. Enforcer."

Isabel wanted to laugh. It was completely absurd. Enforcers were the thugs used by gangsters to twist people's arms meta-phorically, which meant to break them in reality.

"She said I was an *enforcer*?"

He nodded. "She said you were a subtle one."

"Well, at least that's something," said Isabel. "I should hate to be thought of as some sort of *mafiosa*." She wondered whether Italian had a feminine form of *mafioso*. Presumably not, as the Mafia was traditionally a male organisation.

"She said that you specialised in ruining reputations," Jock continued. "She said that you could kill a professional reputa-tion stone-dead. Through smears."

"I see."

"Yes. And she said that you were going to make sure that I didn't get my partnership here." He cast a quick glance over his shoulder. "This is a fairly conservative firm, as you may know. It wouldn't be helpful for the partners here to know that I had . . .."

"Had an affair with another man's wife?" prompted Isabel. "Particularly a man as well-connected as Gordon?"

"Yes. And she said that you could ruin me in other ways. She didn't say how."

"I suppose there are ways," said Isabel. "But not being an enforcer, I wouldn't really know."

He sat back in his chair. "So I tried to contact you. To tell you that I was dropping my claim to Roderick. I didn't get you and so I telephoned Margaret and asked her to pass on the mes-sage to Minty that I was out of it. Altogether. Completely. She wouldn't hear from me again."

Isabel was listening, but as she did so she was trying to master what had happened. It was very neat. Minty had used her to give Jock Dundas a fright. She could have made the threats herself, but it might not have had the same effect. To hear that somebody else had been engaged—particularly somebody portrayed as being ruthless—gave a subtle twist to the situation. It was considerably more frightening, bringing in two enemies instead of one.

"May I ask you something?" Isabel said.

"Yes."

"If I tell you that this is complete nonsense," she said. "If I tell you that I spoke to you the other day purely as a favour for Minty and with no intention at all of intimidating you. If I told you all this—and if you believed me—would you still give up your claim to Roderick?"

"Yes."

"For career reasons?"

It took him some time to speak. "All right. Yes. You won't approve of that, will you?"

Isabel remembered T. S. Eliot. This was a clear case of doing the right thing for the wrong reason. But she said nothing about that.

"I think it's the right thing to do," she said. "It really is."

She rose to her feet and offered her hand. "I think we should shake hands. We don't have anything else to say to one another really." But then she thought that in fact she did.

"We have both been wronged by the same woman," said Isabel.

Jock Dundas looked thoughtful. Then he nodded his agreement. "Yes, we have."

"And I hope that you find somebody else," said Isabel. "Maybe somebody with a child, or children. It's a good thing to be a stepfather, you know, even if you can't be a father. It's a good thing."

They shook hands. Isabel noticed how soft his hands felt, like the hands of a woman, a young girl. She noticed, too, that he was wearing some sort of cologne—sandalwood, she thought. She had bought Jamie a bottle of something like that the previous Christmas, but he had left it on a shelf in the bathroom with the top off and it had evaporated. She had asked him, "Was that a mistake, Jamie? Or did your subconscious prompt you to do it because you don't want to use it?" And he had looked at her, smiled, and said, "Why must you complicate everything, Isabel?"

It had not been an argument, merely a discussion about why things are done, or not done, the way they are—or are not.

CHAPTER FOURTEEN

SHE LEFT THE OFFICES of McGregor, Fraser & Co. and walked the short distance into Charlotte Square itself. It was a little after noon, and she felt at a loose end. Grace had been left in charge of Charlie until two, and was taking him out to lunch with one of her spiritualist friends, Annie, a woman whom Isabel had not met but of whom she had heard a great deal. Annie, who came from the Isle of Mull, was said to have a particular gift of second sight. "A lot of people from the islands are like that," said Grace. "They see things we don't see. Annie often knows what the weather is going to be like. It's uncanny."

Isabel had been about to suggest that Annie might perhaps watch the weather report, but checked herself. She had discovered that there was no point in engaging with Grace on these issues, as her housekeeper usually interpreted even mild disagreement as a direct challenge to her entire *Weltanschauung*. Not that Grace felt undermined by such exchanges. "You'll find out," Isabel had once heard her mutter. "You'll find out once you cross over."

Isabel had thought about this. She was open-minded enough to recognise that the self—or the soul, if one wished—

might have an extra-corporeal existence that might just survive the demise of the mass of brain tissue that appeared to sustain it; the rigid exclusion of that possibility could be seen as much as a statement of faith as its rigid assertion. That is what she believed, and it allowed her to concede that Grace could be right. It also allowed her to find room for spirituality in its attempt to give form to a feeling that there was something beyond what we could see and touch.

"I've never asked you this," Jamie had once said, as they sat together one summer evening on the lawn. "Do you believe in . . ." He looked at her and spread his hands to create a space.

And that space, she thought, might be God. "In God? Is that what you're asking?" She assumed so, although he could very easily have been about to ask, "Do you believe in Scottish independence?" or "Do you believe in pouring the milk in first when you make a cup of tea?" Both important questions, but not ones that would necessarily lead to much.

He picked a tiny blade of grass and idly began to strip it down; how complex—and perfect—the construction of even this little piece of vegetation. "Yes. I suppose that's what I want to know."

"And you?" she asked.

"You first. I asked you." Children dared one another in this way: you jump first, no you, no you go, then I will.

She lay back on the grass. The night was warm as was the lawn itself, warm, breathing out into the darkening air. The earth breathes, she thought.

"I don't know," she said. "Not in the white-bearded sense. But I *sense* something that is beyond me. I'm not sure I would give it the name *God*. But one could, if one wanted to."

He listened carefully, and she realised, turning her head

slightly so that she could see him, that for him this was one of the most intimate conversations they had ever had. To talk about sex was nothing to talking about God; the body stripped bare was never as bare as the soul so stripped. "And what about you?" she asked gently.

"I don't think about it very much. It's not really the sort of thing that I think much about."

The answer pleased her. She would not have wanted him to reveal a certainty concealed up to this point. And there was something unattractive about a belief that excluded all doubt.

"But you're not an out-and-out atheist? You don't deride people who do believe in God?"

Again his answer pleased her. "No, not at all. People need some idea . . . some idea of where they are."

"Exactly."

He had been lying down too, and now he propped himself up on an elbow and faced her. "And there's Mozart."

She encouraged him to explain.

"Mozart, you see," he said, "is so perfect. If there can be music like that, it must be tied in some way to something outside us—it has to be. Some combination of harmony and shape that has nothing to do with us—it's just there. Maybe God's something to do with that. Something to do with beauty."

Something to do with beauty. Yes, she thought, that was one way of expressing it. Moral beauty existed as clearly as any other form of beauty and perhaps that was where we would find the God who was so vividly, and sometimes bizarrely, described in our noisy religious explanations. It was an intriguing thought, as it meant that a concert could be a spiritual experience, a secular painting a religious icon, a beguiling face a passing angel.

But that was on the lawn and this was in Charlotte Square. She looked at her watch again. The meeting with Jock Dundas had resolved itself well—in a handshake that had amounted to an act of reconciliation. Yet in another sense it had left her angry and disturbed. She had been used by Minty Auchterlonie, and had she not gone to see Jock Dundas, she might never have discovered that fact. It should not surprise her, of course. Peter Stevenson had spelled it out for her: Minty was, quite simply, wicked. Of course she would use people, as she had just used Isabel.

As she began to walk round the square, thinking of having lunch somewhere but not yet decided, Isabel found her anger mounting. Anger was like that, she knew: one did not necessarily feel at one's angriest in the first few minutes after some act of provocation by another—one's anger slowly grew as the implications of what had happened sank in. And there was a physiological basis to this too: levels of noradrenaline peaked in the system some time after the event. Anger of the moment was often less vivid than the anger that came later, once one got home and reflected on what had happened.

She stopped walking and stood quite still, closing her eyes. I am a philosopher, she told herself. I shall not allow myself to be overcome by this emotion of anger. I shall not. She opened her eyes. She took a deep breath, held it, and then exhaled. Her heart rate slowed. That's better, she thought. That was the way to deal with noradrenaline. Minty is . . . Minty is nothing. But she was not nothing. There was no comfort to be obtained in thinking something so patently false. No, she is not nothing, she is simply a manipulative psychopath. But even that was not very satisfactory; labelling another may help, but not always. A label which one can preface with the word *poor* is capable of putting things in perspective and defusing antagonism, but we did not say *poor psychopath*.

She took another deep breath and began to walk again. She was now outside the National Trust for Scotland café on the south side of Charlotte Square. It was just what she needed: the National Trust stood for stability, for reason, and for conservation of what had gone before. The Trust looked after castles and gardens and stretches of coastline. It was synonymous with peace and calm, and Isabel decided she would order a bowl of soup in the café—there was nothing quite like soup as a comfort food—and she would have a sandwich or two and perhaps a glass of wine. All of which, she imagined, would remove any remaining traces of anger-inducing noradrenaline as surely as a glass of something rich in antioxidants will mop up circulating free radicals.

She went in and took a seat at one of the tables. She looked about her. A waitress was coming towards her, smiling, bearing a menu, and behind her was another waitress holding a plate of food. She looked in the other direction. The café was not crowded; only one or two tables were occupied as it was not yet the lunch hour. But the table next to hers was taken, and at it was sitting Minty Auchterlonie.

IT IS HARD to ignore the other people in a room when there are only a few of you. You can try, of course, and some people make a passable job of acting as if others are just not there. Grace had once recounted such an experience when she had found herself in a small room with two other candidates for a part-time job in a hotel. One of the others had acknowledged her presence and smiled encouragingly; the other woman, "putting on airs" said Grace, pretended that nobody else was in the room and looked everywhere but at her companions—up at the ceiling, at the pictures on the wall, at her wristwatch. Isabel relished the thought: Grace in combat was glorious.

"And what happened?" asked Isabel.

"When I walked past her I stood on her toe," said Grace. "Deliberately."

Although Isabel would have preferred not to encounter Minty in the National Trust café, the other woman was none the less there, and was looking in Isabel's direction.

"Isabel!"

Isabel looked up from her feigned scrutiny of the menu; it had been upside down anyway.

She smiled at Minty, who rose from her table and crossed the floor towards her.

"Are you by yourself?" Minty asked brightly.

Isabel had no alternative but to welcome Minty to the empty seat on the other side of her table.

"I very rarely come to this place," said Minty. "I usually have lunch at my desk. I send my assistant out for a sandwich. Of course there are business lunches, and I have my places for those. What about you?"

Isabel waved a hand airily. "Oh, just like you. A sandwich. A bowl of soup. Mostly at home."

"You're so lucky," said Minty. "Not to have a job."

Isabel's eyes narrowed; she would not be condescended to by Minty. "Actually, I do have a job. As you know, I edit a journal."

Minty seemed hardly to hear the reply. This was not a real job as far as she was concerned. "Of course."

Isabel glanced at the menu. The soup was Tuscan bean. "Tuscan bean," she began to point out, but was cut short by Minty. "I was going to phone you this evening," she said. "This is fortuitous."

Isabel looked at Minty evenly. "Yes, I wanted to talk to you too."

"Well, here we are," said Minty breezily. "Tell me, how did—"

Isabel decided that it was her turn to interject. "I've just seen Jock Dundas," she said. "I went to his office."

Minty was silent. Isabel saw a muscle on the side of her face twitch slightly; it was almost imperceptible, but she saw it.

"Yes," Isabel continued. "I went round to McGregor, Fraser and talked to him."

"A good firm," said Minty. "We occasionally use—"

Isabel was aware that any conversation with Minty was a struggle for control. Again she cut in. "He told me something quite extraordinary. He said that Margaret Wilson had been speaking to him."

Minty frowned. "Margaret Wilson? The Margaret Wilson at the bank? That one?"

"Yes. Your Margaret Wilson. And what she told him has effectively frightened him off."

Minty shook her head in puzzlement. "I've never mentioned you to Margaret. Never."

Isabel watched her. Minty would have no difficulty, she thought, in denying any knowledge of this. But she was determined to persist.

"Margaret Wilson is a friend of yours, I believe."

"She isn't," snapped Minty. "She works at the bank, yes, but I don't know her all that well. And let me repeat what I've just said—she and I have never discussed anything to do with you. We just haven't."

"Doesn't matter," said Isabel. "I'm afraid that I think that you have. The significant thing is that she told Jock Dundas that you had set me on to him and that I was some sort of . . . 'enforcer.' She said that my job would be to ruin him."

Minty's eyes opened wide. "What?"

"And Jock Dundas believed her. He's very concerned about a partnership in the firm. He thought he wouldn't get it if a scandal blew up."

Minty seemed to be listening very carefully. "Even if . . ."

"Even if that means giving up Roderick."

Minty sat back in her chair. Isabel found herself feeling surprised over her adversary's reaction. She had anticipated a flat denial from Minty, which she would simply discount. But what she saw now was something quite different. There had been an initial denial—at least with regard to Margaret Wilson—but that had been followed by a reaction that was altogether more calculating.

Minty now leaned forward. "Well, I must say that this is very satisfactory, Isabel," she said. "At least from my point of view. As for this . . . this ridiculous story that Jock came up with—who knows where he got that from. He probably made it up."

"Why? Why would he make it up?"

Minty shrugged. "I haven't the faintest idea." She paused for a moment. "To get back at me? Probably. A parting shot. Yes, why not? People get pleasure from harming others . . . after it's all over. Hell hath no fury—you know the expression."

"Like a *woman* scorned," Isabel continued. "That saying rather focuses on women, as I recall."

Minty laughed. "Oh, come on! Men are just as bad as we are. A man can be as vituperative as a woman any day. Are you telling me that men don't go in for revenge?"

"They do, I suppose."

"Well," said Minty. "There you are."

Isabel needed to find something out. "I take it that you ended the affair? It wasn't the other way round?"

Minty did not answer immediately; she glanced away. "It was me. Yes. I became a little bit bored, frankly. Some men— these good-looking ones—are really rather, how shall I put it delicately, disappointing. You'll know that, of course."

Isabel caught her breath at the naked effrontery. Minty had seen Jamie and was obviously including him in this category of disappointing good-looking men. *You'll know that, of course.*

"I'm not sure I know what you mean," she said icily. "Perhaps I've just been luckier."

They stared at each other. Isabel felt her dislike for Minty well up; simple, pure dislike. Is this what hate is? she asked herself. Or is hate something even stronger? Is hate the desire to annihilate, to stamp out—to *annul* the other? She could not recall hating in that sense—ever—but perhaps this is how it started.

The intensity of her antipathy worried her, and she briefly closed her eyes. Unbidden, a line of poetry came to her: *Let hatred not distort us / nor make crooked our ways.* She could not place it; it was dredged from some deep place in her memory, detached from its reference, its anchor. But she would heed it, wherever it came from.

"I suppose it's possible," she said. "I suppose he might wish to harm you."

Minty sensed a small victory. "Yes," she said, simply. "As I told you."

Yet it still seemed implausible to Isabel—why would Jock Dundas bother? And she remained puzzled by Minty's reaction. If Minty had indeed set the whole thing up, then surely she would have taken more trouble to protest her innocence. She had not even bothered about that, as if she did not care at all whether or not Isabel believed her.

Isabel's appetite had disappeared, and even had she still felt hungry and in need of soup, she could not face the prospect of lunch with a triumphant Minty. She looked at her watch. "I'm not sure that I have time for lunch after all," she said. "I have to see somebody."

Minty smiled sweetly, almost conspiratorially. "Somebody interesting?"

"Very," said Isabel. I'm married, she thought. Or almost— and you know it. It was Charlie—she would go home and wait for him. She would make him a warm chocolate drink, which he loved, even on a sunny day. She would settle him for his afternoon rest and hold his hand while he went to sleep. Charlie belonged to a world of innocence and truth—not to the world of lies and deception inhabited by Minty.

"I'm grateful to you," said Minty. "I can't tell you how relieved I am. Everything's changed now. You helped, and I owe you."

Isabel looked at her watch once again—unnecessarily—and began to rise from the table.

"I really am grateful," Minty said. "If there's ever anything . . ."

Isabel tried to smile. "Thank you," she said. "One never knows."

"No," said Minty. "One doesn't."

Isabel started to leave, but Minty suddenly stood up and reached out for the sleeve of her jacket; she felt her fingers around her arm, surprisingly tight.

"A final thought," said Minty.

Isabel moved her arm slightly, causing Minty's grip to loosen.

"You know something? I think that Jock had no real interest in Roderick at all. None at all."

Isabel waited for her to continue, although she wanted to leave now; she felt that she was becoming entangled in an unpleasant end-of-affair squabble. Shots were being exchanged, recriminations, and all the parties wanted in such circum-stances was to enlist your support, to hear you say: "Yes, you're right, how terrible, how badly you've been treated."

Minty seemed to warm to her theme. "He doesn't care, does he? This business with Roderick was just to put me on the spot, to exert pressure on me. And then, when push comes to shove, he drops the claim like that—just like that. No man who really loved his son—*really loved him*—would choose professional promotion over the boy himself. He just wouldn't, would he?" She pressed her hands together in a curious gesture that Isabel could not interpret.

Isabel said nothing. Her earlier belief that Minty had lied was now being undermined by the apparent logic of what Minty said. What Minty said *could* be true. In fact, as she thought about it, it seemed to her that she was very probably right. But if this was so, then she had misjudged Minty again, and that con-clusion made her feel foolish. It was as if she was swithering this way and that, quite unable to make up her mind—a reed blown in the wind. "Don't you think I'm right?" asked Minty.

Isabel started to leave again. But not before she said, "Yes, you may be."

GRACE WAS LATE in bringing Charlie home, but was apologetic. "Annie didn't draw breath," she said. "That woman! Talked and talked, which meant that lunch was late. I was getting hungrier and hungrier."

Isabel thought of the contrast with her own lunch.

"Mind you," Grace continued, "she had a lot to say. It was very interesting."

"She's *seen* something, has she?"

Grace nodded. "She said there's going to be trouble."

"Where?"

"She didn't say."

Isabel was silent for a moment. "But there's always going to be trouble, isn't there? Whichever way one looks at it? It's like saying it's going to get dark tonight. It always does. It's the same with trouble. It's always brewing."

Grace put on a pained expression. She had explained these things to Isabel on numerous occasions, and her employer just did not seem to grasp them.

"It's just that if people like Annie," Isabel continued, "would be a bit more *specific* in their predictions it would be helpful. But they tend to vagueness, don't they? Look at Nostradamus. He's so opaque: those strange quatrains can be interpreted to cover anything. Why don't these people say things like: 'Next Tuesday at four in the afternoon there'll be an earthquake'? Why do they have to be so Delphic?"

Grace sighed. "When you see something, you don't see the details," she explained.

"Why?" asked Isabel. "If one has good eyesight in this dimension, so to speak, then why should one's eyesight be different in the other dimension?"

"You're not taking it seriously," said Grace.

"I am," protested Isabel. "Look, I am. It's just that . . ." She trailed off. There was something else that she wanted to ask Grace. "Do you mind if I change the subject?"

Grace made an indistinct gesture of assent; in her view, Isabel would never understand these matters—how could one ever see something that one was determined not to see?

"Do you think," began Isabel, "that a man who loved his son would agree never to see him again? Let's say that he had to choose between his career and his son?"

Grace gasped. "Jamie?"

"No, certainly not. Not Jamie. Somebody else."

Grace looked out of the window. "Well, I'm glad it's not Jamie. But if you want to answer that question, just apply it to Jamie. Imagine that it's Jamie you're thinking about. We know how much he loves Charlie. Would he do that?"

Isabel answered immediately. "Of course not."

"Then there's your answer," said Grace.

CHAPTER FIFTEEN

EVERY BIT THE ANGEL OF DEATH, Billy McClarty, scourge of foxes, chairman of the Dalkeith and Bonnington Model Railway Association, father and husband, stepped out of his van and made his way down the driveway to Isabel's front door. He was carrying a metal-barred cage, heavy enough to give him a curious, unbalanced gait. The cage was surprisingly small if it were to accommodate a fox, but not built for comfort, of course. For most foxes finding themselves trapped within, this would be the condemned cell in which they would be incarcerated with their last meal—half a chicken, perhaps, or, if Billy's advice had been heeded by the householder, a gamy portion of pheasant.

It was five o'clock, and Grace had gone home. Jamie had just returned and was having a shower, while Charlie and Isabel were playing with a set of building blocks that had been passed down to Charlie from a boy over the road who had outgrown them. Charlie was learning to balance one block upon another, three high, and then knock them down. He appeared to find this endlessly amusing; not much different, thought Isabel, from slapstick humour, from the antics of silent-film actors, from those flickering scenes where people stood up and then fell over, and we all laughed.

When the bell rang and she realised that it could be Billy McClarty, Isabel lifted Charlie and deposited him in his play-pen with a couple of his bricks for diversion.

Billy McClarty was wiping his shoes when she opened the front door. Isabel glanced at the cage. "Mr. McClarty."

"That's me," said Billy. "Sorry I'm a bit later than I thought, but there was a wasp bike in Morningside—a big one—and I had to get up on someone's roof."

Isabel assured him that it did not matter. As she spoke, she noticed the tattoo across his right forearm—the Hand of Ulster, with *Ulster is British* in shaded lettering beneath it. It was well executed, the hand itself in red and the motto in blue. I was right, she thought: Billy McClarty is an Orangeman, a follower of William of Orange, who had put the Catholic James VII to flight. That might have happened in the dying years of the seventeenth century, but it was not too long ago to be a very live issue for some, the symbol of the securing of a Protestant monarchy. And that, in due course, became all tied up with freedom from being told what to do and think by priests—a cause that at least was about liberty, at any rate from Billy McClarty's perspective. Catholics, of course, thought otherwise.

She led Billy McClarty round the side of the house to the garden. "We last saw him in those bushes over there," she said, pointing to the deep bank of rhododendrons. "He may still be there, but I'm not sure."

Billy McClarty took a step forward and peered into the undergrowth. "Good place for one of these fellows," he said. "Dark. Private. Good place."

"Like us, they need shelter," said Isabel.

"Aren't like us at all," said Billy. "Aren't like anything, these boys. Just foxes."

"That's not exactly what I meant," said Isabel. "I meant that they have the same needs as we do. That's what I meant."

Billy McClarty sniffed at the air. "They don't have the same needs," he said. "Not at all."

He took a step forward and crouched to get a better view of the ground under the rhododendrons. "He's been burrowing down there," he said. "I cannae see him now, but he's been there all right. I'll put the trap in there, I think. He'll be by."

"It won't hurt him, I take it," she said.

Billy McClarty reassured her. "The most that can happen—the most—is that he gets his tail stuck in the door. That's all." He stood up again and gestured towards the trap. "You got that chicken?"

"A pheasant," said Isabel. "It's in the kitchen."

"Even better," said Billy McClarty, looking in the direction of the house. "You fetch it and we'll set this up."

She went into the kitchen and took the pheasant from the fridge, a whole bird, roasted for Brother Fox. When she returned to the garden, Billy McClarty had positioned the trap under the outer foliage of the rhododendron. He took the pheasant from Isabel, sniffed at it with approval and pushed it into the trap, up against the back. Then he pulled back on the small spring arm that would trigger the closure of the door once Brother Fox had succumbed to temptation.

The trap armed, Billy McClarty took a step back and inspected his handiwork. "Aye, that'll do." He turned to Isabel. "And then?"

"When he's safely in there, I'll call the vet."

"And then?"

Isabel found herself irritated by Billy McClarty's manner. It was condescension, of course—the condescension of a man who assumes superiority simply because he is a man. "I shall call the vet," said Isabel. "I have already told him about this, and he'll come out and treat his wound."

Billy McClarty looked sceptical. "Foxes nip," he said. "How will he be able to look at him without getting nipped?"

"I assume that he has a . . ." Isabel was not sure, but she was not going to let Billy win. "I assume that he has gloves. And a sedative."

Billy McClarty shrugged. "I don't know why you bother," he said. "Nature, you know."

"Because he's suffering," said Isabel. She stared at this man with his red Hand of Ulster tattoo and his tobacco-stained fingers. "Suffering, Mr. McClarty. Suffering calls for us to do something about it. Don't you think that too?"

He stiffened. "You can't fix everything."

"No. You can't. But you can fix some things." She paused. He was looking at her with what amounted to a sneer. She would not tolerate that.

"I suspect you think that I'm just a sentimental woman," said Isabel. "You do, don't you?"

Billy McClarty shook his head. "No. Not me." He was grinning like a schoolboy denying the obvious. Of course he did, and he did not care that she should know it.

"Yes, you do. I can tell what you think. And I can also tell that sometimes you can't tell that people know what you think. Am I right?" She smiled as she said this, as if to indicate that the comment was not entirely hostile.

"I don't know what you're talking about," said Billy Mc-Clarty defensively.

"Exactly," said Isabel. She felt her heart pounding within her; any confrontation, even a small one, did this to her, brought on anxiety and its physical symptoms.

She indicated that they should go back towards the house, where she said she would pay him his one hundred pounds, fox or no fox. He looked sullen, but accepted the money quickly, and made his way down the driveway back to his van, tucking the twenty-pound notes into the side pockets of his trousers. Where the taxman will never see them, thought Isabel as she returned to Charlie's playroom.

Jamie, freshly out of the shower, his hair still wet and ruffled, had removed Charlie from his playpen and was lifting and lowering him in controlled fall, a game which he called Aviation Boys, and which made Charlie shriek in high-pitched delight. Charlie had eyes only for his father now, and she smiled and left them to their game.

In the corridor she stopped for a moment, lost in thought, staring down at the floor as if transfixed by the pattern of red and blue lozenges on the Baluch rug. Her smile went away. *I should not have spoken like that to Billy McClarty. It was wrong.* He had condescended to her, not casually or inadvertently, but with intent. Even so, she should not have tried to put him down, as she had done, using her skill with words to derail him. Those who had words might on occasion use them against those who did not have them, but only with caution. It had been a cheap victory over a man whose life was much harder than hers, for all his bravado and his Orangeman posturing, and she felt embarrassed and ashamed, as anybody should feel after humiliating another, even when such treatment seemed richly deserved.

"SO," said Jamie. "Minty."

They were sitting in the kitchen after dinner, a quiet time in the day that they both relished. The evening at this stage could go either way—into a companionable state of relaxation, or into a final period of work, during which Isabel attended to the affairs of the *Review,* or Jamie might practise in the music room or transcribe pieces for his students.

It was as yet undecided how this evening would develop. Isabel knew that she had submissions to read—articles sent in for publication in the *Review*—but she felt that she could not face them now and that tomorrow would do. So when Jamie enquired about her lunch with Minty she was ready to talk.

"Where did the two of you eat?" he asked.

"I didn't," said Isabel. "She put me off my food."

She explained what had happened, and at the end, with some reluctance, she admitted to Jamie that she might have misjudged Minty—yet again.

"If you have to keep changing your view of whether somebody's telling the truth," he said, "then that means she's a liar." He looked at Isabel quizzically. "What did you say Peter said about her?"

"He called her wicked."

"Then she probably is," said Jamie. "He's usually right about people."

"He must get it wrong sometimes," she replied. "And if people are wicked, will they necessarily be liars?"

Jamie was not sure. Isabel, though, was having further thoughts about her own question. The answer lay in character:

if one's character was base, then one did base things across the board. But that did not mean that one might not be good in some parts of one's life: one might show loyalty, for instance. Gangsters were loyal to each other—some of the time at least—and could be loyal to their country too. But was loyalty always something to be admired, or did it require a good object? It was no good being loyal to the Mafia or the KGB; loyalty in itself was neutral—it only showed its colours when you saw what somebody was loyal to.

Of course, if one . . . She stopped. A strange yelp came from the garden, followed by a rapid, high-pitched barking sound. She looked at Jamie, who spun round to face the window. "Brother Fox?"

"Yes." He stood up, but he was taking his lead from her. This was Isabel's plan, not his. "Now what?"

Isabel crossed the room to take a torch from a drawer. "We investigate. And then we call the vet."

They went out into the garden. With the lights still on in the kitchen, the lawn was partly illuminated. Some light carried to the cluster of rhododendrons in which the trap had been concealed, but only some. Now the beam from Isabel's torch played on the outer fringes of the vegetation and, as Jamie held aside the branches, into the dark interior of the shrubs.

Brother Fox's eyes were two small headlights, yellowy discs moving behind the bars of the cage. And beyond that, the red of his coat, half in shadow, half revealed in the swinging torchlight.

Crouching down, Isabel spoke to him in a low voice. "Don't be afraid. You know me, don't you? You've seen me before. I won't hurt you."

Jamie joined her, crouching too. "Should I move him?"

"Yes."

There was a metal handle on the top of the cage. Jamie reached out to take hold of this and began to pull the cage from under the boughs of the rhododendron. In the confines of his prison, Brother Fox twisted himself round and snapped at Jamie's arm. But the bars prevented his doing anything other than snapping at air—and at metal. "He can't get you," said Isabel. "Poor thing—he must be terrified."

"He thinks we're going to kill him," said Jamie.

Isabel bent down over the cage. Moving the beam of the torch across the fox's body, she found the site of the wound. She thought she could smell it too—a rancid smell, the smell of infection that is only one step away from the smell of corruption. She looked at her watch. "Simon told us to ring whatever time we needed him. Will you keep him company while I go and phone?" Simon was a vet whom Isabel knew; she was sure that he would never ignore an animal's pain. She was right. "I'll look after him," he had said. "A fox is an unusual patient, but I'll do my best."

She went into the house and made the telephone call. Simon was in, and agreed to come immediately. "Try not to stress him too much," he said. "I don't think foxes are easy patients at the best of times."

She rang off and went to join Jamie in the garden. Jamie had moved away from the cage in the hope that Brother Fox would calm down, but it did not seem to have made much difference. Every few seconds a whimper came from the caged animal— a whimper that sounded like a plea—and this would be followed by a yelp or a howl. There was no mistaking the distress in the sounds, and Isabel wanted to block them from her ears. "I can't bear it," she whispered to Jamie. "He's appealing to us to help him."

Jamie reached out and took her hand. "Which is what we're trying to do," he replied.

"I know."

She felt the pressure of his hand on hers, joined in an intense moment of understanding. It was a little drama being enacted—a tiny thing in the context of the ocean of suffering that the world bore every single day; incessant suffering—but for Isabel it was immediate, and vivid. She returned the pressure of Jamie's hand; he looked down at her and kissed her on the cheek, as if he might kiss away her pain, and with it the pain of Brother Fox.

Simon did not live far away and it was only a few minutes before they saw the lights of his car coming down the street. Isabel left Jamie with Brother Fox and went to the front gate to meet him. As she opened the gate to the vet, a particularly loud yelp came through the darkness.

"Sounds unhappy," remarked Simon. "Poor chap."

They walked round the side of the house. Simon had a bag with him, which he now put down and opened. From it he extracted a pair of thick gauntlets—rather like gardening gloves, but heavier and providing more protection for the wrists. He looked up at Jamie. "I could use these," he said. "But it might be better if you could keep him under control while I sedate him. Let him bite on one of them and use the other to hold the scruff of his neck. I'll give him a jab while you're doing that. Can you do it?"

Isabel felt that she had to protest. "Jamie needs his fingers to play the bassoon," she pointed out. "Let me do it."

Jamie objected. "No. I'll be fine."

"What if he bites through? I can edit the *Review* with a bandaged hand. You can't play the bassoon like that." She reached for the gloves. "Here, I'll take them."

Jamie knew better than to argue with Isabel once she had decided upon something, and so he watched as she slipped on the gloves. While she was doing this, Simon extracted a syringe and ampoule from his bag and attended to that; now they were ready.

"All you have to do is engage his jaws," said Simon. "Then I'll pop the needle in."

He was calm, and his calmness seemed to be having an effect on Brother Fox; the yelping had stopped and he was cowering on the floor of the cage, watching them. Isabel moved forward and carefully opened the door. Then she advanced a gloved hand towards Brother Fox. "Gently," said Simon.

She felt the pressure of his bite through the glove's thick material. It was not as hard as she had imagined it would be; perhaps he was weakened by the infection—Simon had said that was likely to be the case. It was the first time that she and Brother Fox had touched—the fact struck her forcibly. He had lived in her garden, or at least passed through it every day—it was his corridor, perhaps—and they had seen one another but were like neighbours who remained strangers, never exchanging greetings or doing any of the other things that neighbours do. But now they were face-to-face, not as the friends that she thought they were, but, in his eyes at least, she as an assailant who was trying to kill him.

Simon was quick. Isabel hardly saw his hand as he reached in and slipped the needle into a fold of the fox's skin. Then

Simon withdrew, and she noticed, curiously, a tiny drop of blood on the tip of the needle—vulpine blood, the blood of Brother Fox. The blood of another creature seems always so alien; stranger to us than our own blood, the bearer of the biological secrets of the species.

"That should calm him down," said Simon. "Give it a few minutes and he should be as docile as a lamb."

Isabel looked at Brother Fox, who looked back at her. His jaw slackened and she released him. For a moment she thought that she saw puzzlement in his eyes, replacing the fear that had been there before. Then he shook his head, as if trying to clear it; the sedative was clearly having its effect. His head drooped, and then he collapsed to the floor of the cage.

"That's him," said Simon. "Now we can bring him out."

The vet reached into the cage and took hold of Brother Fox's front paws. There was no resistance. Once he was outside, lying on the grass, Simon reached beneath him and picked him up. "The kitchen might be the best place," he said.

They took Brother Fox into the house. In the kitchen, Isabel covered the table with newspapers, copies of the *Scotsman* that Grace saved for the weekly recycling collection. Brother Fox lay prone across a front-page picture of the First Minister of Scotland. He is in your hands too, thought Isabel; this creature, this fox, is one of yours too—not one to whom you have ever said anything, but one of your constituents.

Simon washed his hands, dried them carefully and put on a pair of latex gloves. Then, very gently, he probed at the wound on Brother Fox's flank. It was not a large wound; a cut of some sort, he said, that had become infected. He took a pair of scissors from his bag and snipped the fur away around the wound;

there was congealed blood on the fur, a blackness. Then with a small scalpel he cut at what looked like small bits of string around the wound; dead tissue, he explained. Isabel watched, but Jamie turned away in his squeamishness. "I'm sorry," he said. "I don't like this sort of thing."

"It won't take long," said Simon.

Isabel had moved a lamp over to the table and was holding it above Brother Fox so that Simon could see more clearly. He worked nimbly, and was soon ready to suture the top part of the wound. "I'll leave this lower part open to act as a drain," he said. "And then all we need to give him is a big shot of antibiotic and that'll be it."

Now Isabel studied Brother Fox on the table. She stared at the pads of his feet—rough and scarred—and the imperfections in his coat. His fur was rough and unkempt, but thicker than she had imagined. His tail, she thought, was beautiful; she had admired it so many times when she had seen him walking along the top of the high wall that surrounded the garden at the back, as firm-footed and assured as . . . as a funambulist. Bruno. She had not thought of Cat's fiancé recently as she had been too preoccupied with the Minty issue. Now he came vividly to mind, and she imagined him, absurdly, on her garden wall, walking along in his elevator shoes with Brother Fox behind him.

Simon spoke. "Something amusing?"

She shook her head. "No. Just thinking about something else."

"Isabel's mind works in wondrous ways," contributed Jamie, from behind her.

Isabel half turned to Jamie. "I was thinking about our friend Bruno," she said.

Jamie smiled and raised an eyebrow. Now that Simon had finished attending to Brother Fox's wound, he was taking the opportunity to study the animal at close quarters. "He's lovely," he said. "He really is."

"They're interesting creatures," said Simon, standing back from the table. "They might have become domesticated way back—like dogs—but kept their independence. They're survivors." He moved forward to pick up Brother Fox, whose eyes opened briefly, but then shut again. "We can leave him out under the bushes," Simon went on. "It's a nice summer night. He'll come to in due course and wonder whether he dreamed it all."

"He's going to be all right?" asked Isabel.

"I would have thought so," said Simon. "He's tough, and he's got a bit of fat on him. Some of these chaps are half-starved, but he's been getting a reasonable diet." He paused, looking enquiringly at Isabel. "You?"

"Perhaps," said Isabel. She knew that there was a view that one should not feed wild creatures as it interfered with the balance of nature, but how could she not give Brother Fox the occasional treat?

"I'm sure he appreciates it," said Simon.

Isabel and Jamie followed Simon as he took the limp form of the fox out of the house and laid it carefully under the rhododendron bush. Then they accompanied the vet back into the house to retrieve his bag, and while Jamie went to check on Charlie, Isabel saw Simon to his car. "Will you send the bill?" she asked. "Or just let me know how much I owe you."

"Nothing," said Simon.

She looked at him. "You don't have to," she said gently.

"I know. But why should I charge you for looking after a wild creature? He belongs to nobody. And there's no point sending him a bill."

Isabel laughed. She imagined Brother Fox hiding a purse away somewhere, a purse with a few gold sovereigns, perhaps—his life's savings.

"You're very kind," she said. It was true. People who looked after animals were by and large kind people; they simply practised kindness, unlike those who made much of it. Thus, thought Isabel, are virtues best cultivated—in discretion and silence, away from the gaze of others, known only to those who act virtuously and to those who benefit from what is done.

She went back into the house to find that Jamie, having checked on Charlie, was clearing up in the kitchen. As he removed the newspaper on which Brother Fox had lain, a small piece of fur fell to the floor. Isabel picked it up. "A memento," she said, handing it to Jamie. "The Victorians loved putting hair in jewellery. I could put it in a locket."

Suddenly she smiled, and Jamie, for whom smiles were as infectious as yawns, grinned. "What are you thinking about now?" he asked.

"I suddenly remembered something that I hadn't thought about for a long time."

"Tell me."

Isabel looked doubtful. "It's silly."

"Life's silly."

"All right. A long time ago, when I was a student, I volunteered to work for a month in France. It was during the summer. A gorgeous, sultry August."

She had told him about this before. "The place for kids from Paris? The children who'd never seen a cow?"

"Yes."

He looked at her expectantly. "And?"

"And there was another girl there. There were three of us, in fact—all Scottish, as it happened. There was somebody in Edinburgh who recruited volunteers for this place. Anyway, there were the three of us. Me, a rather frightened-looking girl called Alice, and Jenny. Jenny was the one I was thinking of." She smiled again at the memory.

"What about her?"

"Well, she had a boyfriend," Isabel continued. "And she talked about him non-stop. He was called Martin. Martin says this. Martin says that. Martin and I went to Germany once. Martin will be visiting his aunt right now, as we speak. I wonder if Martin is all right. And so on. All the time. She was so annoying."

"Maybe she loved him," said Jamie.

"That's putting it mildly. But it drove me up the wall. Alice was too timid to say anything, and so she just sat there and listened to the Martin stories. I switched off."

Jamie shrugged. "People get . . . how should one put it, fixated?"

"Yes," said Isabel. "You could say that. But it was not so much her talking about him that I was thinking of. It was the mention of mementoes."

"She had a memento of Martin?"

Isabel's smile widened. "Yes. His boxer shorts. She slept with a pair of his boxer shorts under her pillow. We all shared a room and I saw them. They were a sort of red check. She took them out from under the pillow before she went to bed, waved them about a bit and then put them back under the pillow before she got into bed. Stupid girl."

Jamie burst out laughing. "How touching."

"She was so stupid," said Isabel. But then she thought: Was she? People fell deeply in love, and the clothing of a lover can so easily become symbolic of the object of that love. She glanced at Jamie. She could easily talk about him, just as Jenny had talked about Martin. Just as easily. And would she sleep with his boxer shorts under her pillow? Yes, she thought, I could. Yes. Like a silly schoolgirl, I could.

"Actually, she wasn't stupid," she said. "Not really. I shouldn't have said that."

Jamie reached out and touched her gently. "I have an old pair of boxer shorts if you'd like them," he said, in mock seriousness.

"But I have *you*," she said.

"Of course."

SHORTLY AFTER THREE that morning, Jamie woke up and slipped out of bed. Half-awakened, Isabel watched him drowsily from her side of the bed. He had gone to the window and had drawn back a curtain sufficiently to look out on to the garden.

"What are you doing?"

He replied in a low voice, not much more than a whisper. "I wonder how he is."

"He'll be off. Simon said a few hours."

Jamie moved back from the window. "I'm going to go and check."

She said nothing, but watched him as he moved naked across the room.

"I'll just be a minute." And he was gone.

She sat up in bed, suddenly and for no reason concerned. What if something happened to him? What if he were taken from her? Boxer shorts. She would have just his boxer shorts. Absurd! Don't even think like that. You think like that just because it's dark—that's all.

She got out of bed and crossed the room to the window. She looked out. He was there, on the lawn; there was nobody to see him, just her. She watched. He was so beautiful—she kept telling herself this, and now she told herself again. This was a neoclassical painting—a Poussin perhaps—with the naked athlete in the sylvan setting. She drew back from the window. She should not think in this way because it was . . . No, there was no reason why she should not think it, because beauty was to be celebrated, and that it occurred before her eyes, that it dwelt within her tent, was the greatest of possible good fortunes; like being vouchsafed a vision for which others are waiting but which has come to you of all people, descended to you.

He returned shortly, and she was back in bed.

"Gone?"

"Yes," he said. "He's off on his fox business, whatever that is." He slipped under the sheets. "Will you tell me a story about a fox?"

"I'm so tired. It's three. Do you really . . ."

He took her hand. "Please. I do."

"All right." She thought for a moment. "Fox went out; prowled about."

"Yes," he prompted. "I can just see him."

"Moonlight night; quite all right."

He pressed her hand. "Yes. All safe."

"Shadows dark; foxes bark. Saw the moon; above the toon. Fox went home; shouldn't roam. Warm as toast; tasty roast. Fox, good night; moon night-light."

Her voice had become drowsier, and now she was silent. Jamie held her hand gently, and then moved it, laid it carefully by her side, and lay still, looking up at the ceiling in their shared darkness.

CHAPTER SIXTEEN

ISABEL'S DREAMS that night might have been about Brother Fox, or foxes in general, but it was Minty Auchterlonie of whom she dreamed: Minty in her garden, talking about something that she could not quite make out; Minty at a table in a restaurant pointing a finger at her, jabbing at the air to emphasise her point. And then, quite suddenly, Minty was no longer there, and Isabel found herself in a place that she thought might be Mobile, Alabama. She was with an aunt in a garden shaded by oak trees, and her aunt, whom she hardly knew, was talking about her sister, Isabel's mother: "Such a pity she had an affair and your poor father was so upset by it." Isabel felt embarrassed, and ashamed for her mother, and was about to protest that the affair was long ago and should not be talked about, when her aunt suddenly and severely said, "We must finish what we begin, Isabel. Your mother should have taught you that, but clearly has not. Too busy having an affair perhaps."

Jamie touched her lightly on the shoulder. "Isabel?"

The garden in Mobile disappeared. "Oh."

"You were having an unpleasant dream."

"Yes."

"You were muttering, you know. It was quite loud."

She sat up. There was light flooding into the room through the chink in the curtains. Glancing at her watch, she saw that it was almost seven; Charlie would have had Jamie up already. She looked at Jamie, who was standing beside the bed, having leaned over to touch her; he was already dressed, in dark trousers and a lightweight navy-blue jacket.

She got out of bed. "I was dreaming of Minty Auchterlonie," she said. "Minty—of all people."

Jamie moved across to the dressing table. He picked up a silver-backed clothes brush and used it cursorily on his jacket. The brush had belonged to Isabel's mother, and she wondered: *What would she have thought about Jamie?* She would have approved; Isabel's mother had only wanted her to be happy, and Jamie made her happy. She would have understood.

Jamie spoke without turning round. "That woman. You know what I think?"

Isabel retrieved her dressing gown from the back of the door. "What do you think?"

Jamie turned round now. "I think that she's not going to go away."

Isabel frowned. "Meaning?"

Jamie's eyes met hers. "I think that she's like a piece of unfinished music. It wants to resolve, but the notes aren't there. So it goes round and round in your head until you work out an ending for it."

She fumbled with the cord of her dressing gown. It was frayed and she would need to replace it. The dressing gown was beginning to look shabby, but she still loved it. She looked up. Jamie's words hung in the air between them; one of those observations that on occasion comes out as an accusation.

"You think I should do something?" It was not what she expected; whenever Jamie offered her advice in this sort of situation, he usually told her to do nothing, to avoid further involvement.

"Normally . . ."

"Normally you wouldn't."

"No. I mean, yes, you're right, I wouldn't. But it seems to me now that this Minty person has really got under your skin."

It was a good way of describing it. Minty had indeed got under her skin, like one of those little jigger creatures that one found in the American South; her aunt, the one she had dreamed of, had complained about those in the grass of her lawn. "Like a jigger," said Isabel.

"Those parasite things?"

"Yes. My mother used to talk about how she took them out from under her skin as a child. With a pin."

Jamie shuddered. "Maybe. But you need to sort out what you think of her. You can't leave things up in the air, as they are. Many people could—but you can't. You're too much of a worrier." He paused. "Use a pin."

Isabel listened carefully. Why should she be surprised that Jamie thought of her as a worrier? Was she really?

"Do you think that I should . . . ?"

"Have it out with her again?"

"Yes."

He hesitated before replying. "Maybe. Just tell her what you think of her. Tell her that you don't believe a word she says, and leave it at that. If you don't do anything, she's likely to draw you into something again. You don't want that, do you?"

She thought about this. Charlie, who was in his playpen downstairs, had begun to cry. He would have thrown one of his soft toys out of the playpen confines, like one prisoner helping another to escape over the prison fence, and now he was regretting it.

"Fine. I'll do it."

She thought: he's right. And he often is.

He seemed pleased with her response. "Do you want me to come with you?"

She did not. He had done enough: he had pushed her in a direction that she might have gone in anyway, and she was confident that she could manage by herself. And she did not want to expose Jamie to Minty; she was not sure why, but she felt somehow that Minty was a threat to him, and that he was vulnerable.

AFTER BREAKFAST, Isabel went to her study. There were letters that she had to write, some personal and some connected with the *Review*. Edward Mendelson had written from New York, and her reply to him was late. As Auden's literary executor, he had been trying to trace a school magazine in which Auden had written an article when he taught at a small private school in the west of Scotland. A woman on the Isle of Mull, hearing about this, had written to say that they had no knowledge of the magazine, but had a typescript which they thought was Auden's original draft. "My grandfather," wrote this woman, "was on the staff of the school when Auden was there. He was friendly with him and he gave him a box of papers to look after, which he forgot about and never claimed." The woman was happy for them to be looked at, but would not allow them out of the house, even on a promise of return.

"I don't like to impose," wrote Edward, "but could you possibly go and take a look at them? Perhaps she'll allow you to photograph them. And, as for the typescript, you can tell straight away whether Auden typed it. He never put a space after a comma—it's as if it's a signature. If you see that, then that's almost certainly by him."

Isabel wrote back and said she would do this. They would all go—Jamie and Charlie too—and look for crowded commas.

Then there was a letter from Steven Barclay, a friend who had a flat in Paris. Steven wanted Isabel and Jamie to spend a weekend with him in Paris. There was a hotel, he said, whose staff would love Charlie and it was not far from his place in the Latin Quarter. "I'll take you to my favourite restaurant, La Fontaine de Mars," wrote Steven. "It's in the seventh arrondissement on rue Saint-Dominique, close to the Ecole Militaire—so you'll be quite safe! And you've always been so keen on Vuillard—I can take you and Jamie to the place where Vuillard stayed when he was in Paris. And you can look at the Vuillards in the house of somebody I know. Vuillards that nobody else sees. Just you. Isabel, you've got to come."

She wrote to Steven and assured him that she would. Then, musing on a life that included such calls to Mull and Paris, she turned her attention to *Review* correspondence. This was largely mundane, although she had to write to one author to inform him of a negative assessment of an article submitted for publication. "I'm sure that you will understand," she wrote, knowing that authors often did *not* understand. Months, possibly years, might have gone into the turned-down article, and more than a few hopes might be dashed by rejection. For an untenured professor somewhere in the reaches of a university system looking for savings on salaries, the rejection might precipitate the end of a career. That worried her, but she saw no way round it. The world could be a hard place—as hard, even if in a different way, for philosophers as for salesmen or miners or anybody who lived on the edge of unemployment and financial ruin.

By eleven o'clock her correspondence was finished. She printed out and read through the last letter, to the *Review*'s printers; she noticed that in the final sentence of the last paragraph she had used unspaced commas—,thus, —and on impulse she left them. She would do that too, from time to time, as an act of homage, and because little rituals like that gave life its texture. Big Brother, masked as the intrusive state or the political censor of thought and language, might force us to do this and that, but we could still assert ourselves in little things—private jokes, commas without spaces, small acts of symbolic subversion.

She rose from her desk. She had decided what to do next, and she would do it without prevarication. She would pay a call on George Finesk, Minty's wronged investor, and then she would go to see Minty, seek her out in the lair of the leopardess.

IT WAS NOT DIFFICULT to find where George Finesk lived. There were two Finesks in the telephone book—one in Tranent, a former mining town in East Lothian, and an unlikely place for a wealthy investor to live; another was in Ann Street, a highly sought-after Georgian street that was known for its elegant, if somewhat cramped, terraced houses. That was the number she dialled, and it was answered by a rather warm, welcoming voice.

She gave her name, and the warmth immediately disappeared; it was as if a window at the other end of the line had been opened to admit a chill blast.

"You said that you were Isabel Dalhousie?"

"Yes."

There was silence at the other end. "And you wanted to speak to me? May I ask why?"

Isabel had been taken aback by the change in tone and took a moment to recover. "It's about Minty Auchterlonie."

A further silence ensued. Then, "I thought it might be."

This puzzled Isabel. Why would George Finesk associate her with Minty? It would be unlikely that Peter Stevenson had said anything—he would never mention anything confidential.

Isabel resumed the conversation. "I think it might be best for us to discuss this matter in person, rather than on the phone. Easier."

George Finesk agreed, even if he sounded reluctant. Yes, she could come down immediately, if she wished. He would have to leave the house in about an hour, so he could not give her very much time. With that, he rang off, after the most cursory of goodbyes. He had not put the phone down on her, she thought—he was obviously too polite for that—but it felt to her as if he had.

Isabel went into the kitchen. Although it was a Saturday, Grace was there, making up some time ahead of her holiday. She was giving Charlie an early lunch, crushed peas with fried fish fingers—quintessential nursery food. The smell tempted Isabel, and she reached forward to sample a morsel.

"Please," Grace reprimanded her. "We mustn't take the food out of his little mouth."

Charlie, strapped into his feeding chair, looked up at his mother. Then he looked down at his plate and reached for a small fragment of fish finger. He offered this to her.

"Why, thank you, darling," Isabel said as she accepted the

offering, glancing at Grace. "I can't refuse his little present, you know."

Charlie watched solemnly, and then offered a similar scrap to Grace, who frowned before she took it.

"We must be grateful for small mercies," said Isabel, smiling.

Grace, tight-lipped, turned to Charlie. "You must eat up your food, Charlie," she said. "Mummy and Grace have their own. We don't really need yours."

ISABEL TOOK A TAXI to the other side of town, getting out at the top of Learmonth Terrace and walking down the hill to the point where Ann Street joined the larger road. It was a part of town that she knew quite well; her art historian friend Susanna Kerr lived there, as had her father's cousin, a clever, bird-like woman who had been an expert in palaeography and Celtic place-names. Cousin Kirsty had spoiled Isabel as a child with overly generous presents and regaled her with sanitised snippets of Edinburgh gossip, which her father claimed were exaggerated, or even untrue, but which he liked to have passed on to him anyway. When Isabel had been eleven, Cousin Kirsty had slipped on her highly polished kitchen floor and lain there unattended, in the cold, and died, which meant the end of Isabel's visits to Dean Terrace. She had sobbed and sobbed over Kirsty's death, her first real loss; and the second, and much greater one, had come not long afterwards, with the loss of her mother.

She found the house almost at the end of the street. The front garden was well tended, as were all the neighbouring gardens, and colourful too: there was California lilac, climbing roses and a small square of lawn at the side of which a stone bench had been placed. The bench was covered with silver-grey lichen; it did not look well used.

George Finesk was slow to answer, but eventually the front door opened. Isabel found herself standing before a grey-haired man wearing a loose-fitting white jacket, a pair of gold-framed spectacles tucked into the top pocket. He looked her in the eye briefly, but then his gaze fell away. He was a tall man, somewhere in his fifties, she thought, with an aquiline nose and blue eyes that seemed to be a small area of space, an area of nothing. She had seen such eyes before, in the north of Scotland; eyes that seemed to reflect the sky and its emptiness.

The drawing room in an Ann Street house would not be on the ground floor, she realised, and George Finesk, without speaking, motioned for her to follow him up the flight of narrow stairs that gave directly off the entrance hall. As they went up, Isabel noticed the paintings on the staircase walls and on the landing at the top. A portrait by Henry Raeburn, a woman against a background of rich greens and reds; a still life by Cadell; and a mezzotint print of a great Indian durbar.

"I have a Cadell too," she said. "Rather different. One of those women in hats."

He was still in front of her, and he did not turn round. She felt snubbed, and angry. She would not accept this rudeness; she would not.

"Mr. Finesk," she said sharply. "You are clearly not at all happy to see me. However, may I remind you that I am a guest in your house. You said that you'd see me and you owe me the basic decencies that a host should offer."

He stopped immediately, and spun round. He looked at her for a moment, as if speechless. "How dare you?" he said.

She held his gaze. There was outrage in the pale eyes.

"What do you mean?" she said. "What do you mean, 'How dare you?' "

He narrowed his eyes. As he spoke, he spluttered slightly, as if the indignation he was experiencing was too much for him. "You write to me with that crude threat—a threat I was almost minded to take to the police—and then you have the audacity to come to my house. That is why I said 'How dare you?' And I would say it again. You . . ." Isabel's astonishment must have made an impression on George Finesk, as he faltered towards the end of his tirade.

"I think we need to talk about this," said Isabel. "There's obviously been a very major misunderstanding."

He led her into the drawing room and gestured to a chair. A subtle change had occurred in his manner now, and a natural politeness seemed to be reasserting itself.

"Now, what is this letter?" Isabel asked. "I have never written to you, you know."

He stared at her. "But you . . ."

"I repeat what I said. I have never written to you."

"Then . . ."

"Then any letter purporting to come from me will be a fake." She felt in command of the situation now, and was able to glance at the paintings on the wall. Another Cadell, she observed, and a Redpath Mediterranean hillside, viewed through a window.

Her gaze reverted to her host. "What did this letter say?"

"That you have been engaged by Minty Auchterlonie to look into incidents at her house. You went on to say that you have photographic evidence linking me with these incidents and that you would be passing these on to Minty's solicitors for action unless . . ."

"Unless what?"

"Unless what you call 'commercial disagreements' are brought to an end."

"What *I* call 'commercial disagreements'?"

Isabel's irritation had a yet further effect on George Finesk's manner. Now he became apologetic. "Sorry. It's what the letter said. Maybe not you."

"Certainly not me," said Isabel forcefully.

"Very well."

It interested Isabel that George Finesk should have been so quickly mollified. He did not know her, and he had no means of telling whether she was speaking the truth—and yet he appeared to have made that assessment remarkably quickly. And then she realised what it was: they both *belonged*. The thought made her feel slightly uncomfortable: it was precisely the sort of assumption that led to unfairness in society, to that state of affairs where social cosiness brought special considera-tion and the conclusion that somebody who *belonged* would be incapable of lying or cheating, or, as in this case, writing a letter like the one that George Finesk had received.

They talked. Isabel told him about the approach from Minty and the request that she should help her in "another matter"— she did not reveal what it was. Minty had misrepresented her on that matter, she said, or so she suspected; and now it seemed that she had done it again.

"It's clear to me what happened," she said. "And I must say I find it hard to believe. Minty wanted to scare you off. She used me to do that by cooking up this letter."

"But why?" asked George. "What's the point?"

"It covers her tracks," said Isabel. "If you're threatening somebody, it's usually better, I'd have thought, to get somebody else to do your threatening for you. It's more sinister, of course, but safer. You're not implicated in the paper trail, so to speak."

George Finesk looked down at the floor. Isabel waited for him to speak, but he merely gazed mutely at his feet. "Could you tell me what happened between you and Minty Auchterlonie?" she asked.

He looked up. His face had coloured. "She's a thief," he said. "It's as simple as that."

Isabel waited for him to continue.

"You evidently don't believe me," he said.

"You haven't told me much," she said. "It's difficult to reach a conclusion when you don't have the facts."

George stared at her, as if in disbelief that she could be unaware of something very obvious. "You know that she runs an investment bank?"

Isabel nodded. "She's quite high-powered, I've been told."

He cast his eyes upwards. "So is an electric chair. And about as pleasant."

Isabel smiled. She was picturing Minty wired into the mains, sparks of malice coming from staring eyes.

George now began to explain. "I bought shares in that bank of hers. Quite a lot. The shares were part of her own holding in the bank. Then, a few weeks after I had agreed to the purchase, she went and sold some of the bank's assets. Some of the things she got rid of were pretty ordinary investments, but one of them was a major holding in a company that had a renewable energy licence. This was quite valuable."

Isabel asked what a renewable energy licence was.

"In this case, it was the right to position turbines on a bit of seabed," George said. "The coast of Scotland has very strong tides."

Isabel remembered the Corryvreckan whirlpool. "Jura," she said. "The Corryvreckan."

"Exactly. Not that anybody was proposing to put a generator there. But think of the energy—just imagine it." He paused. "It's a big thing these days. If we could get even a quarter of our energy needs from renewable sources, then . . ."

Isabel prompted him to return to the subject of Minty. "Yes, of course. But should she not have sold that company?"

George coloured again. "Oh, you can sell assets all right. Banks are doing that all the time. But if you sell them to yourself, you have be very careful. You have to sell them for the proper value, for a start."

Isabel frowned. "She sold them to herself?"

"Yes, using the money she had raised from the sale of her shares in the bank. In other words, the money I'd paid her. And then it transpires that the company in question had a licence that nobody knew about. Or so she claimed. That licence suddenly became very valuable and so Minty Auchterlonie ended up with something that was worth a lot of money. It would have been completely different had she told me that she was going to dispose of those particular assets. But she didn't."

He gazed out of the window, over the garden, as if searching for some visible manifestation of the outrage he was describing. Then he turned to face Isabel again. "She claims, of course, that she was unaware of the licence when she bought the shares. Lies." He spat the word out. "Lies."

For a few moments neither said anything. The word *lies* hung in the air between them, infecting the room with vituperation. Anger serves no point, thought Isabel. It happened—of course it did—and it was humanly understandable, but it disfigured us.

Then Isabel broke the silence. "Do you have a legal claim?"

George sighed. "We took counsel's opinion. And the answer was that it would be very difficult to prove that she knew of the licence. So I was advised not to pursue it. The advocate told me, though, that he felt I had a strong moral claim. Some consolation. A moral claim means nothing to a woman like that. Less than nothing."

"Moral claims depend on a shared sense of morality," observed Isabel. "And that is something we do *not* share with psychopaths." She paused. "Do you mind if I see the letter?"

He did not, and he went to fetch it, returning a few minutes later with a folded piece of cream-coloured stationery. Isabel read the letter quickly and stared for a moment at the signature at the bottom of the page. It was hers. She looked away, then looked at it again and thought: *the visitors' book.* Minty showed attention to detail—even unnecessary detail.

"And this came with it," said George, handing Isabel a photographic print of a shot from a security camera.

Isabel studied the photograph. It showed George Finesk against a background of lawns and trees. There was a time printed at the bottom of the picture; the camera recording the moment that he had crossed its line of vision.

"Where is this?"

George Finesk glanced at the photograph. "Taken outside her house. I admit I did go there—but I went to see her. I wanted to ask her about the transaction. She wasn't there. That's all."

"And this date?"

"It was the day on which one of the incidents occurred. I chose a bad day to go."

Isabel nodded. "So it seems."

She saw the pulse in his throat; a small movement under the skin. His eyes were fixed on hers. "But I didn't set fire to her greenhouse, or whatever it is that she accuses me of doing."

"Of course not." Isabel paused. "But she's persuaded you to give up your . . . campaign against her?"

"Yes. I can't risk the scandal of a police investigation—even if it's for something I didn't do."

Isabel told him that she could understand that. Edinburgh was a small place when it came to reputations; what was said at dinner parties would be believed by some, and repeated, even if it was untrue—and demonstrably so.

She rose to her feet. He stood up, his natural politeness fully restored. "Please let me get you some tea," he said.

She thanked him, but explained that she had to get on her way.

He demurred. "I'm so sorry," he said. "Please forgive my rudeness."

"Of course. I can understand how you felt."

She began to walk to the door, and as she did so a woman appeared from the landing outside the drawing room. She was a tall woman and Isabel noticed immediately that she had very similar eyes to George's—*sister*, she thought.

George introduced them. "My wife, Angela," he said.

Angela shook hands with Isabel. "I think I know who you are," she said, and mentioned a mutual acquaintance.

"When we lived in India, we lived outside a village," George Finesk said. "Now we come home and we find ourselves living *in* a village."

"Yes," said Isabel, smiling. "It sometimes feels like that,

doesn't it?" She felt the other woman's eyes upon her. There was something disconcerting about her gaze. It was not hostile, or even reserved; rather it was a look that indicated that there was something that she wanted to say.

"I'll show Isabel out," Angela offered. She spoke in a slightly peremptory way, to which George meekly acceded. Isabel thought, *She makes the decisions.*

They left the room and made their way downstairs, Angela leading the way.

"Are you married?" Angela asked in the downstairs hall.

It was an unexpected question, posed out of the blue, almost rude in its suddenness. "Engaged, as it happens," Isabel replied.

Angela nodded. "Then you'll understand what I mean when I say that there are certain faults that one just has to live with. You feel that, I think, with a fiancé as much as with a husband. You see your way past them."

Isabel nodded. "I suppose that you find out more about them as you go along."

"You do." They were at the front door now, and Angela fumbled with the lock. "I must get this thing attended to. It's always catching." She gave the door a tug and it opened.

Outside, in the garden, Isabel was struck by the musky scent of a flowering shrub. The fragrance lay heavy on the air, like a coating. They began to walk down the path; Solomon's Seal, Isabel said to herself, looking down at the delicate rows of suspended white flowers.

The older woman took Isabel by the arm, pressing hard. Isabel looked down at the other woman's hand: there was an aquamarine set in a wide ring; a bracelet too—gold. There were sunspots on her hand—the Indian sun, presumably.

"I know why you came," Angela said. "I know about your letter."

Isabel started to explain. "Well, that's not what it seems—"

Angela cut her off. "Please. Please let me tell you something. George didn't really intend to do what he did. That's just not his style—it really isn't."

She was puzzled. "To do what he—"

Angela interrupted again. "He should never have caused that damage—or done any of the other things he did. It's just that he was so livid over what that woman did. He is a fair-minded man, and he couldn't bear the thought of that woman sitting there with impunity. I think something snapped inside him. Of course he knows that violence and threats are no solution, but . . . well, he's human—as are we all."

She looked at Isabel. There was pleading in her eyes.

"Please don't do anything that will cause difficulties for George," she whispered. "I'm asking you woman to woman. Please don't. He won't do anything like this again—I promise you that."

CHAPTER SEVENTEEN

IN HER DREAM, her aunt from Mobile had told Isabel to finish what she began. Isabel realised that this was wise advice, of course, of the sort that we started to give to children the moment they understood what the words *finish* and *begin* meant. She realised, too, that the advice given to us by people inhabiting our dreams was really advice from ourselves to ourselves. Somewhere within herself, then, was a self that wanted to advise another self about what to do—which suggested that the self was bifurcated, split between the wise self, cautious and prudent, and another self, lazy, flawed, headstrong perhaps.

No, she thought, I shall not be drawn into *that*. There were conflicting desires—that was all; there was only one Isabel Dalhousie, one self, but it had to weigh options and make choices. Any other view would take one down some ridiculous and dangerous path of multiple personalities, and Isabel was not going in that direction. Although . . . although how convenient it would be to have two *personae* and to be able to choose to inhabit one at this time and another at that time. We are all compartmentalised to an extent: there was the private self, the person we were when there was nobody about, and then there was the public self, the person we were when others were watching. For most, the differences between the two were small—ideally the two selves should be exactly the same—but for others there was usually some distinction. Even a saint might in private be irritable, or might swear sotto voce should he stub his toe; even the great and dignified might be silly at times when not in the public eye, might give the inner child the chance to romp.

Driving out that evening to Minty Auchterlonie's house off the Biggar Road, Isabel told herself that at least she was finishing what she had started—or planning to do so. She knew that not only was this the correct thing to do, it was what Jamie wanted as well. He was right about that, as was her aunt in her dream; Minty was a ghost that had to be laid to rest. And yet she was not quite sure what she should do. Should she tell Minty that she knew that she had been used, and then demand an apology? Or should she simply upbraid her, thus showing her that she—Isabel—would not tolerate being implicated in whatever proxy lies or threats Minty might resort to in order to get out of difficulties? A third possibility presented itself—that she should drive as far as Nine Mile Burn and then turn round and head back to Edinburgh, forgetting about the whole thing. She almost did that; almost, but then Nine Mile Burn flashed past and she had not even slowed down very much and a new stretch of country revealed itself; at the edge of it was Minty's house, now to be glimpsed, just, in the distance, a small block of white put down amongst the folds of the landscape, and beyond it the blue of the distant hills, and more blue.

Minty knew that she was coming, as Isabel had telephoned

in advance. As Isabel made her way up the drive, the car wheels crunching the expensive gravel mix below—pink and grey—she saw Minty appear at the front door. She was carrying something in her hands, a magazine or a sheaf of papers—it was difficult to tell at that distance. She went back in, deposited the papers somewhere, and came out again just as Isabel brought the car to a halt in front of the house.

Minty's manner was warm. "I know better than to offer you something to drink," she said. "That's one thing about living in the country—people have to drive out to see you and so your drinks cupboard rarely has to be stocked up."

Isabel smiled weakly. "I like tea," she said, "if that's on offer."

"Of course it is. Anything."

Isabel instantly regretted her request. She did not want her visit to be transformed into a social meeting conducted over a cup of tea. She knew that this would be a danger with Minty, who would use her considerable skills to forfend any threat to her command of a situation. "Actually," she said, "I'm not sure that I even want a cup of tea."

Minty started to frown, but obviously thought better of it, and the incipient frown became a smile. "It would be no trouble."

They were still standing outside, and Isabel, sensing that Minty was about to invite her in, looked over her shoulder at the expanse of rough-cut grass behind her. "It's such a warm evening," she began. "Couldn't we go for a walk down there? The view must be stunning."

Minty looked over Isabel's shoulder, towards the hills. "It looks like rain's heading our way."

Isabel was insistent. "But not just yet. Come on."

Minty conceded, and they began to stroll over the grass

towards the bank of shrubs at the end of the garden. Beyond the shrubs there was a field, and beyond that more fields, woods, and, in the distance, the hills themselves.

"I hope you'll hear me out in what I have to say," Isabel said. "You may not like it."

Minty was all innocence. "Not like it? Why? What could you say that I wouldn't like?"

Isabel went straight to the point. "I know that you've used me," she said. "You've deliberately misrepresented me . . ."

She did not finish. "Misrepresented?" snapped Minty. "I explained to you, remember. I told you in the café. I told you what happened."

"And George Finesk? The letter you wrote?"

They did not stop walking. It was easier, Isabel felt, to utter these lines while walking.

"George Finesk?"

"You know perfectly well what I'm talking about."

Minty hesitated. Then: "George Finesk carried out a totally unwarranted attack on our property. And I have the evidence to support that."

"But you didn't tell me about that," retorted Isabel. "You led me to believe that it was Jock Dundas. Yet you knew all along that it was George."

"So? So what?"

Isabel stopped walking. She took a step to the side so that she was now standing directly in front of Minty. "You used me," she said again. "You forged my signature." She was looking directly into Minty's eyes, hoping to see the effect of truth upon them. But there was none. Minty stared back at her, bemused. She controls even her gaze, Isabel thought.

Minty spoke. "I haven't caused you any harm, have I? I've

had to deal with two . . . how shall I put it? Two little problems. And I've done it—with some assistance from you, I admit, for which I really am grateful." She paused. "Two women helping one another deal with troublesome men. But if it's payment you're looking for, I can certainly . . ."

"I don't want money," Isabel hissed. "I want . . ." What did she want? "I want an apology."

Minty did not hesitate. "Of course. Sorry. Yes, I'm very sorry if you've been offended by my somewhat unconventional tactics. But you must admit, surely, that they seem to have worked."

Suddenly Minty took a step backwards. "Do you mind? I feel a little bit claustrophobic when I'm too close to people."

"Because you're forced to see them as real?" asked Isabel.

"I don't know what you mean."

"You do. You know exactly what I mean."

Minty looked at her watch. "Look, it's almost eight. I really have to get on with things. Gordon . . ."

Isabel looked past Minty towards the house. There was a light on in one of the rooms to the front of the house, and she saw a figure move across a window, silhouetted. It occurred to her that it would be very easy.

"Gordon doesn't know."

Minty, who had also turned, spun round. "What?"

"I said that Gordon doesn't know about your affair with Jock . . ."

For a moment Minty said nothing. Isabel saw her colour though, saw the flush of anger, or was it fear?

"You'd tell him?" Minty's voice was small—constricted by something.

Isabel was aware of the moment's significance. It was a

strange feeling—having somebody in your power and completely at your mercy. One might relish it, if one were insecure or perverted, or simply cruel.

Minty spoke again. "You wouldn't tell him? You gave me your word, you know."

She had to decide, and now, at this extreme moment, she found it remarkably easy to choose. There was no self within her saying, *Go on, go ahead and threaten her;* all that she heard was the self that said, *It would be wrong; what you have to do is forgive her.*

"I told you that I wouldn't tell him, and I won't."

Minty's relief was palpable. "Good."

Isabel watched her. "I notice that you said *good* and not *thank you.*"

"Thank you," said Minty.

"An afterthought."

Isabel swallowed. Her heart was thumping again, as it always did at these moments. Minty's heart, she thought, will not be thumping, or turning somersaults, or doing any of the things that the hearts of normal people are said to do.

"One final thing," Isabel said. "You have wronged me, but you have wronged others—George Finesk included."

Minty stared at her. "George Finesk? Let me tell you something. That man has a dispute with me. A simple business disagreement. He's the one who's taken it nuclear."

Isabel held her gaze. "But I know what happened. And it seems to me that you should have told him that you were going to sell the bank's holding in that company."

Minty's expression now showed amusement. "But I did. I told him about it. There was complete disclosure."

"He says there wasn't."

Minty waited for a few moments before she replied. "He's a liar." She paused, watching the effect of her words on Isabel. "Can't you tell when somebody's lying?"

No, thought Isabel. I don't seem to be able to do that at all.

She looked away, unsure as to whether she would have the courage to challenge Minty. "People tell a lot of lies, don't they? So what if I were lying when I told you that I wouldn't tell Gordon about your affair? What then?"

Minty froze. She opened her mouth, but said nothing. Isabel felt her eyes upon her; cold rays.

"Well, I wasn't lying when I said that. But tell me something—have you heard of the liar paradox?"

Minty looked uncertain. It was what Isabel wanted; she had forced the other woman on to her own territory.

"It's something that philosophers talk about," said Isabel. "A Cretan says 'All Cretans are liars.' But he's a Cretan, you see. More to the point, though, I might say to you, 'All Scots sometimes tell lies,' which is probably true. There can't be anybody, really, who hasn't told a lie—even a little one—at some point in life, particularly as a child. So what this suggests is that you shouldn't always believe what a Scottish person tells you. And, of course, I'm a Scot . . ." She smiled. "What a ridiculous conversation, though. Please don't pay too much attention to what I say. I'm a professional philosopher, you see, and we go on about things rather a lot. Strange, unrealistic speculation, and so on."

Minty was watching her, but Isabel now felt confident. Wickedness was tawdry when you came right up against it—as she felt she was doing now. It was tawdry and banal. There was nothing impressive or frightening about Minty Auchterlonie; she was very ordinary.

"Yes," Isabel went on, "I love philosophical speculations. So I might ask myself, for example, whether in a case like this it would be appropriate for one person to compensate another. What do you think, Minty—do you enjoy speculating about that sort of thing?"

Minty remained quite still. "I understand what you're saying," she said. "I will. I'll do something."

Isabel watched her. No, she thought, she's lying. Again. But she had played with her enough. It was not for her to punish Minty.

"I don't think you will at all," said Isabel. And then, rather reluctantly, she added, "And I don't think that you really understand me. So let me reassure you. When I said that I wouldn't say anything to Gordon, I meant that. You can trust me."

IT TOOK HER TIME to calm down as she drove back, but by the time she reached the turn-off for Flotterstane she felt normal again. Her visit to Minty Auchterlonie, she decided, had not been a waste of time; nor had she allowed herself to become angry. She found herself wondering what would have happened had she yielded to the temptation to force Minty to make amends to George by threatening to tell Gordon of the affair. Again, she had made the right decision, as to do otherwise would have been to play by Minty's rules, and Minty, she suspected, would always win in any such game.

She looked out of the car window, down towards Roslin and Dalkeith beyond. The evening air seemed to have applied a wash to the countryside, like the layer of faint blue that a watercolourist will use to blur the details. It gave the land that feeling of peacefulness, of near somnolence, of a country getting ready for the darkness that was still an hour or two away. She loved that view; she loved that bit of land, which, when she turned the next corner following the road that curved round Hillend House, would become the city.

Charlie had been put to bed by the time she arrived at the house.

"I would have kept him up for you," said Jamie, "but he was ready to drop."

They crept into Charlie's room together, and she bent down and kissed him gently, imperceptibly, on the side of the head. His hair smelled of baby shampoo, and beside him was his stuffed fox staring up at the ceiling with the patience that only stuffed animals seem capable of. It made her think of Brother Fox, who must be better by now, she thought, unaware of why it was that his wound had stopped aching. That was the best way of doing good, she thought; do it when the person for whom you are doing the deed is under heavy sedation and will never remember. So might one leave presents for others— while they were asleep or otherwise unaware of what you were doing.

They went downstairs. Jamie had prepared an elaborate salad, which they would eat with wild Scottish salmon steaks and boiled new potatoes. She poured a glass of New Zealand white wine for both of them, chilled and dry. Then she told him what had happened that evening.

"That's the end of that," he said. "Odd ending, though."

She found herself agreeing. It had indeed been an odd ending, but it was, she felt, exactly right. "If it had ended any other way I think I would have felt uncomfortable," she said. "I just would."

He thought about that, and after a few minutes he agreed. "You have done nothing wrong."

"In fact, I've done virtually nothing," she said. "Everything happened without my really doing anything. I was a complete pawn in Minty's hands."

"I suppose so," he said. "But then you showed her something at the end."

"Did I?"

He was quite sure. "I think you did. She may take no notice, but she may have learned something. May have."

He took the salmon steaks from the fridge and prepared the pan.

"I love you in your apron," she said, looking across the room at him from her chair at the kitchen table. "Why is it that men look so good in aprons?"

Jamie had no idea. He did not think of himself as looking good; he was without vanity.

"Oh," he said, remembering something as he dropped the steaks on to the surface of the pan. "Guy Peploe phoned."

She looked up. "About that portrait?"

Jamie nodded. "He left a message, since he was going to be in London tomorrow and might not be able to speak until he came back. He said his view of that painting has been confirmed. It's not the lost one. It was done by an Italian, I think he said."

"By Dupra. I see." She felt a pang of disappointment. "He told me that was probably the case. I still like it, though. And I'm glad we bought it."

"Well, there you are," said Jamie. "I've often thought about the value that we give to things that are authentic. Does it matter if something is not made by the person we'd like it to be made by? If a violin plays like a Strad, does it matter if it's by a lesser maker?"

Isabel was about to answer "Not really," but then she realised that sometimes it did matter. "It matters if we're interested in where things come from," she said. "Maybe it doesn't matter if it's just utility we're bothered about."

"So if I composed something that sounded like Mozart, would it count for as much as the real thing?"

Isabel smiled. "It would to me," she said.

He averted his gaze in momentary embarrassment, but soon turned round again and smiled at her. "Thanks," he said.

Jamie returned to the stove and Isabel crossed over to the kitchen window. She stared out into the garden. A clump of valerian stood along the wall, a curious, light purple plant, a faithful returnee whom she had never had to encourage. It brought sleep, she knew, like the poppy. *Baldrian,* she thought; *Baldrian* in German. A German visitor, a professor of philosophy from Frankfurt, had seen it in her garden and called it *Baldrian.* She had asked why, and he had replied that it was named after a Norse god called Baldur—"so good and so true that the light shone forth from him." There were people like that, not just gods—but only a tiny handful. How many in Scotland? Ten? Twenty?

Her thoughts returned to the picture and to Guy's call. Things were not what they seemed to be; sometimes that mattered, while other times it mattered not at all. It was not important that the picture of Bonnie Prince Charlie was not what she had hoped it would be; the prince himself was probably not what so many people had hoped he would be. He was a military failure, he was proud and seemingly rather vain—as the later

Stuarts tended to be. Minty was palpably not what she claimed to be; nor was George Finesk; nor Jock Dundas. She should not have taken any of these people at face value; she had been naive. But this conclusion, she realised, pointed unambiguously in the direction of cynicism, and she would not be a cynic. It was better to be naive—much better.

The salmon steaks cooked, Jamie served the potatoes and put the salad bowl on the table. "Very delicious," remarked Isabel. She was looking away as she spoke and Jamie could tell that her mind was elsewhere. He assumed that all philosophers were like that—not only *his* philosopher.

"I think we should invite Cat and Bruno back for dinner," she said. "How about next week?" She did not want to do this, but she knew that she had to make an effort. Ill feeling, in what-ever quarter it existed, was like a slow and insidious poison, a weedkiller that strangled the life about it. She would make an effort with Bruno, no matter how hard it might be.

He shook his head. "It might be too late," he said.

"Why?"

He delivered the news in even tones. "Because I don't think they're still together."

Isabel had half expected this. Cat was incorrigible; she was ashamed of her, but she was also pleased. How quickly, she thought, have my good intentions been replaced by delight in the end of Cat's romance. She was human, made up of a will to do good, but also with human failings. It was the end of Bruno, but she resisted any hint of triumphalism, or evident relief, restricting herself to asking Jamie how he had formed this impression.

"Eddie said something," Jamie replied.

Isabel felt her pleasure fading rapidly. Eddie was not always to be relied upon.

"Eddie went to a show on the Meadows," Jamie went on. "It was some sort of sample of what was coming up at the Fringe—the usual thing, actors, jugglers, musicians. And Bruno was doing a tightrope walk."

Isabel could see it. There would be colour and music and the very faint hint of marijuana smoke mingled with cheap perfume.

Jamie continued with his explanation. "Bruno's wire was not very high—about twelve feet or so, Eddie said. But he was doing all sorts of tricks on it—he rode a unicycle across and skipped—you know what these characters do."

Isabel imagined Bruno padding across the wire in his elevator shoes. No, he would take those off and don a pair of soft kid slippers. Did they make elevator slippers? she wondered.

Jamie was watching her. "Are you trying not to laugh?"

She could reply—quite honestly—that she was not. But she sensed that laughter was there, not far away, and that this would spoil all her moral effort, her determination to like Bruno.

"Anyway, he was walking along the wire, and Cat and Eddie were watching from down below. Cat suddenly called out to him and waved—Eddie said that he thought she was really proud of seeing him up there being admired by everybody."

"I suppose so," said Isabel. But she thought: *I wouldn't be.*

"He looked round, apparently, and then fell off. She had distracted him."

Isabel gasped.

"He wasn't hurt, apparently, or not badly," Jamie went on. "He twisted an ankle a bit, but picked himself up and went over to Cat."

"And?"

"And he yelled at her," said Jamie. "Ranted and raved in front of everybody. Then apparently he stormed off. Eddie said that Cat was in tears and nothing's been seen of Bruno since then. No apology. Nothing."

Isabel sat in silence. It was a painful discovery to make, but one very much better made before she married him.

"The end of Bruno," she muttered.

"Yes," said Jamie. He pointed to the salmon steaks on their plates. "Don't let the salmon get cold."

She lifted her knife and fork. Cat had made numerous mistakes, and seemed destined to make more. One day she would stop—she would have to—and take stock of the men she had chosen. Every one of them had been unsuitable, in one way or another, apart from Jamie, that is. But then Jamie had been unsuitable for Cat—principally because he was so suitable for virtually anybody else. Poor Cat: Could she not see the problem?

They exchanged glances. "Let's be honest," said Jamie. "It would have been a disaster. Those elevator shoes."

Isabel was thinking more of his temper, but she agreed that the elevator shoes were a problem too. And the tightrope walking. And the stunts. And *Oil*.

"You're right," she said.

They finished their meal. Then Jamie said, "I composed something today. The words are by somebody else; the music by me. Would you like to hear it?"

Isabel said that she would. She would make coffee and bring it through to the music room. He could go through and get ready.

She ground the coffee, alone in the kitchen, savouring the

smell of the grounds. She thought of Italy, and of the little coffee bar in Siena where she had stood at the high tables and drunk coffee with her friends. That was many years ago, and she was a different person now, and they were scattered to the four corners, as so many of us are. Were they happy? she wondered. For she wanted for them only that—happiness and wisdom, if their hearts were open to these two things, these principal things, that were the foundation of the good. I have been so fortunate, she thought, and Cat so unfortunate. She was grateful for that—for her own good fortune, that is, she was grateful. And she hoped that things would change for Cat, but she feared that they would not. We are condemned to repeat our failures, she thought, and some do so all their lives, to the very end, elderly children who have never learned.

She took the coffee through and put the cups down on the small table beside the piano. Jamie, seated at the keyboard, had his fingers on a chord and played it gently. Isabel sat down and waited for him to begin.

"Go on."

It seemed to her that he was blushing. It was unusual for him to be embarrassed to play before her; they had done that countless times before. "What's wrong?" she asked.

"I'm not sure how it's going to sound."

She sought to reassure him. "It'll sound just fine. It always does." She looked at him. "You don't have to—if you don't want to."

"No, I will."

She asked whether he had given it a name, and he thought for a moment. "No, I don't want to. It's just a tune I've made up. Nothing important."

"What's it about? Olives? Or potatoes dauphinois?"

He smiled. "I suspect nobody's ever written a song about potatoes dauphinois." He played another chord, as if he were looking for something on the piano. "This is about losing things," he said. "About thinking you've lost something, and then finding you haven't."

Isabel sat down next to him, on the piano stool. I would go ten thousand miles for you, she thought; as she was now sure he would for her. That was another song altogether, something about turtle doves.

Jamie began.

What we lose, we think we lose for ever,
But we are wrong about this; think of love—
Love is lost, we think it gone,
But it returns, often when least expected,
Forgives us our lack of attention, our failure of faith,
Our cold indifference; forgives us all this, and more;
Returns and says, "I was always there."
Love, at our shoulder, whispers: "Merely remember me,
Don't think I've gone away for ever:
I am still here. With you. My power undimmed.
See. I am here."

The music accompanying the words was simple, but it followed their mood closely, fittingly, as a well-made garment will follow the shape of the body. When he reached the final sentence, the notes became softer and died away.

Isabel sat transfixed, as did Jamie, and nothing was said for a long time; nor did they move—they were quite still, as they were when they heard the noise outside, the yelping sound: Brother Fox.

Isabel looked anxiously at Jamie. "I hope he's not in distress."

"No," said Jamie. "He's singing."

THE ISABEL DALHOUSIE NOVELS

"The literary equivalent of herbal tea and a cozy fire. . . .
McCall Smith's Scotland [is] well worth future visits."
—*The New York Times*

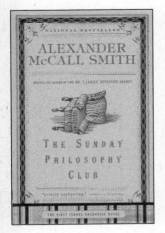

The Sunday Philosophy Club

Isabel Dalhousie is fond of problems, and sometimes she becomes interested in problems that are, quite frankly, none of her business—including some that are best left to the police. Filled with endearingly thorny characters and a Scottish atmosphere as thick as a highland mist, *The Sunday Philosophy Club* is an irresistible pleasure.

Volume 1
978-0-676-97665-6 (pbk)
978-0-307-37040-2 (eBook)

Friends, Lovers, Chocolate

While taking care of her niece Cat's deli, Isabel meets a heart transplant patient who has had some strange experiences in the wake of his surgery. Against the advice of her housekeeper, Isabel is intent on investigating. Matters are further complicated when Cat returns from vacation with a new boyfriend, and Isabel's fondness for him lands her in another muddle.

Volume 2
978-0-676-97666-3 (pbk)
978-0-307-37041-9 (eBook)

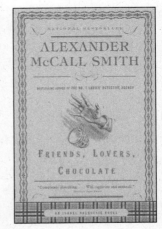

The Right Attitude to Rain

When Isabel's cousin from Dallas arrives in Edinburgh, she introduces Isabel to a bigwig Texan whose young fiancée may just be after his money. Then there's her niece, Cat, who's busy falling for a man whom Isabel suspects of being an incorrigible mama's boy. Isabel is advised to stay out of it all, but the philosophical issues of these matters of the heart prove too tempting for her to resist.

Volume 3
978-0-676-97667-0 (pbk)
978-0-307-37124-9 (eBook)

"No one does understated wit like Alexander McCall Smith."
—The Globe and Mail

The Careful Use of Compliments

There's a new little Dalhousie on the scene, and while the arrival of Isabel's son presents her with the myriad wonders of life, it doesn't diminish her curiosity about other things. While attending an art auction, she discovers a mystery revealed in one of the paintings, launching her into yet another intriguing investigation.

Volume 4
978-0-676-97668-7 (pbk)
978-0-307-37171-3 (eBook)

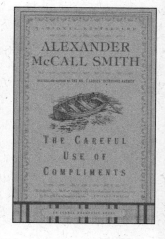

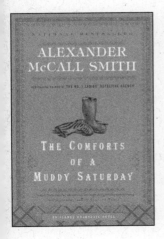

The Comforts of a Muddy Saturday

A doctor's career has been ruined by allegations of medical fraud and Isabel cannot ignore what may be a miscarriage of justice. Meanwhile, there is her baby, Charlie, who needs looking after; her niece, Cat, who needs someone to mind her deli; and a mysterious composer who has latched on to Jamie, making Isabel decidedly uncomfortable.

Volume 5
978-0-307-39700-3 (pbk)
978-0-307-36666-5 (eBook)

The sensational seventh installment in the bestselling chronicles of the irrepressibly curious Isabel Dalhousie

The Charming Quirks of Others

Old friends of Isabel's ask for her help in a rather tricky situation: A successor is being sought for the headmaster position at their alma mater and an anonymous letter has alleged that one of the candidates has a very serious skeleton in their closet. Could Isabel discreetly look into it? What she uncovers about all the candidates is surprising, but what she discovers in herself turns out to be equally revealing.

Volume 7
Coming in October 2010
978-0-307-39956-4 (hc)
978-0-307-39958-8 (eBook)

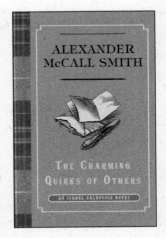

MORALITY FOR BEAUTIFUL GIRLS

While trying to resolve some financial problems for her business, Mma Ramotswe finds herself investigating the alleged poisoning of a government official as well as the moral character of the four finalists of the Miss Beauty and Integrity contest. Other difficulties arise at her fiancé's Tlokweng Road Speedy Motors, as Mma Ramotswe discovers he is more complicated than he seems.

Volume 3
978-1-4000-3136-8 (pbk)
978-1-4000-7766-3 (eBook)

"Truly perfect books to transport yourself someplace else."
—Ottawa Citizen

THE KALAHARI TYPING SCHOOL FOR MEN

Mma Ramotswe is content. But, as always, there are troubles. Mr. J.L.B. Matekoni has not set the date for their wedding, her assistant, Mma Makutsi, wants a husband, and worst of all, a rival detective agency has opened up in town. Of course, Mma Ramotswe will manage these things, as she always does, with her uncanny insight and good heart.

Volume 4
978-0-676-97569-7 (pbk)
978-0-307-37035-8 (eBook)

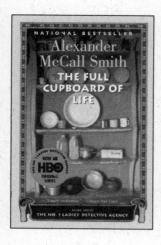

THE FULL CUPBOARD OF LIFE

Mma Ramotswe has weighty matters on her mind. She has been approached by a wealthy lady to check up on several suitors. Are these men interested in her or just her money? This may be difficult to find out, but it's just the kind of case Mma Ramotswe likes.

Volume 5
978-0-676-97571-0 (pbk)
978-0-307-37039-6 (eBook)

"One of the best, most charming, honest, hilarious, and life-affirming [series] to appear in years."
—*The Plain Dealer*

IN THE COMPANY OF CHEERFUL LADIES

Precious Ramotswe is busier than usual at the No. 1 Ladies' Detective Agency when the appearance of a strange intruder in her house and a mysterious pumpkin in her yard add to her concerns. But what finally rattles Mma Ramotswe's normally unshakable composure is the visitor who forces her to confront a painful secret from her past.

Volume 6
978-0-676-97623-6 (pbk)
978-0-307-37126-3 (eBook)

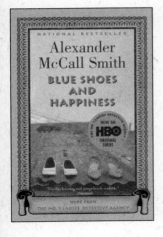

BLUE SHOES AND HAPPINESS

Mma Ramotswe and her inestimable assistant, Grace Makutsi, have their hands full with finding a cobra in their office and investigating the medical clinic and the local advice columnist. But the most troubling situation is in Mma Makutsi's personal life. When her wealthy fiancé misses their customary dinner date, Mma Makutsi wonders if he's having second thoughts about their engagement, but Mma Ramotswe once again steps in with calming, sage advice.

Volume 7
978-0-676-97625-0 (pbk)
978-0-307-37042-6 (eBook)

"A quiet joy, a little gem . . . set apart from the genre by the quality of its writing, as well as by its exotic setting."
—*The Boston Globe*

THE GOOD HUSBAND OF ZEBRA DRIVE

In the life of Mma Ramotswe there is rarely a dull moment, and lately her husband, Mr. J.L.B. Matekoni, has been keeping her occupied above all else. He has been hinting for some time now that he intends to do something special for their adopted daughter, Motholeli, but when his plan hits some snags he finds himself lucky to be married to the ever-resourceful, ever-understanding Precious Ramotswe.

Volume 8
978-0-676-97627-4 (pbk)
978-0-307-37043-3 (eBook)

THE MIRACLE AT SPEEDY MOTORS

Investigating her latest case, Mma Ramotswe has to trek to a game preserve, where she rediscovers the breathtaking beauty of her beloved Botswana. She is there to uncover the truth about an elderly American traveler whose safari proved to be his last journey. What she discovers is a surprise to everyone concerned.

Volume 9
978-0-676-97922-0 (pbk)
978-0-307-37170-6 (eBook)

"One of the most entrancing literary treats of many a year. A tapestry of extraordinary nuance and richness."
—*The Wall Street Journal*

TEA TIME FOR THE TRADITIONALLY BUILT

Mma Ramotswe's white van, in need of repair, is replaced with a new, character-less vehicle by her husband, Mr. J.L.B. Matekoni. She sets out to find the van, unaware that it has been stolen from the man who bought it. Elsewhere, the owner of a local football team has enlisted the No. 1 Ladies' Detective Agency to help explain its dreadful losing streak: surely someone must be fixing the games.

Volume 10
978-0-676-97924-4 (pbk)
978-0-307-37519-3 (eBook)

THE DOUBLE COMFORT SAFARI CLUB

Mma Ramotswe and Mma Makutsi travel to the north of Botswana, to the stunning Okavango Delta, to visit a safari lodge where several unexplained and troubling events have occurred—including the demise of one of the guests.

Volume 11
978-0-676-97926-8 (pbk), March 2011
978-0-676-97925-1 (hc)
978-0-307-37520-9 (eBook)

THE NO. 1 LADIES' HBO® SERIES

Filmed entirely on location in Botswana and coproduced with the Weinstein Company and the BBC, the series began with a two-hour pilot directed by Anthony Minghella (*The English Patient*). The series is now available on DVD.

978-0-307-45663-2 (pbk tie-in)
978-0-307-45662-5 (mm tie-in)

For more information about the series, please visit:
www.hbo.com/no1ladiesdetectiveagency

THE NO. 1 LADIES' DETECTIVE AGENCY BOXED SETS

3-volume includes:
The No. 1 Ladies' Detective Agency,
Tears of the Giraffe, and
Morality for Beautiful Girls
978-0-679-78975-8 (pbk)

5-volume includes:
The No. 1 Ladies' Detective Agency,
Tears of the Giraffe,
Morality for Beautiful Girls,
The Kalahari Typing School for Men,
and *The Full Cupboard of Life*
978-0-307-26158-8 (pbk)

THE 44 SCOTLAND STREET SERIES

**"Will make you feel as though you live in Edinburgh. . . .
Long live the folks on Scotland Street."**
—*The Times-Picayune* (New Orleans)

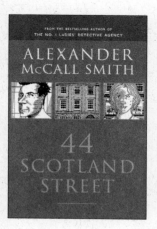

44 SCOTLAND STREET

All of Alexander McCall Smith's trademark
warmth and wit come into play in this
novel chronicling the lives of the residents
of a converted Georgian town house in
Edinburgh. Complete with colorful
characters, love triangles, and even a
mysterious art caper, this is an
unforgettable portrait of Edinburgh society.

Volume 1
978-0-676-97724-0 (pbk)
978-0-307-37033-4 (eBook)

ESPRESSO TALES

The eccentric residents of 44 Scotland
Street are back. From the talented
six-year-old Bertie, who is forced to
arrive in pink overalls for his first
day of class, to the self-absorbed
Bruce, who contemplates a change
of career in between admiring glances
in the mirror, there is much in store as
fall settles on Edinburgh.

Volume 2
978-0-676-97819-3 (pbk)
978-0-307-37125-6 (eBook)

LOVE OVER SCOTLAND

From conducting perilous anthropological studies of pirate households to being inadvertently left behind on a school trip to Paris, the wonderful misadventures of the residents of 44 Scotland Street will charm and delight.

Volume 3
978-0-676-97820-9 (pbk)
978-0-307-37123-2 (eBook)

THE WORLD ACCORDING TO BERTIE

Pat is forced to deal with the reappearance of Bruce, which has her heart skipping—and not in the most pleasant way. Angus Lordie's dog, Cyril, has been taken away by the authorities, accused of being a serial biter, and Bertie, the beleaguered Italian-speaking prodigy and saxophonist, now has a little brother, Ulysses, who he hopes will distract his mother, Irene.

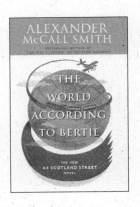

Volume 4
978-0-307-39708-9 (pbk)
978-0-307-37034-1 (eBook)

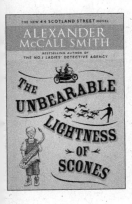

THE UNBEARABLE LIGHTNESS OF SCONES

The Unbearable Lightness of Scones finds Bertie still troubled by his rather overbearing mother, Irene, but seeking his escape in the cub scouts. Matthew is rising to the challenge of married life, while Domenica epitomizes the loneliness of the long-distance intellectual, and Cyril succumbs to the kind of romantic temptation that no dog can resist, creating a small problem, or rather six of them, for his friend and owner, Angus Lordie.

Volume 5
978-0-307-39709-6 (pbk)
978-0-307-37306-9 (eBook)

THREE NOVELLAS FEATURING THE ECCENTRIC AND EVER-LIKABLE PROFESSOR DR VON IGELFELD

Welcome to the insane and rarified world of Professor Dr Moritz-Maria von Igelfeld of the Institute of Romance Philology. Von Igelfeld is engaged in a never-ending quest to win the respect he feels certain he is due—a quest that has a way of going hilariously astray.

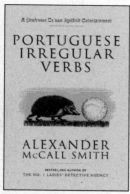

Portuguese Irregular Verbs

978-0-676-97679-3 (pbk)
978-0-307-37037-2 (eBook)

The Finer Points of Sausage Dogs

978-0-676-97680-9 (pbk)
978-0-307-37038-9 (eBook)

At the Villa of Reduced Circumstances

978-0-676-97681-6 (pbk)
978-0-307-37036-5 (eBook)

ALSO BY ALEXANDER McCALL SMITH

LA'S ORCHESTRA SAVES THE WORLD

It is 1939, and Lavender—La to her friends—has fled London for small-town life to avoid German bombs and to escape memories of her shattered marriage. As the war drags on, La organizes an amateur orchestra, drawing musicians from the village and local RAF base, including Feliks, a shy Polish refugee who becomes La's prized recruit.

978-0-307-39812-3 (pbk)
978-0-307-39811-6 (hc)
978-0-307-37465-3 (eBook)

CORDUROY MANSIONS

"Corduroy Mansions" is the affectionate nickname given to a genteelly crumbling mansion block in the vibrant neighborhood of Pimlico in London. This is the home patch of a wonderful new cast of characters and one incredibly clever dog. Filled with the ins and outs of neighborliness in all its unexpected variations, *Corduroy Mansions* showcases the life, laughter, and humanity that have become the hallmarks of Alexander McCall Smith's work.

978-0-307-39908-3 (hc)
978-0-307-37525-4 (eBook)

"**These are pithy, engaging tales, as habit-forming as peanuts.**"
—*Publishers Weekly*

THE GIRL WHO MARRIED A LION and OTHER TALES FROM AFRICA

978-0-375-42312-3 (hc)
978-0-375-42344-4 (eBook)

**Available wherever books and eBooks are sold, or visit
www.alexandermccallsmith.com**